MEET THE MARVEL SUPER HEROES

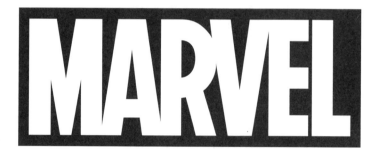

marvelkids.com

TM & © 2013 Marvel & Subs.

Published by Marvel Press, an imprint of Disney Book Group. No part of this book may be reproduced or transmitted in any form or by any means, electronic or mechanical, including photocopying, recording, or by any information storage and retrieval system, without written permission from the publisher. For information address Marvel Press, 114 Fifth Avenue, New York, New York 10011-5690.

Designed by Jason Wojtowicz

Printed in the United States of America

First Edition

1 3 5 7 9 10 8 6 4 2

ISBN 978-1-4231-6142-4

G492-9090-6-13015

SUSTAINABLE FORESTRY INITIATIVE

Certified Sourcing

www.sfiprogram.org

SFI-00993

For Text Only

MEET THE MARVEL SUPER HEROES

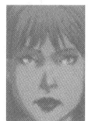

SCOTT PETERSON

Illustrated by **PAT OLLIFFE** and **HI-FI DESIGN**

New York

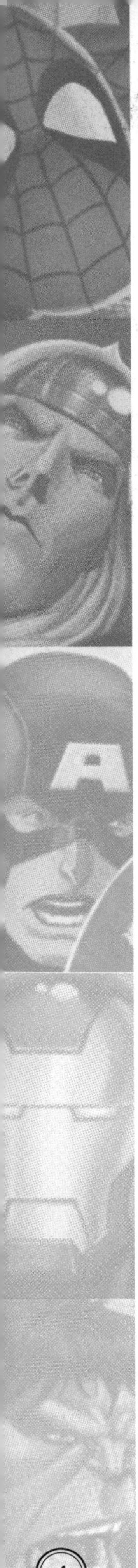

WELCOME TO THE MARVEL UNIVERSE

Within these pages you will learn about some of Marvel's greatest Super Heroes. Some characters you already know, like the Amazing Spider-Man, the Invincible Iron Man, the Mighty Thor, or the Incredible Hulk. But do you know about the futuristic cyborg Cable, the mutant Colossus, or the telekinetic Psylocke? How about Dr. Strange, Jubilee, or Iron Fist? These are just some of the 102 Super Heroes you will meet! From around the world to around the Galaxy; from mutant powers to magic and spells; from alien technology to amazing abilities, these are the heroes of the Marvel Universe!

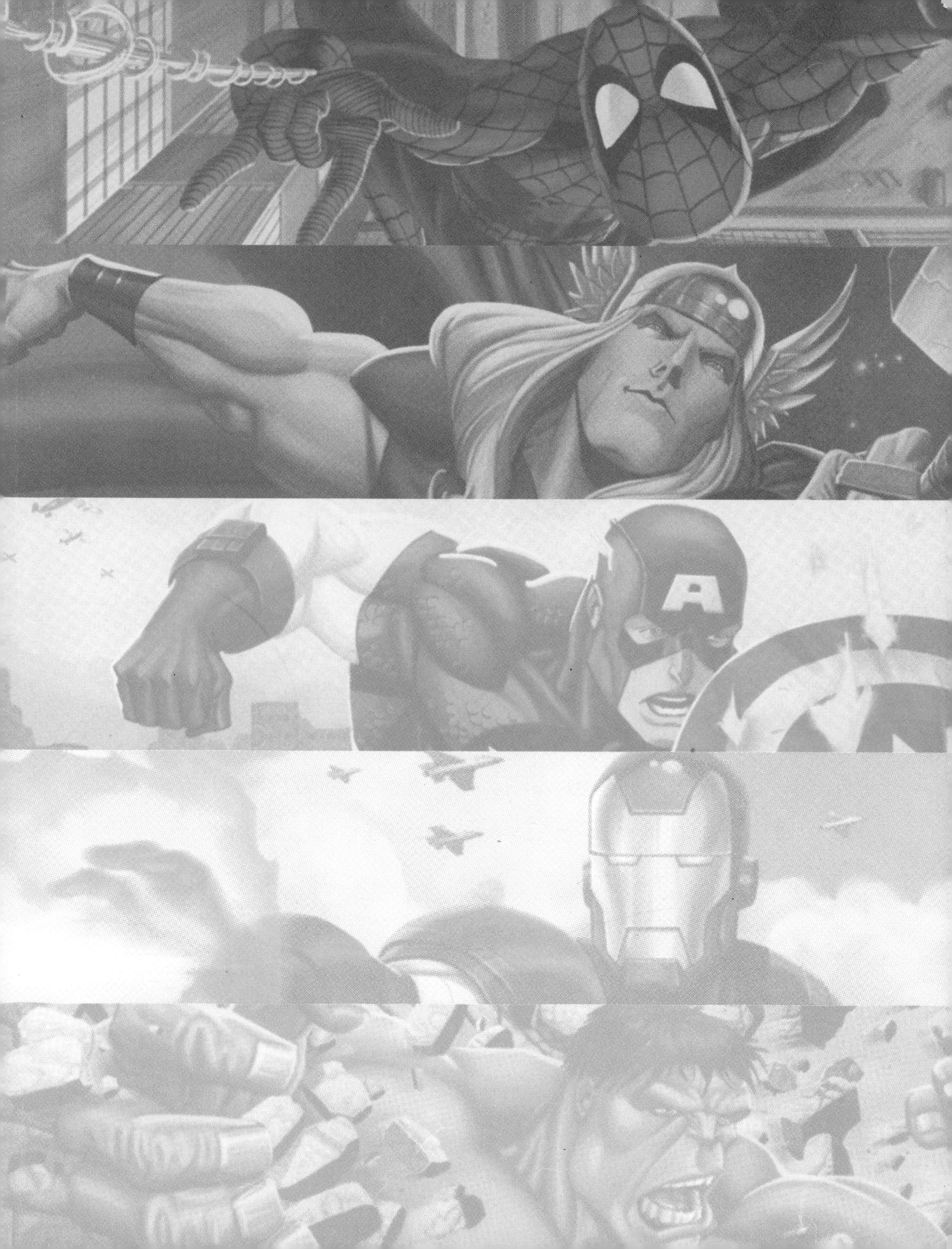

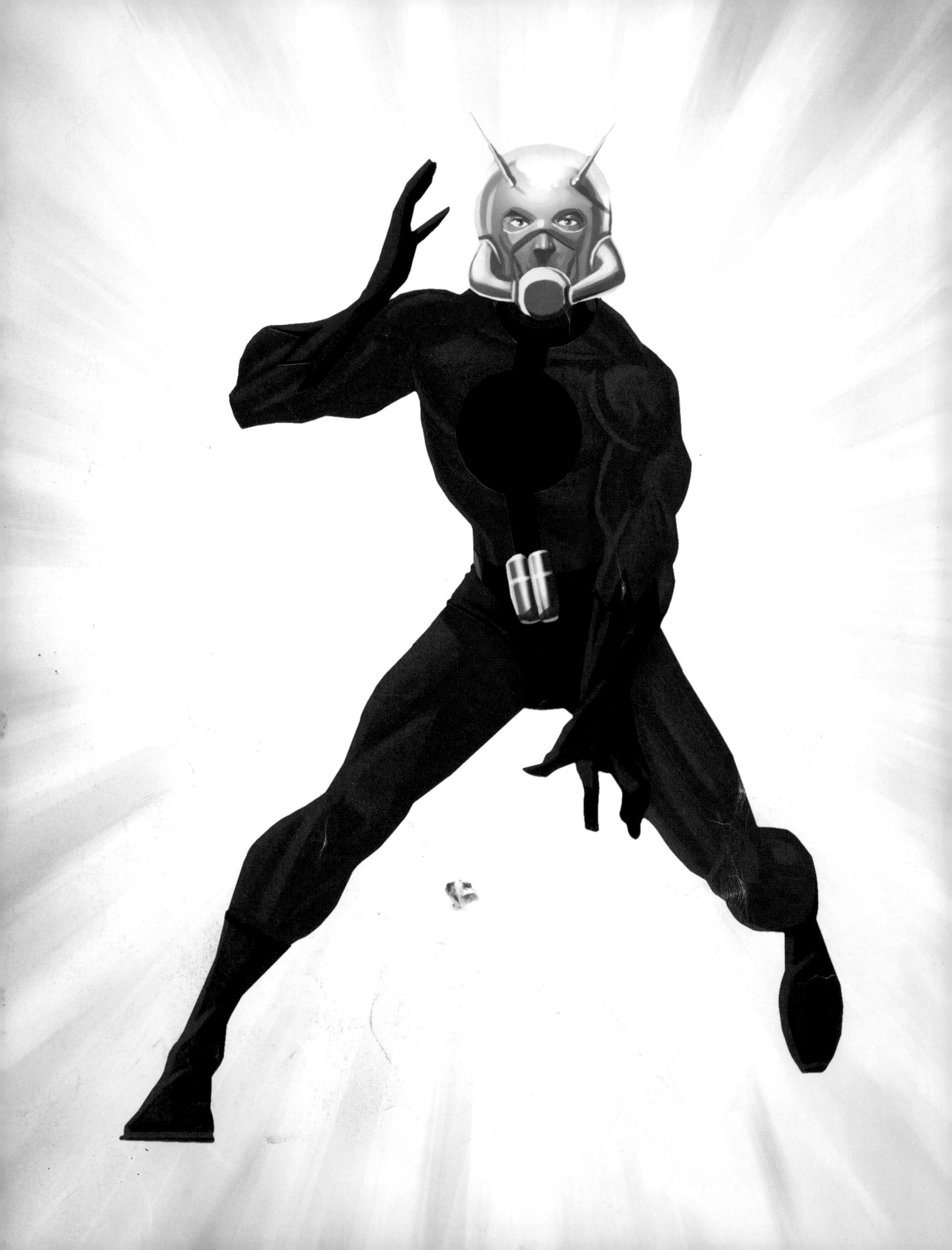

ANT-MAN

HENRY PYM is one of the world's greatest scientists. Henry discovered and harnessed a group of subatomic particles—which have become known as ***PYM PARTICLES***—that allowed him to shrink to the size of an ant or grow to over 100 feet. Taking the name Ant-Man, or Giant-Man, depending on his size, he began to fight crime, first by himself, and later with his wife, the Wasp, as a member of the Super Hero team, the Avengers.

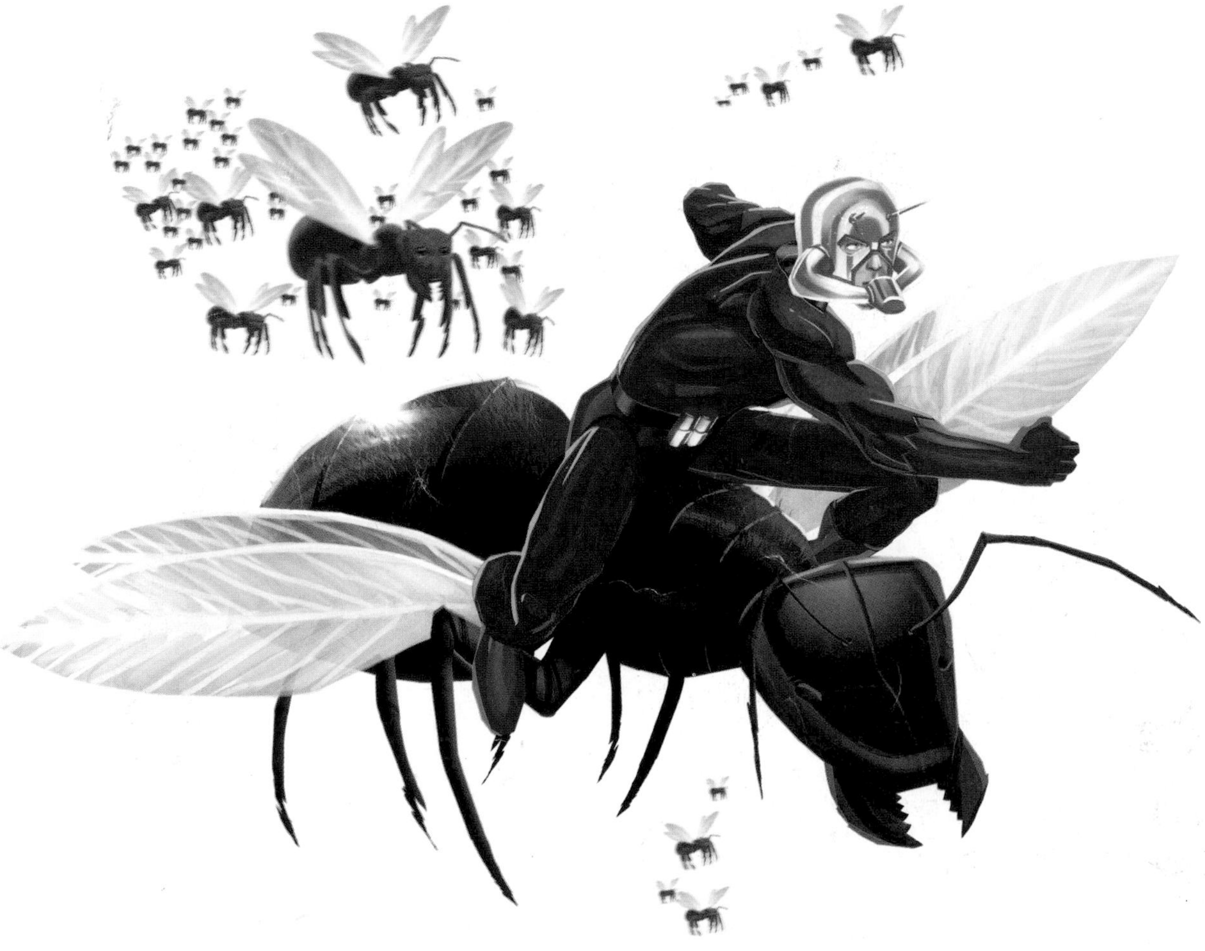

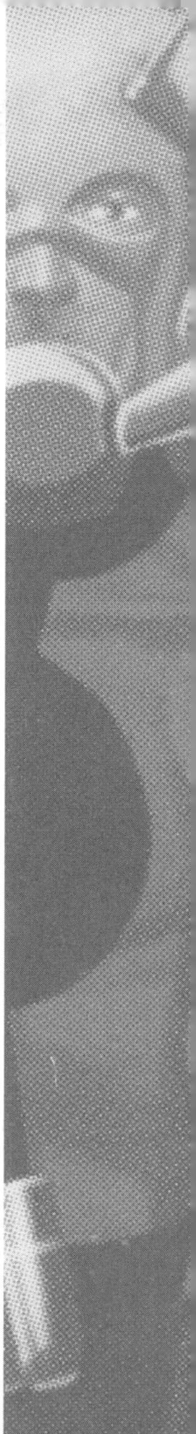

ANGEL

WARREN WORTHINGTON III seemed to be the luckiest kid on earth. He was smart, handsome, popular, and incredibly rich. But what Warren kept hidden from everyone was that he was a mutant.

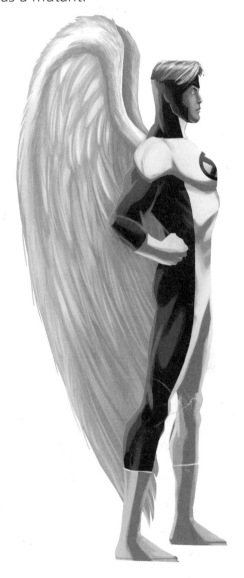

Professor X invited Warren to be one of the first students at his new school for mutants. As an X-Man, Warren can finally **SPREAD HIS WINGS** and help bring a message of peace between mutants and humans to the world.

AURORA

JEANNE-MARIE BEAUBIER didn't know she had a twin brother. Separated at birth, she was raised in a convent. As a young schoolteacher, she was mugged one night. Unfortunately for the muggers, that's when her mutant abilities kicked in. Wolverine saw the whole thing, and shocked Jeanne-Marie by explaining that she was a mutant.

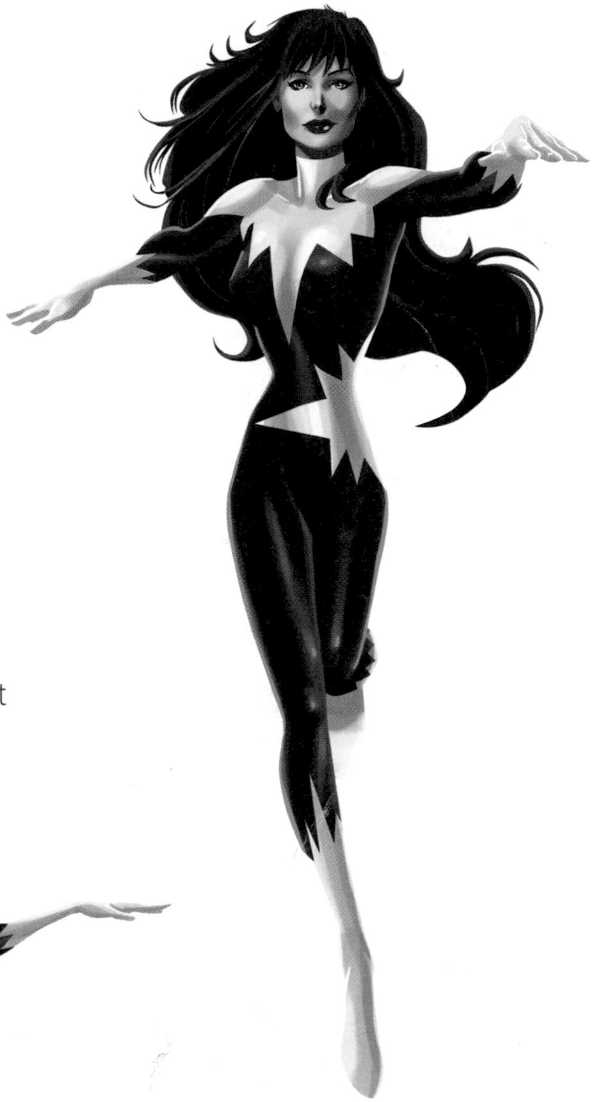

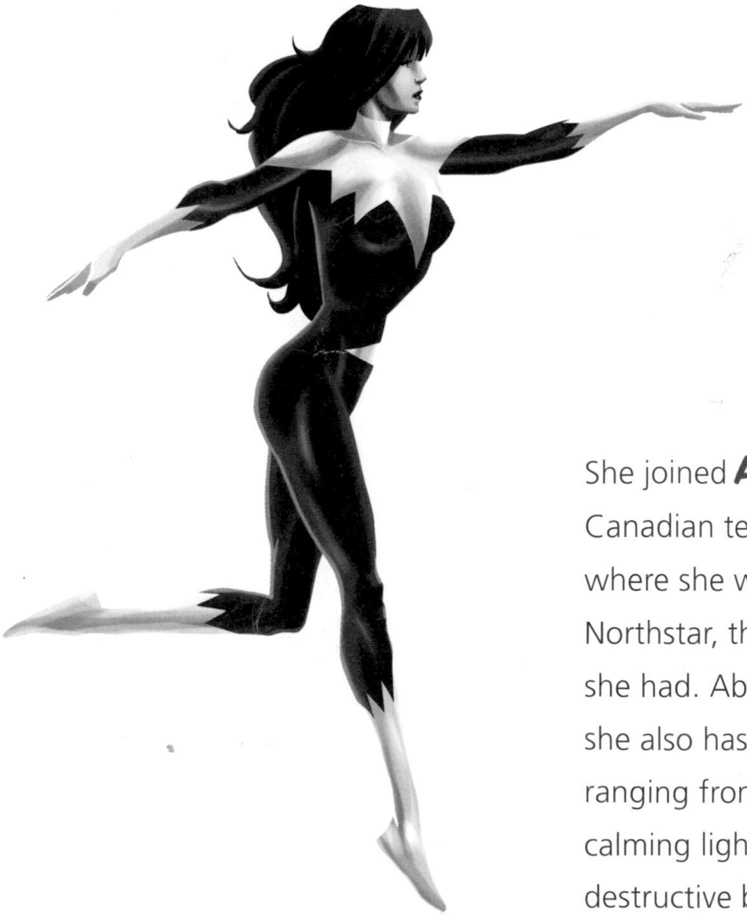

She joined **ALPHA FLIGHT,** a Canadian team of mutant heroes, where she was reunited with Northstar, the brother she never knew she had. Able to move at superspeed, she also has light-based powers—ranging from the ability to create a calming light to being able to fire destructive blasts.

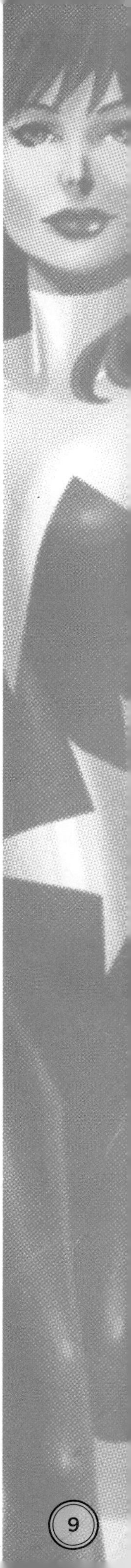

BALDER THE BRAVE

A MEMBER OF THE WARRIORS THREE, Thor's band of trusty companions, Balder Odinson is Thor's half-brother. Like all Asgardians, he is nearly immortal and extremely strong. He is also the **GOD OF LIGHT,** which means he can generate huge amounts of heat and light. With his straightforward Asgardian manner, you're never in the dark around Balder the Brave.

BANSHEE

WHEN PROFESSOR X

learned that a young Irish agent Sean Cassidy had special powers, he invited him to join his School for Gifted Mutants.

Named after the banshees of Irish legend, Banshee can do amazing things with **HIS VOICE:** knock people over, shatter solid objects, and even hypnotize them into doing his bidding. Here's one X-Man you maybe shouldn't listen to.

BEAST

HANK MCCOY always stood out. Not only was he a football star, with the agility of a cat, but he was absolutely brilliant. But what really catches people's eye when they meet him is his **BRIGHT BLUE FUR.** Hank resembles his longtime nickname: The Beast. Even though he stands out among normal humans, the Beast can relax and be himself with the X-Men. One of the very first X-Men, the Beast knows there's at least one place where he fits in.

BETA RAY BILL

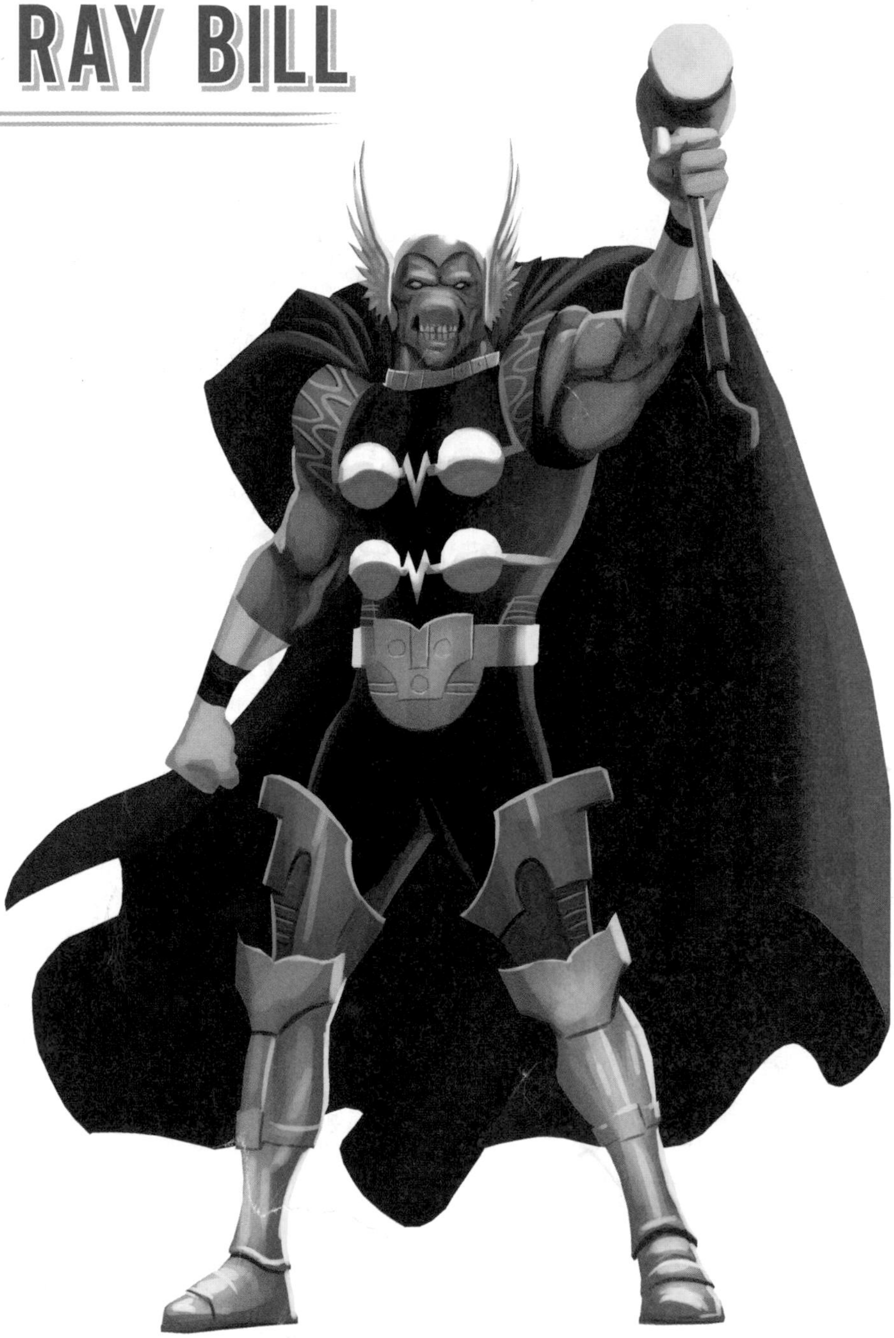

YOU CAN'T JUDGE A BOOK by its cover. Beta Ray Bill doesn't only look like an alien cyborg (which he is), he looks like a monster (which he's not). Instead, he's so noble, he was the first being other than Thor to ever be worthy of wielding the mighty hammer **MJOLNIR.** Nearly as powerful, fast, and tough as the God of Thunder, Beta Ray Bill has turned out to be the best alien invader you could ever hope for.

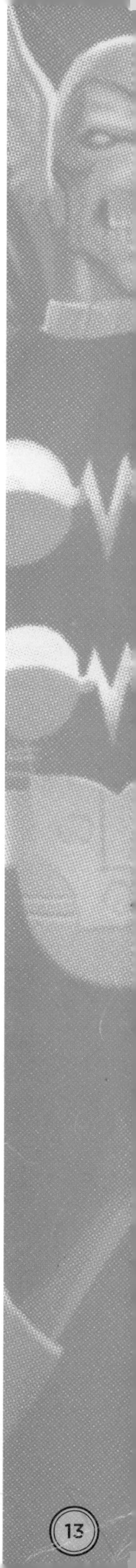

BISHOP

A MUTANT POLICE OFFICER from the future, Lucas Bishop traveled back in time to meet the X-Men, heroes from (to him) the far distant past. Bishop's mutant power is the ability to **ABSORB ANY ENERGY** and redirect it—so if someone's foolish enough to shoot at him, no matter how powerful the weapon, he can turn it right around and back at the shooter.

BLACK CAT

SOME PEOPLE have all the luck. And then there's Felicia Hardy. A cat burglar, she ran into the Amazing Spider-Man during a bank heist. The experience changed her, as she fell in love with the wall-crawler, and decided to go straight.

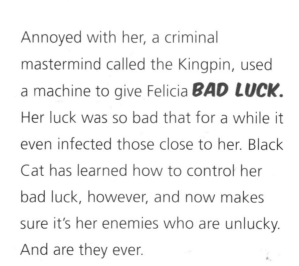

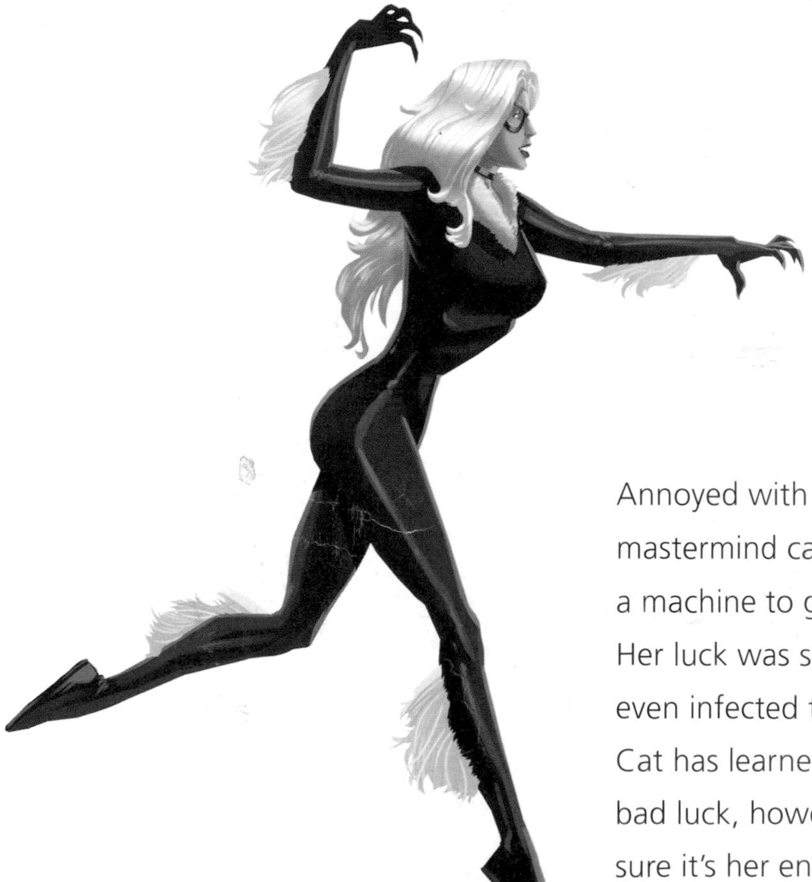

Annoyed with her, a criminal mastermind called the Kingpin, used a machine to give Felicia **BAD LUCK.** Her luck was so bad that for a while it even infected those close to her. Black Cat has learned how to control her bad luck, however, and now makes sure it's her enemies who are unlucky. And are they ever.

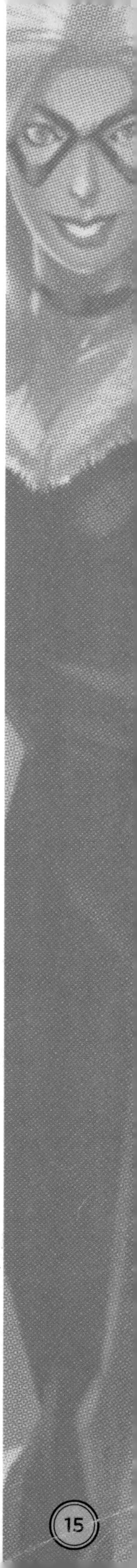

BLACK PANTHER

AS HEIR TO THE THRONE in the African country Wakanda, T'Challa was allowed to eat a special heart-shaped herb which would give him superpowers. T'Challa's senses became extra powerful, so he could hear, smell, and see much better than ordinary humans. He also became far **STRONGER, FASTER, AND TOUGHER.** Although he is the protector of his home country, T'Challa often comes to the United States as the Super Hero the Black Panther, where he is a member of the Mighty Avengers.

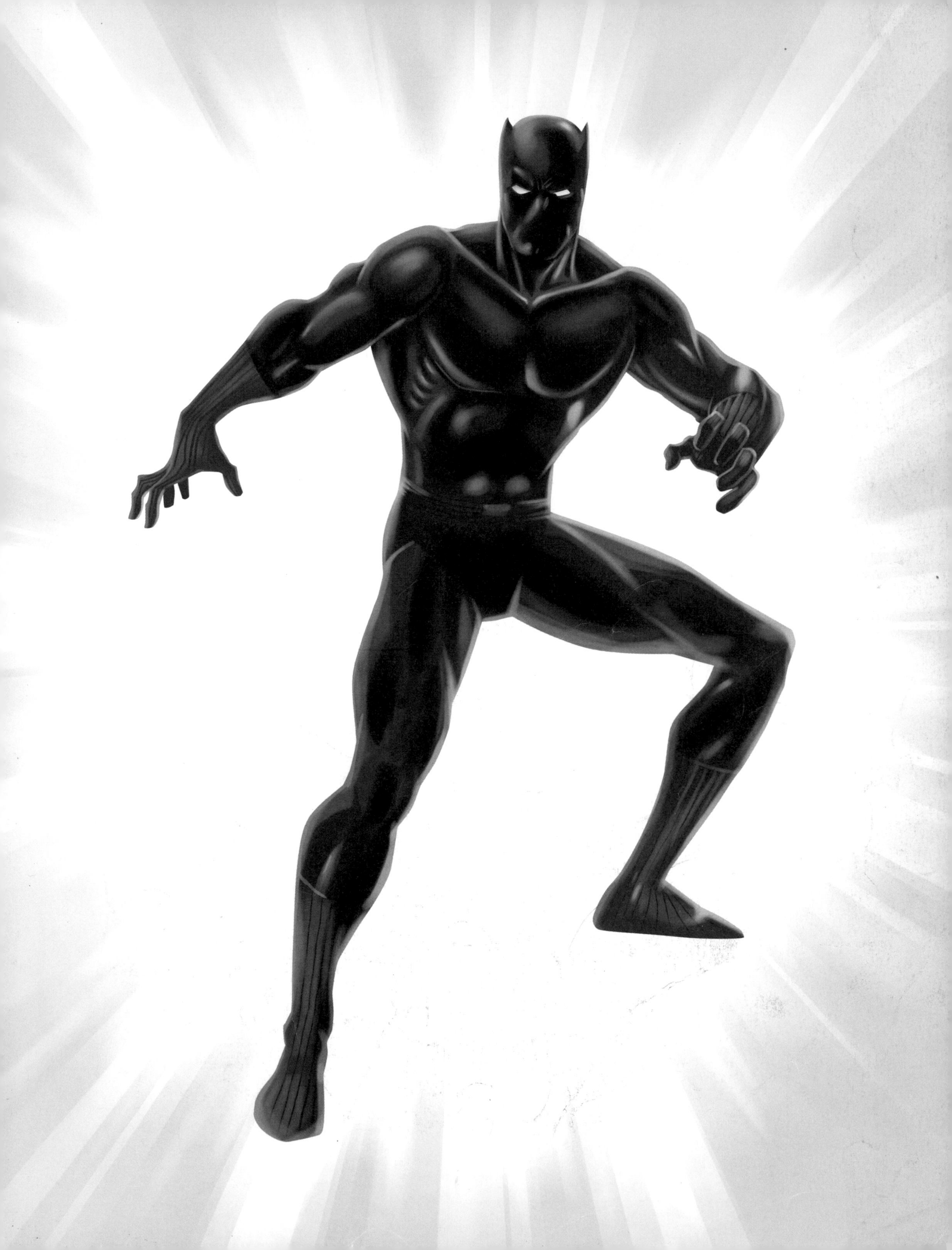

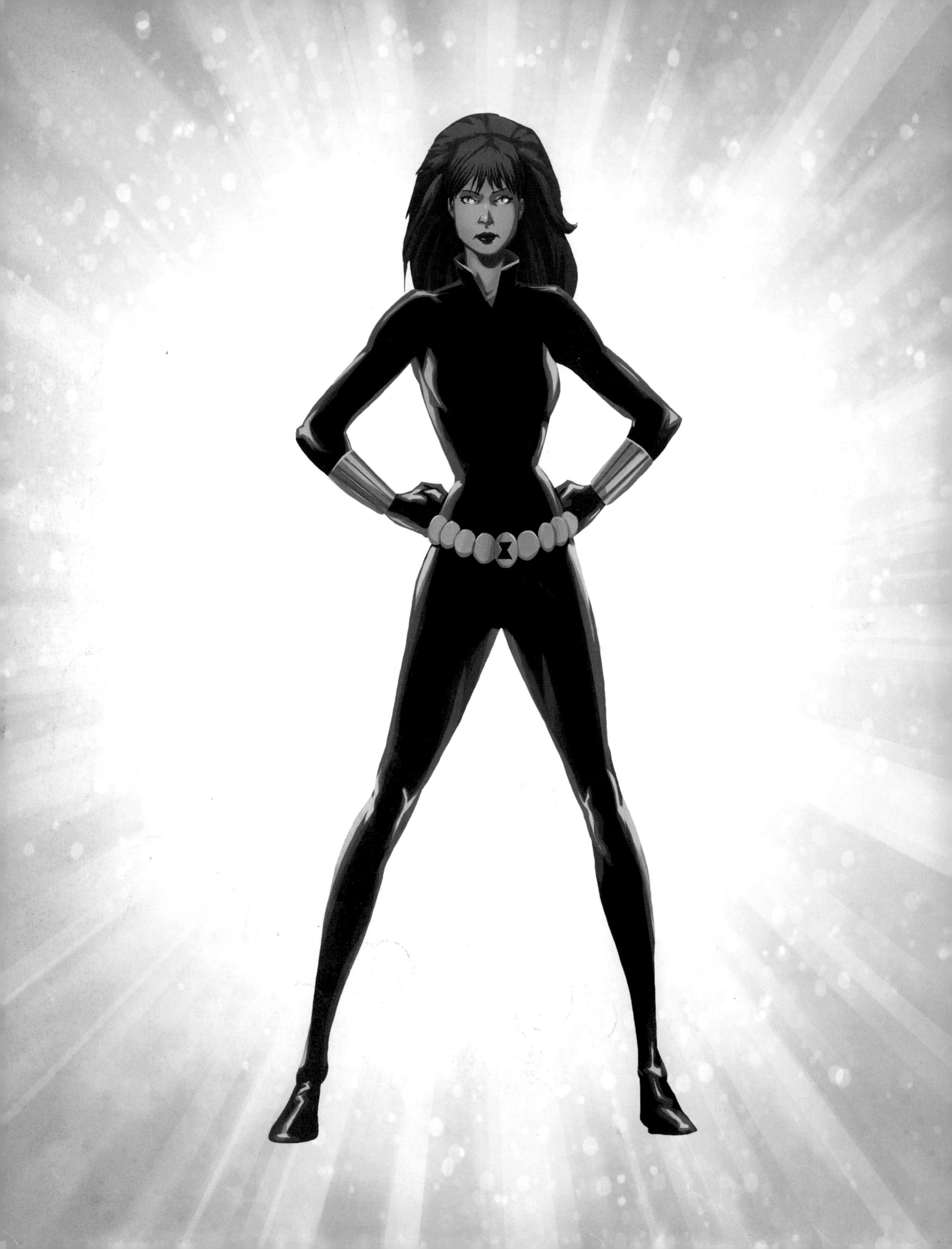

BLACK WIDOW

NATASHA ROMANOFF was born in Russia and raised to be a super spy. Due to her intense training, Natasha developed **EXTRAORDINARY STRENGTH, SPEED, AND STAMINA.** Betrayed by the spy school that raised her—they kidnapped her brother—so she fled to the United States in search of help. When she broke into a S.H.I.E.L.D. base, she met Nick Fury. Seeing some good in her, he decided to help her rescue her brother – with some help from the Mighty Avengers of course. Now a part of the team, S.H.I.E.L.D. agent Black Widow fights alongside her fellow Super Heroes to help those in need.

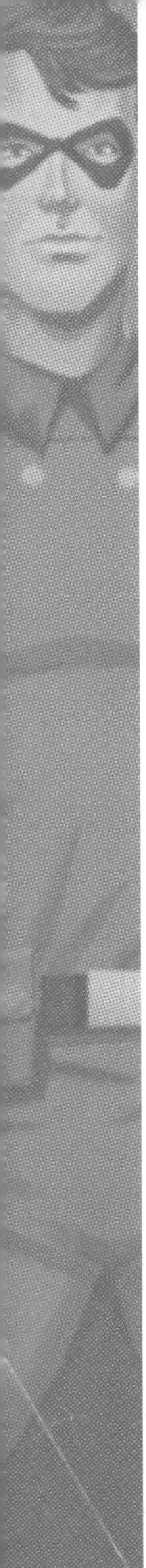

BUCKY BARNES

JAMES BARNES was born an orphan in Indiana. Adopted by the U.S. Army, he unofficially became the camp's mascot. Given the nickname 'Bucky', he eventually donned a uniform and took on the life of an Army man. That's when he met a clumsy soldier by the name of Steve Rodgers and soon they became best friends. One day, Bucky discovered that Steve was actually the Super-Soldier, Captain America! ***TOGETHER, THEY SERVED THEIR COUNTRY AND FOUGHT ALONGSIDE ONE ANOTHER IN WWII.***

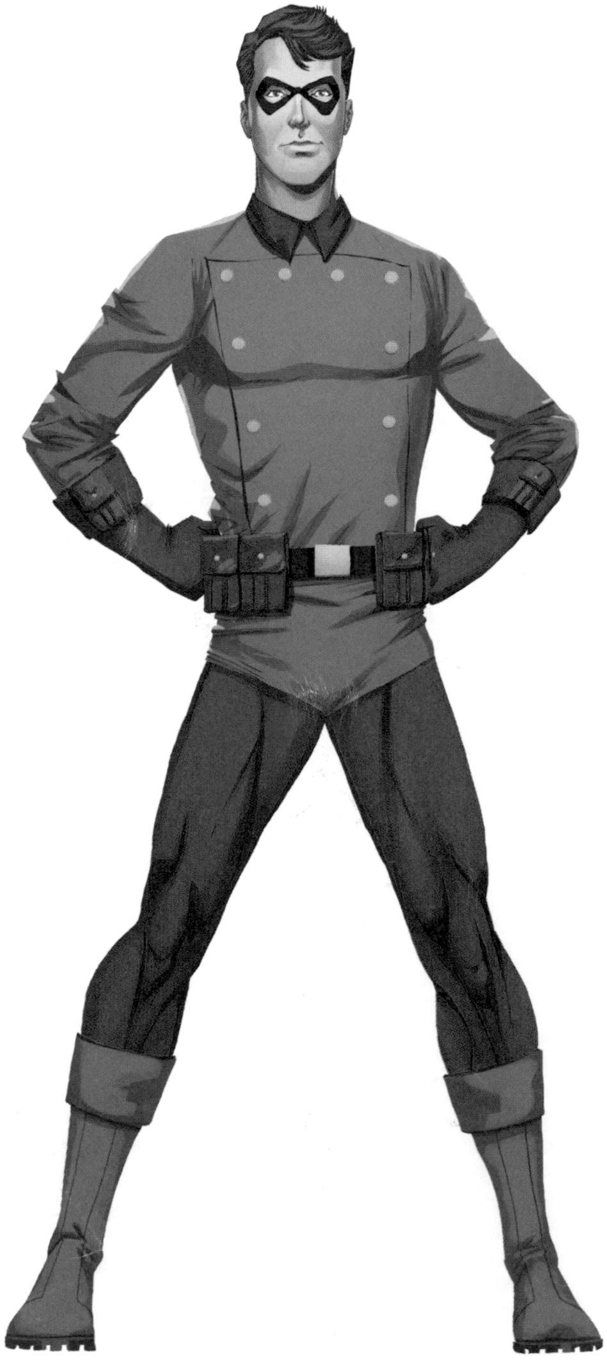

CABLE

THE SON OF THE X-MAN CYCLOPS, Nathan Summers was infected with a virus as a baby. Cyclops believed that the only way to save his son was to send him into the future, where they might have a cure for his illness.

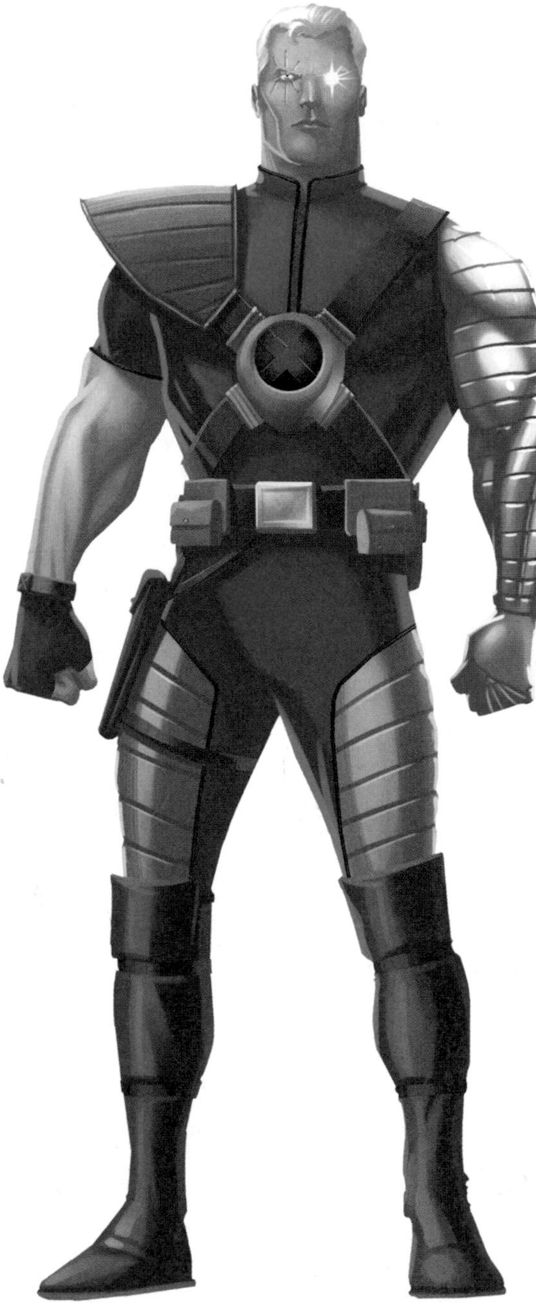

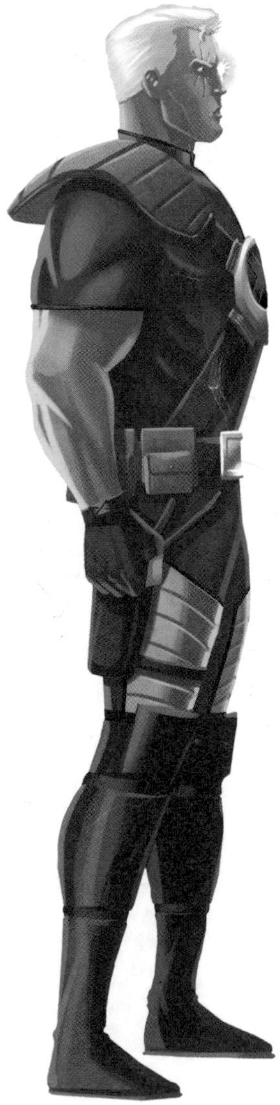

Nathan returned to our time as an adult called Cable—coming back to help save the world. **ONE OF THE STRONGEST TELEPATHS IN THE WORLD,** Cable is also a cyborg—a result of the cure he received—making him strong in body and mind.

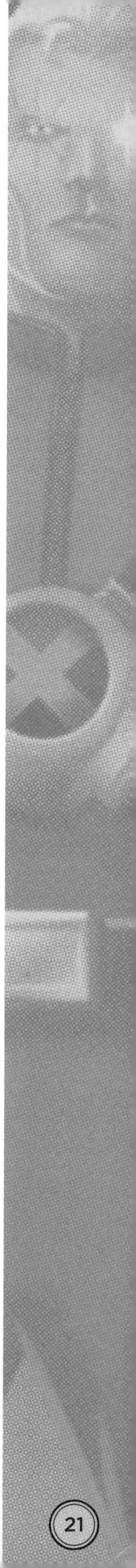

CANNONBALL

THE OLDEST SON of a large Kentucky family, Samuel "Sam" Guthrie discovered his mutant ability—the power to fly at high speeds while surrounded by a force field—when he was trapped in a coal mine.

Once a member of the X-Men, Sam, now known as Cannonball, also founded **THE NEW MUTANTS.** Cannonball has even learned how to expand his force field to cover others, making him a great guy to have around when a mountain is collapsing on top of you.

CAPTAIN AMERICA

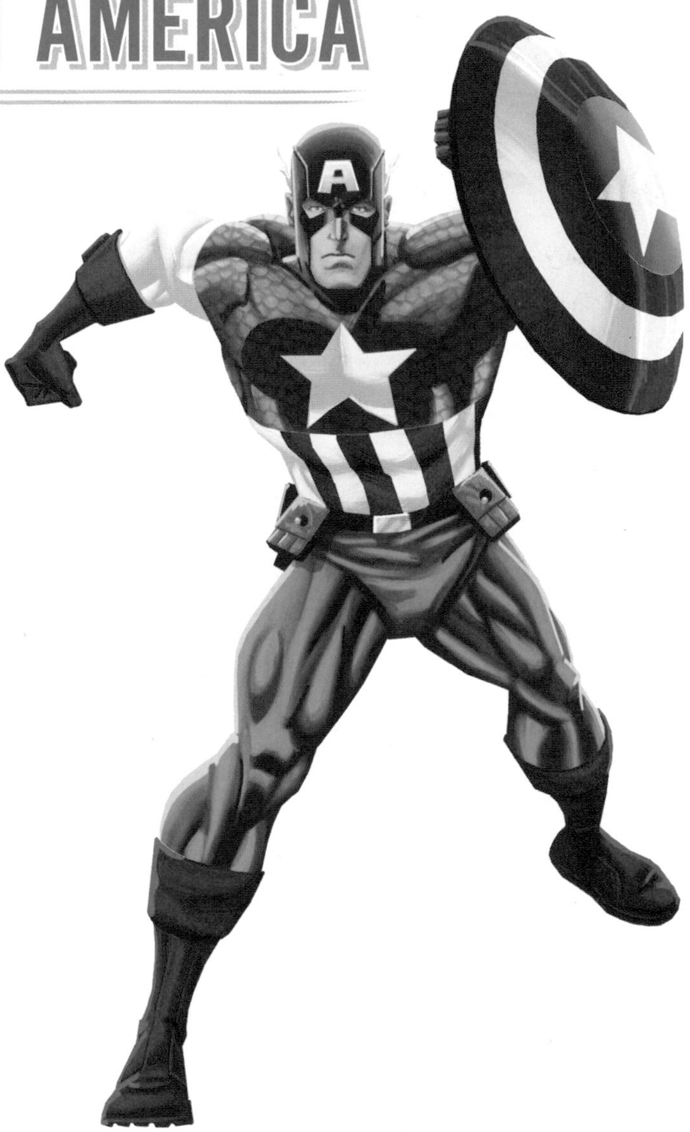

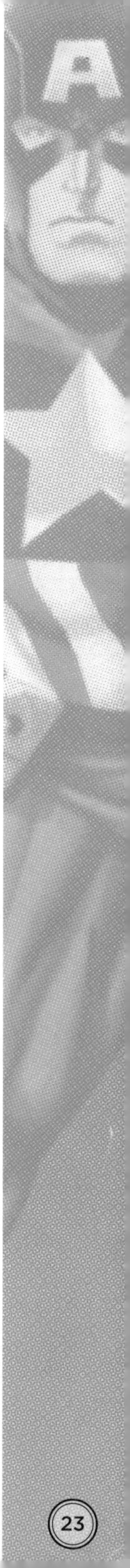

THERE IS NOTHING Steve Rogers wanted more than to fight for his country. Unfortunately, Steve was very, very small and very, very weak—much too small and weak to get into the Army. He tried again and again . . . and again and again they said no. Finally, a mysterious doctor noticed Steve and offered him a chance to take part in a top secret experiment. After being given the ***SUPER-SOLDIER SERUM,*** Steve suddenly grew very tall and very, very powerful. Now he was much stronger and faster than other men. Armed with his indestructible shield, a fantastic military mind, and a code of morals as strong as his body, he became Captain America: a true hero who comes to the rescue whenever his country needs him.

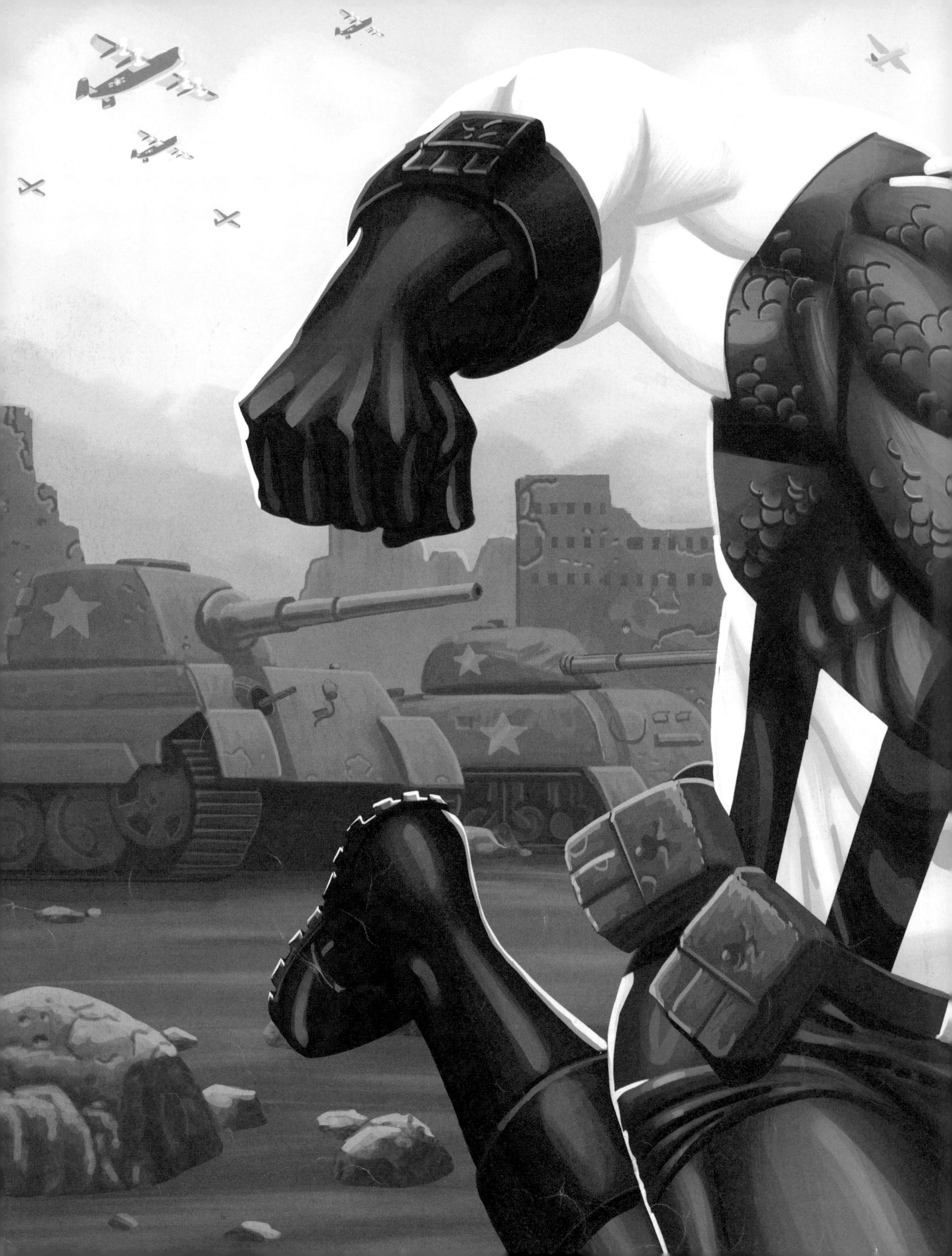

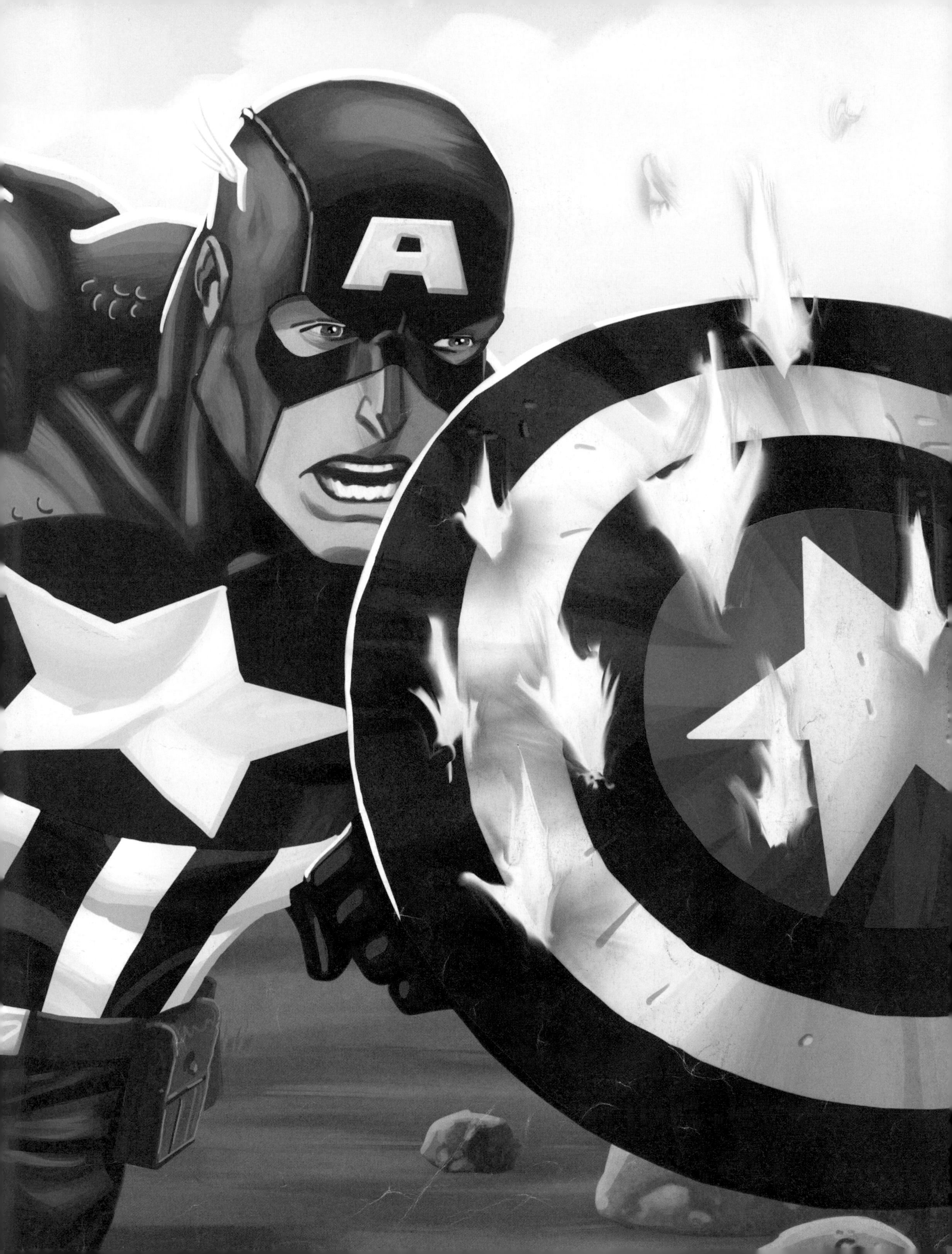

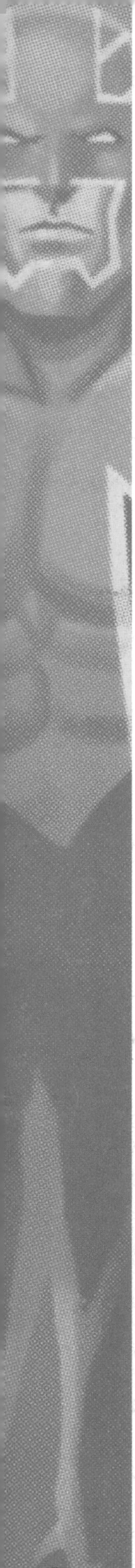

CAPTAIN BRITAIN

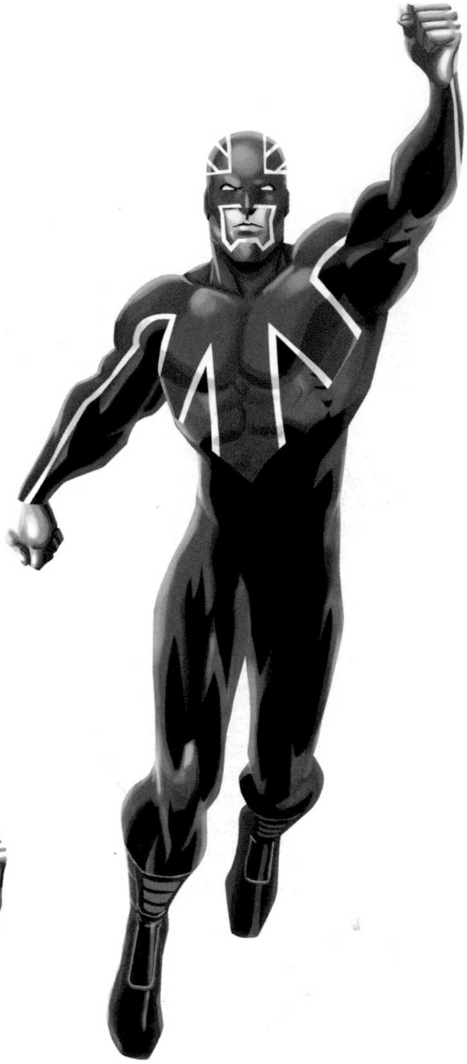

BORN IN A SMALL British town, Brian Braddock was a shy young man—the only thing he enjoyed, other than the company of his parents and siblings, was science. When the laboratory at which he was working was attacked, Brian jumped on his motorcycle to get help as fast as he could.

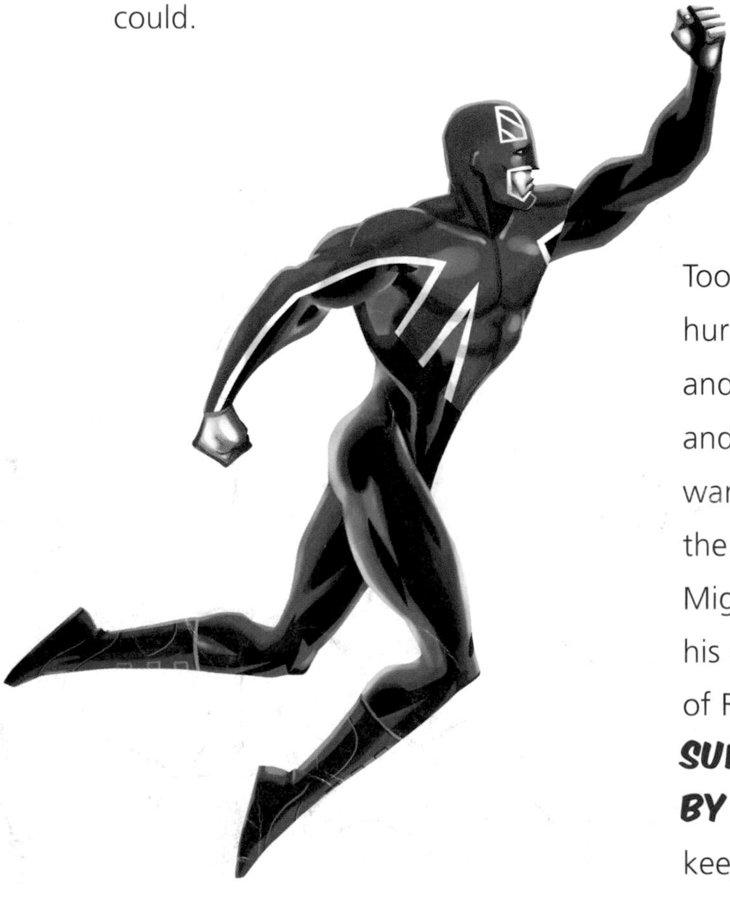

Too fast, in fact: he was in such a hurry he crashed his bike. Merlyn and his daughter, Roma, appeared and offered Brian a choice: if he wanted to live, he could have either the Amulet of Right or the Sword of Might. Feeling a sword wasn't really his cup of tea, Brian chose the Amulet of Right. **SUPERSTRONG, WITH SUPERSPEED AND PROTECTED BY A FORCEFIELD,** Captain Britain keeps all of England safe.

CAPTAIN MAR-VELL

SURE, THE ALIEN RACE known as the Kree are perhaps Earth's most dangerous enemy. But that doesn't mean they're all bad, right? Sent to Earth as a spy, the Kree known as Mar-Vell found himself using his superstrength **TO SAVE HUMANS** in need of help again and again. Realizing humans were not an enemy, Mar-Vell stayed on Earth to help those who need it—a job made easier by his ability to predict the very near future.

CLOAK

BECAUSE HE COULDN'T SPEAK without stuttering, Tyrone Johnson had trouble revealing his true feelings to others. Running away to New York City, he quickly became friends with another runaway named Tandy Bowen. Afraid Tandy was falling in with bad people, Tyrone tagged along—which is how he and Tandy both ended up having an experimental drug tested on them. The drug brought out Tyrone's mutant abilities. **NOW NAMED FOR THE MAGICAL GARMENTS HE WEARS,** Cloak can disappear or pull people and things into his cloak and make them go away . . . forever.

COLOSSUS

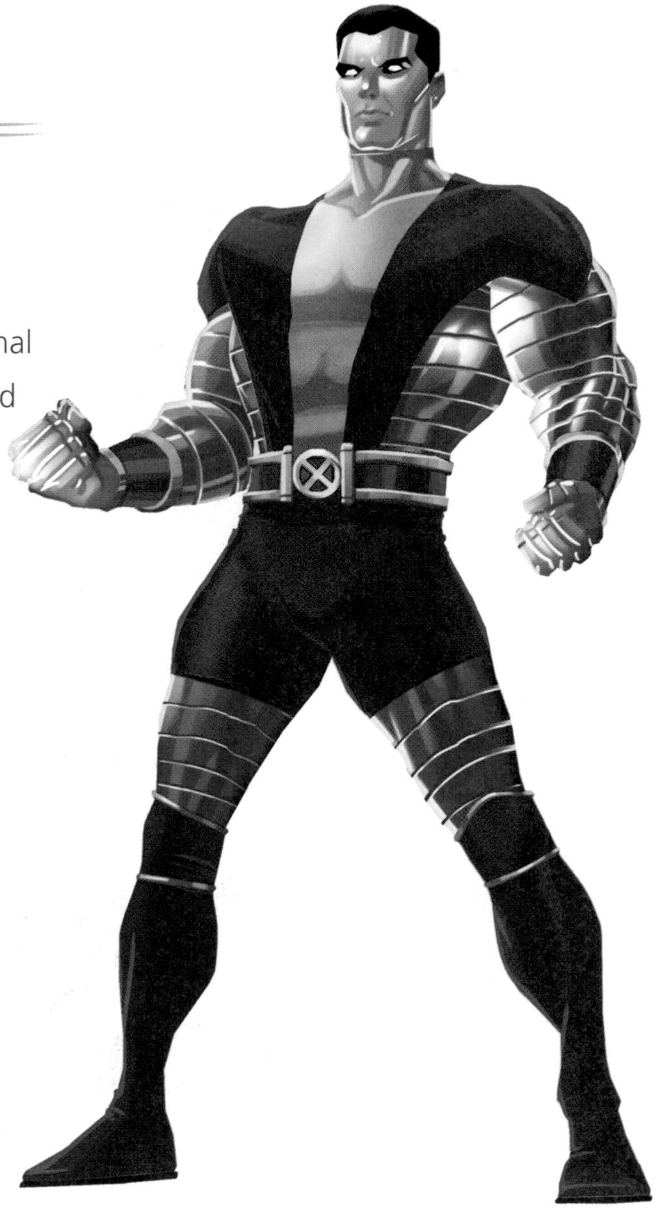

BORN A FARM BOY in Russia, Piotr Rasputin was asked by Professor X to help rescue the original X-Men from Krakoa, the living island that had trapped them.

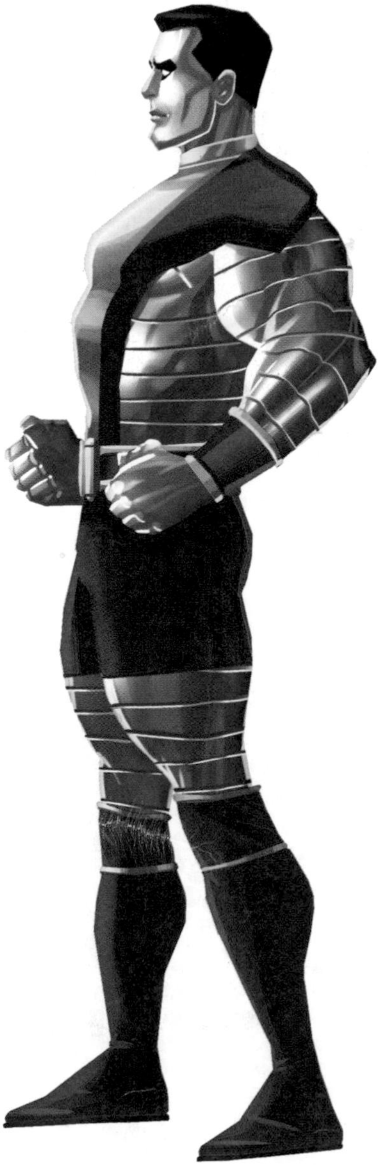

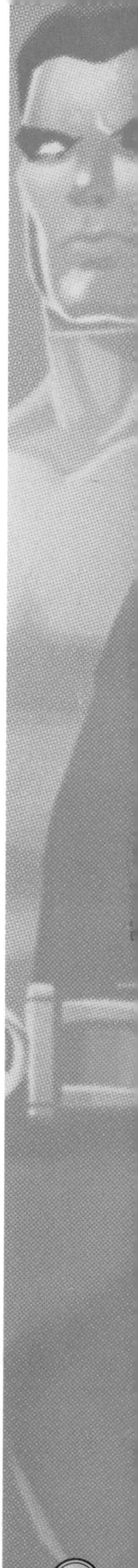

Piotr's ability to ***TURN INTO STEEL,*** making him invulnerable and superstrong, came in handy, and earned him the nickname Colossus. After helping to save the day, Colossus decided to stay in the United States as a member of the X-Men.

CYCLOPS

PROFESSOR X'S right-hand man, Scott Summers, is usually the leader of the X-Men when the professor is not around. Scott's mutant ability is to shoot **SOLAR ENERGY BEAMS** out of his eyes. The beams are powerful enough to instantly destroy a mountain. Given the name Cyclops, Scott can't control these beams, so he has to always wear a special ruby quartz visor which blocks them. A natural leader, Scott wants there to be peace between humans and mutants more than anything, despite the way humans have often treated him and his fellow mutants.

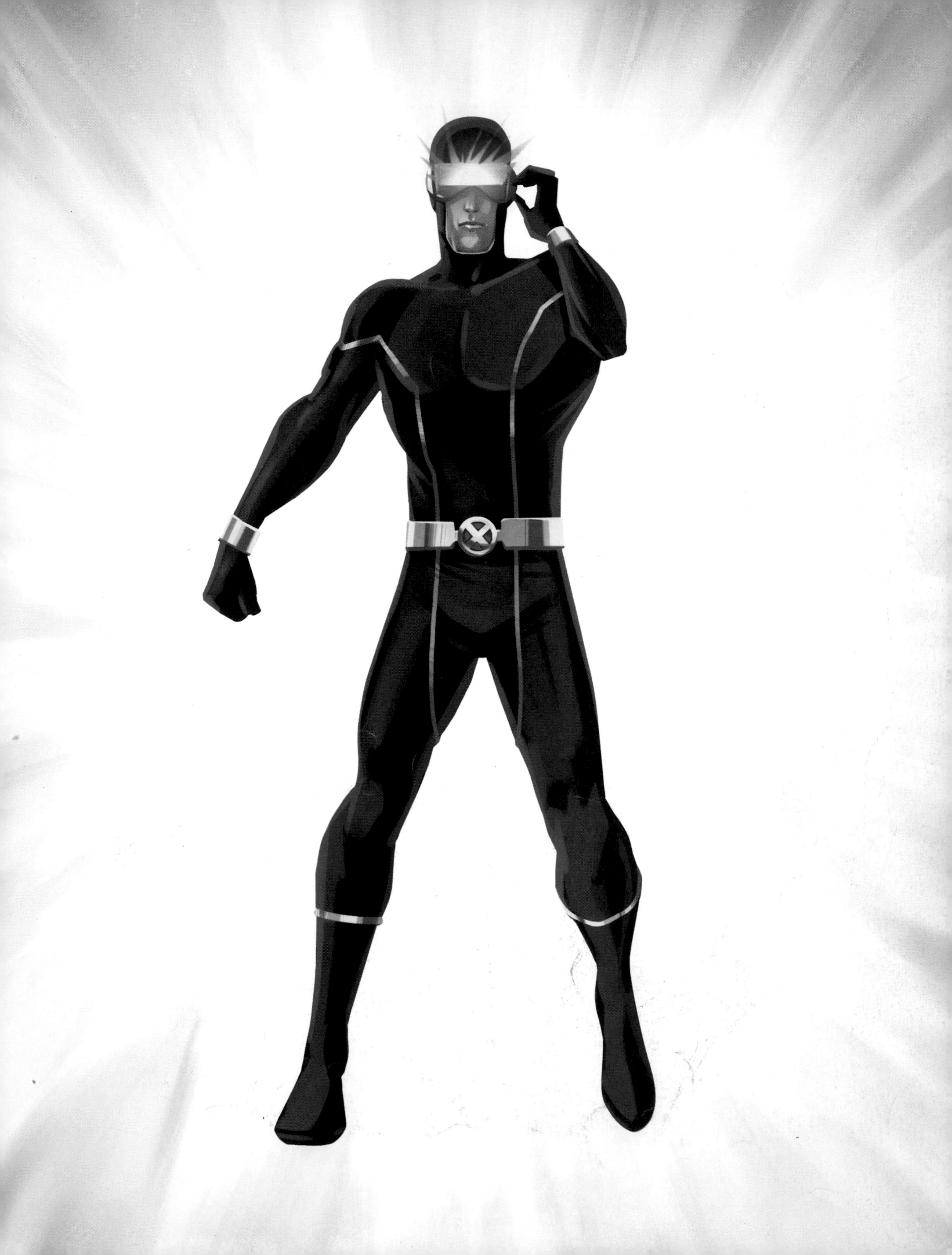

DAGGER

TANDY BOWEN ran away to New York City, where she was lucky enough to make friends with Tyrone Johnson. Too trusting of strangers, Tandy was shocked to find herself injected with an experimental drug. The drug brought out her mutant powers. Now known as Dagger, for her ability to create and throw **DAGGERS MADE OF PURE LIGHT,** she and Cloak try to make sure no one other mutant has to go through what they went through.

DAREDEVIL

AS A YOUNG BOY, Matt Murdock was hit by a truck carrying dangerous radioactive materials. The chemicals spilled on Matt, causing him to lose his sight—but they also made all his other senses much, much stronger. He could now hear a person's heartbeat and read just by feeling the tiny bumps of ink on a page—or follow a person down a busy street by their smell. His extra strong senses enable Matt to move almost as though he has superpowers. While Matt is a lawyer during the day, at night he fights crime as Daredevil, **THE MAN WITHOUT FEAR.**

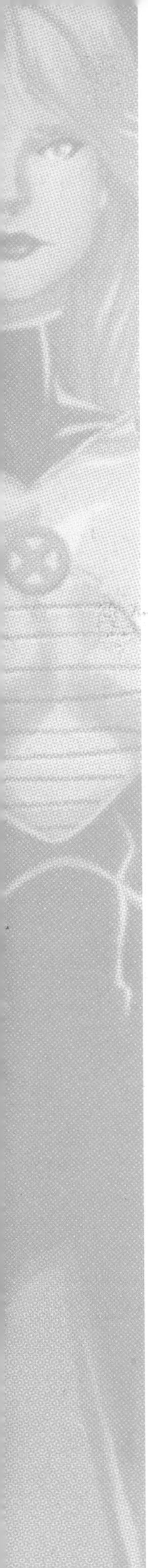

DAZZLER

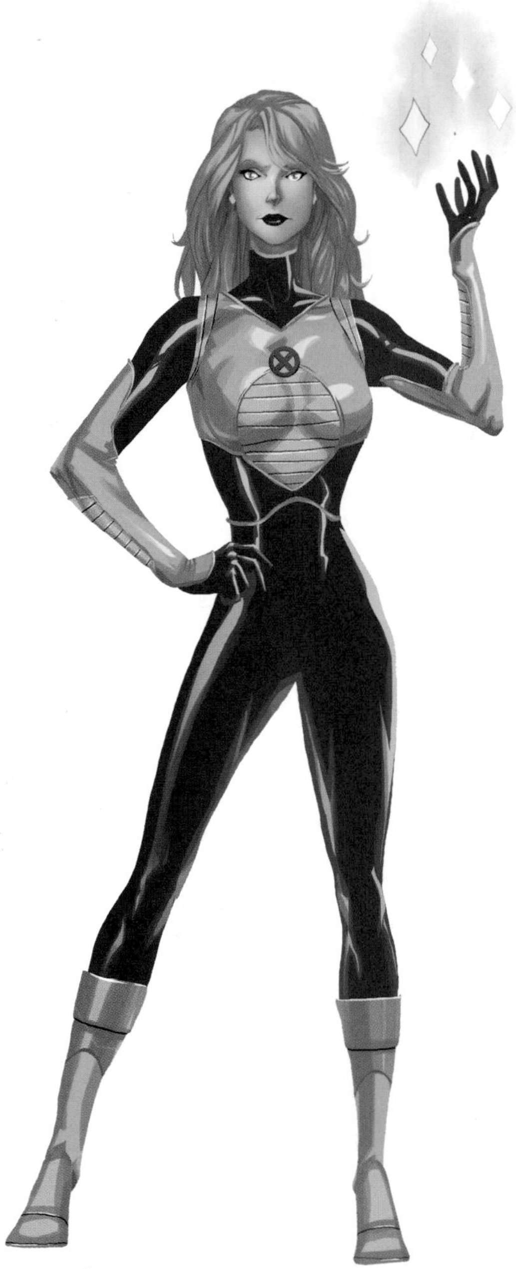

ALTHOUGH HER FATHER didn't approve of the idea, Alison Blaire wanted to be an entertainer. Her mutant ability to turn sound into light made her a star—but it also drew other kinds of attention.

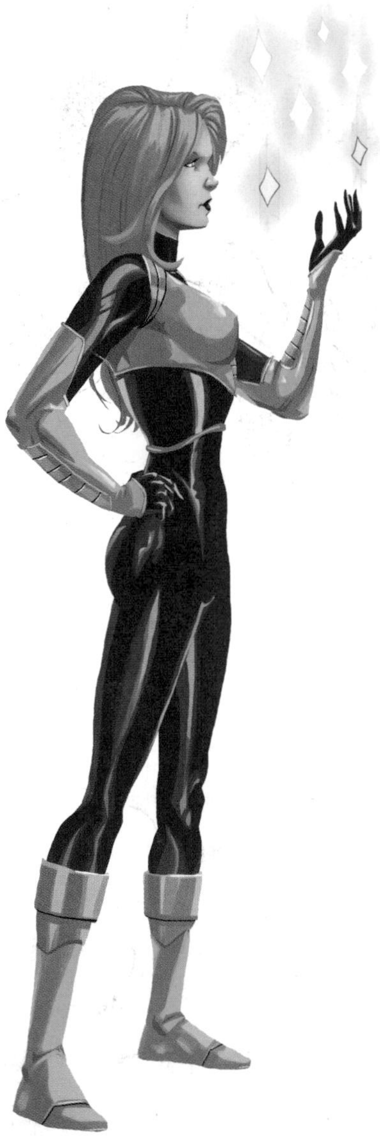

Both the X-Men and an evil group of mutants wanted her to join them. Alison just wanted to sing. But forced to choose, she joined the X-Men and decided to use her powers for good as Dazzler, the **HUMAN LASER-LIGHT SHOW.**

DR. STRANGE

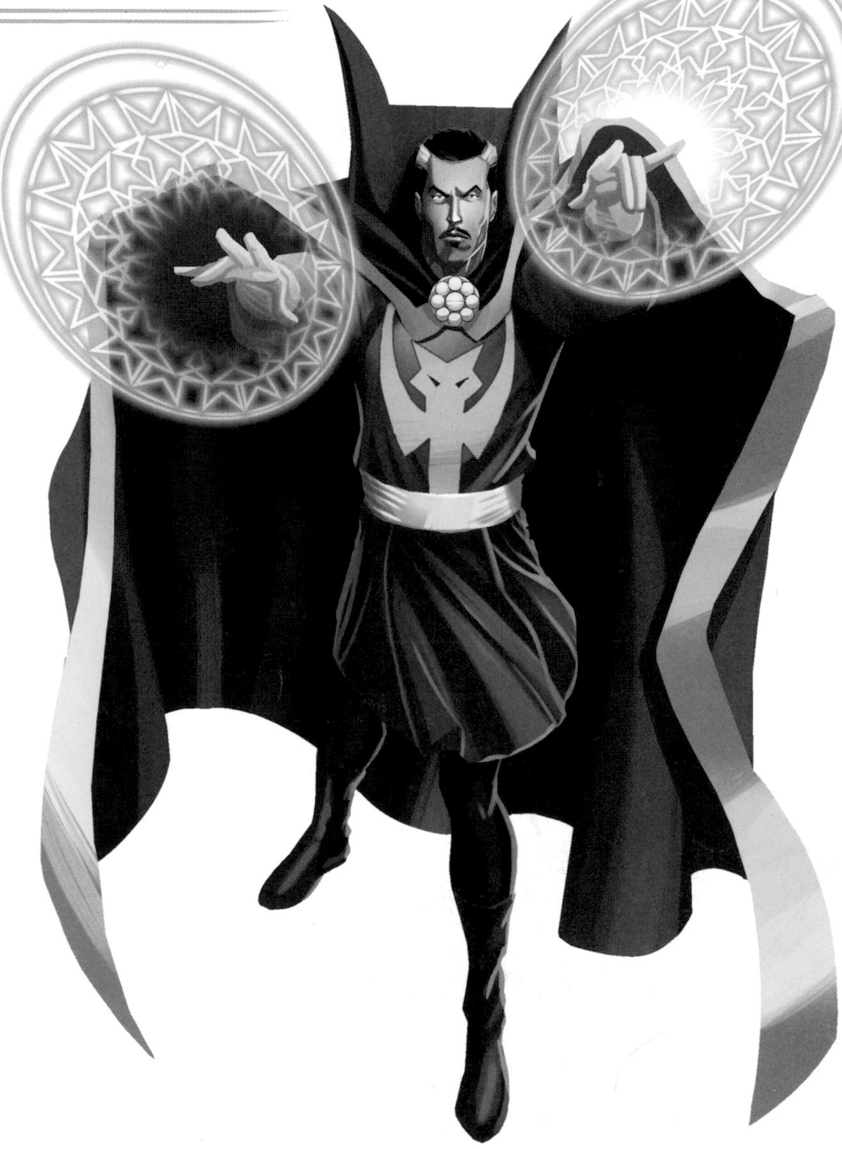

STEPHEN STRANGE was always an unusual child. Mystics predicted he would be the next great sorcerer, and sent dangers his way to try to stop him when he was still young. Even though Stephen didn't realize what was happening, he always managed to easily defend himself. Later, he became a famous doctor. But then his hands were injured in an accident. Refusing to believe he couldn't be a surgeon anymore, Stephen tried and tried to find a cure—and ended up discovering his natural talent for magic instead. He studied the **MYSTICAL ARTS** and now fights for good as the sorcerer Dr. Strange.

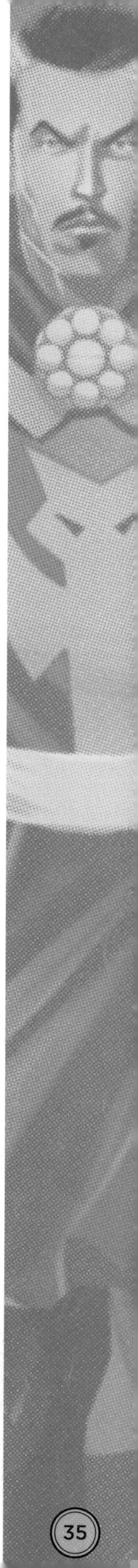

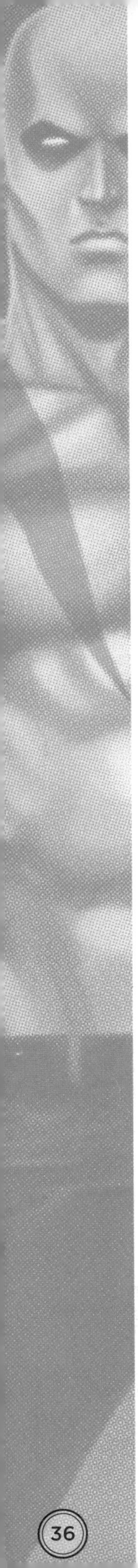

DRAX

SOMETIMES you're just in the wrong place at the wrong time. Arthur Douglas just happened to see Thanos—so the Super Villain destroyed Arthur's car, with Arthur still inside. Fortunately, the father and grandfather of Thanos—Mentor and Chronos—stepped in. They created a new body for Arthur. Dubbed Drax the Destroyer, he uses his new **SUPERSTRONG AND INDESTRUCTIBLE FORM** to fight Thanos and other evildoers as a member of the Guardians of the Galaxy.

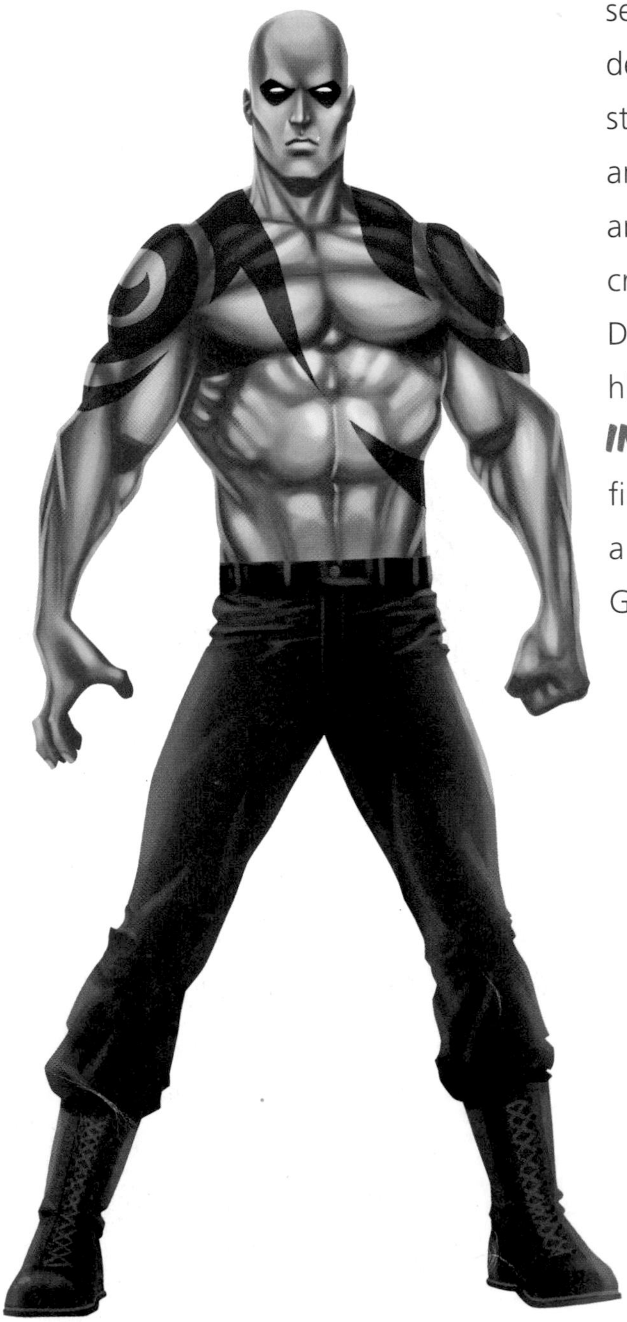

ECHO

MAYA LOPEZ never lets anything stop her. Born deaf, she has developed the amazing ability to perfectly **DUPLICATE SOMEONE ELSE'S MOVEMENTS.** This has enabled her to become a concert pianist, a top ballerina . . . and a Super Hero.

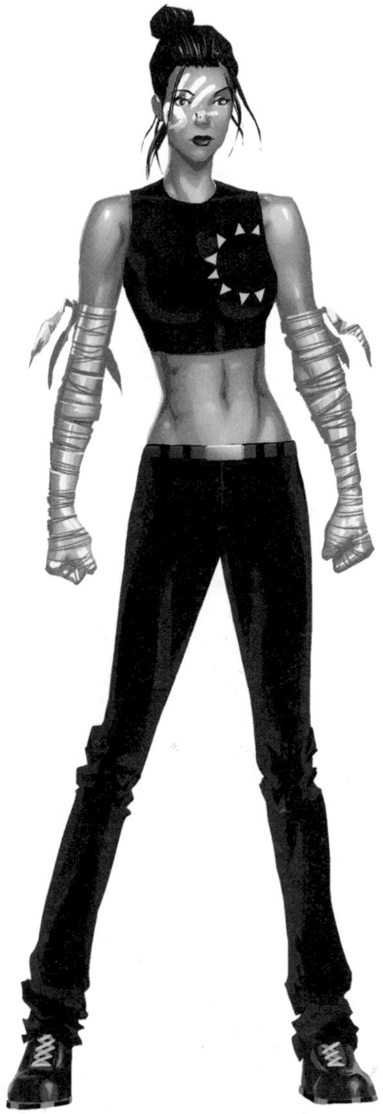

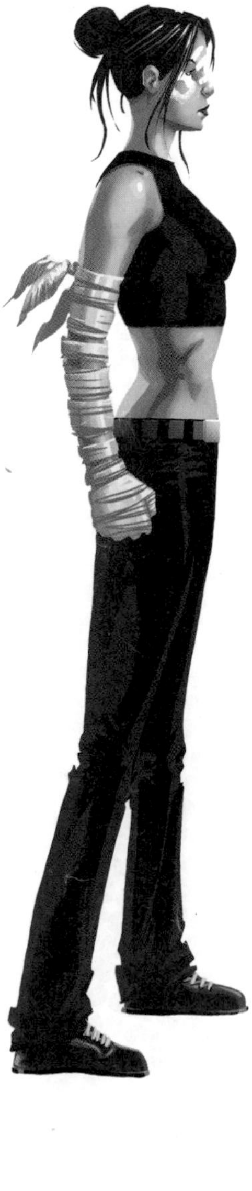

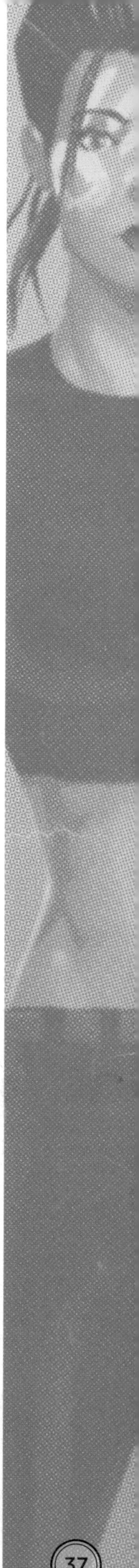

Maya was raised by her father's best friend, the criminal known as the Kingpin, who told her Daredevil had killed her father. **DETERMINED TO GET REVENGE,** she studied Daredevil, learning all his moves and becoming his equal as a fighter. But she soon learned that the Kingpin had actually killed her father. She switched sides to fight evil as a member of the New Avengers.

ELEKTRA

THE DAUGHTER of an assassinated Greek diplomat, Elektra Natchios swore revenge on those who took his life. She traveled to Japan, where she became one of the most **SKILLED NINJAS** in the world. Sent to the United States on a mission, she was reunited with Daredevil, her former boyfriend. Realizing her true nature, Elektra vowed to fight on the side of the angels.

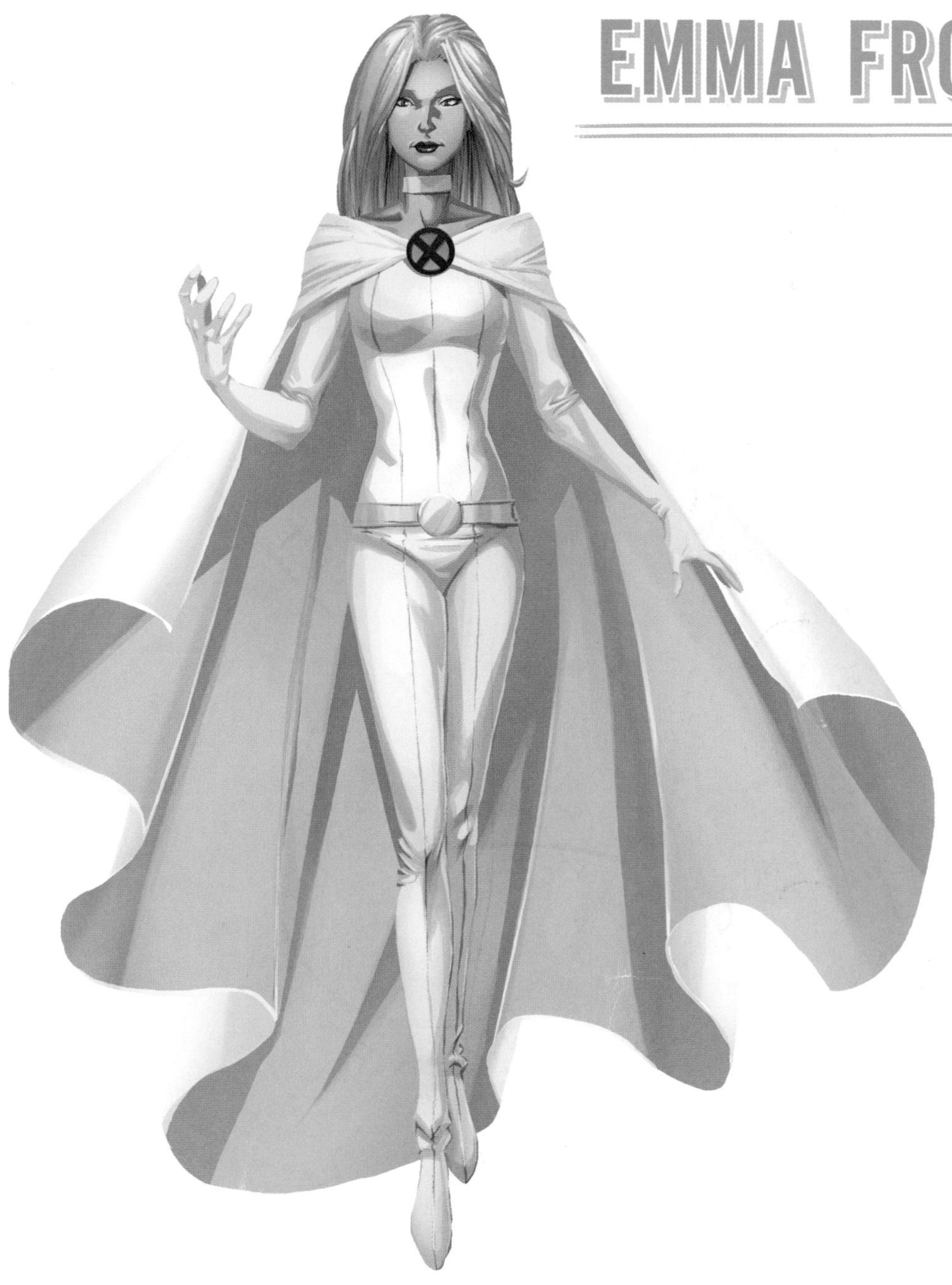

EMMA FROST

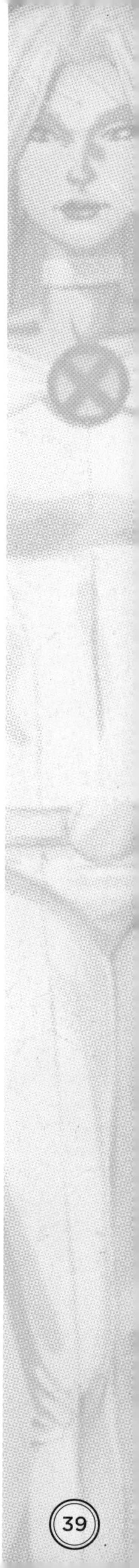

ONE OF THE MOST POWERFUL TELEPATHS in the world, Emma Frost was never sure who or what she really was. Drifting from place to place and job to job, she always seemed to be searching for something. Emma became one of the X-Men's greatest enemies. But the patient and generous example set by Professor X made her choose the right path, and she became a proud member of the X-Men.

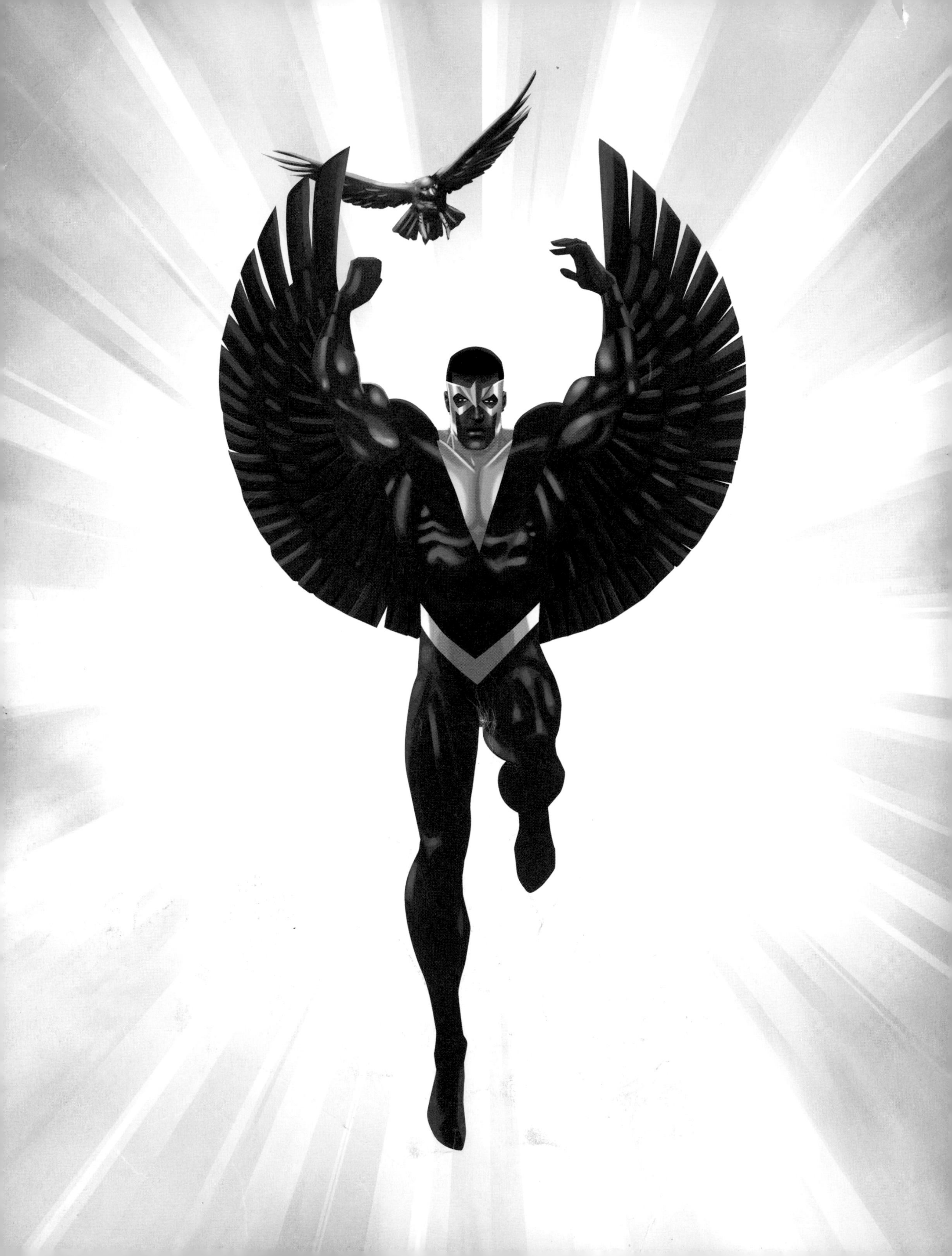

FALCON

SAM WILSON LOVED BIRDS so much, he had the biggest pigeon coop in Harlem. A plane crash stranded him on a Caribbean island, where he ran into the Red Skull. Hoping to gain his loyalty, the Red Skull used the Cosmic Cube to give Sam the **ABILITY TO COMMUNICATE WITH BIRDS.** When Captain America showed up, Sam quickly realized which side he wanted to be on. Together they defeated the Red Skull. Now, with a suit designed by the Black Panther, and the ability to see through the eyes of his trained falcon, Red Wing, Falcon can not only talk with the birds, he can fly with them, too.

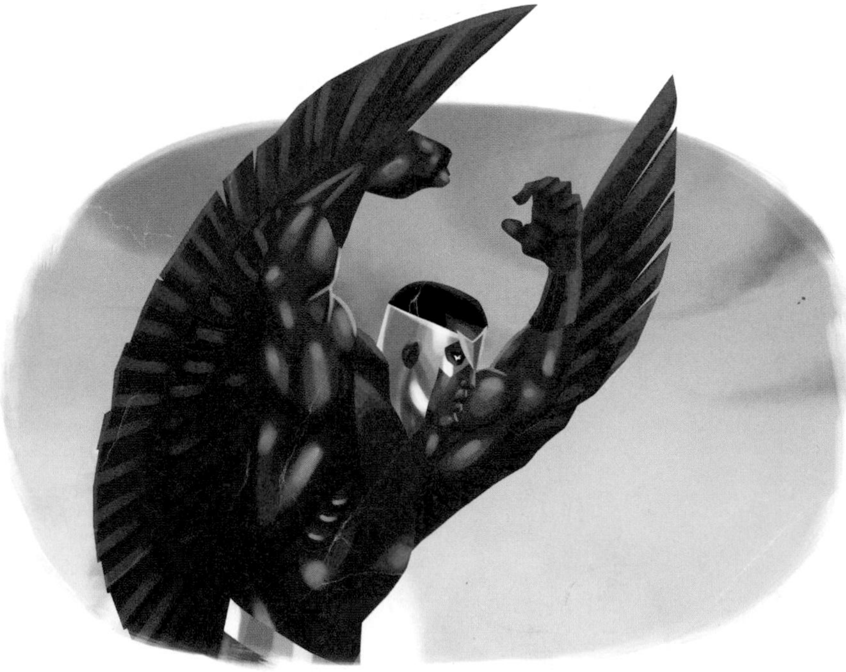

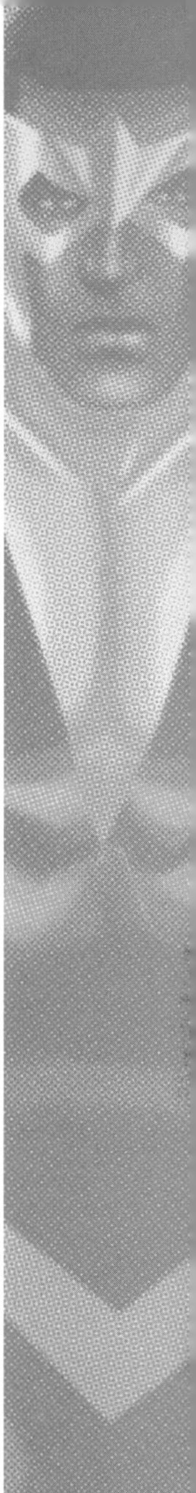

FANDRAL

THERE ARE SOME who claim that he's the original Robin Hood. Others think he's the smoothest warrior in all of Asgard. Something everyone agrees on: this member of the Warriors Three is one of Thor's best friends and most trusted allies. Like all Asgardians, he's superstrong and has superspeed, but Fandral **IS ALSO UNUSUALLY GIFTED WITH HIS SWORD.**

FIRELORD

BORN ON THE PLANET XANDAR in the Andromeda Galaxy, Pyreus Kril was a starship captain unlucky enough to run into Galactus, the devourer of planets. Agreeing to serve as Galactus's herald if he'd spare Pyreus's friends, Pyreus became Firelord.

Now possessed with **THE POWER OF A MINIATURE SUN,** Firelord is superstrong and can fly—even through space—as well as shoot fire. His blasts can burn through any known substance, other than adamantium or Captain America's shield.

FIRESTAR

ANGELICA JONES'S father wanted the best for her. So when her mutant abilities kicked in, he wanted to send her to a special school to help her get them under control. Eventually Angelica—now calling herself Firestar—joined the Avengers. Now she uses **HER POWER OVER ENERGY WAVES**—firing both energy and heat bursts—disrupting electronics, as well as the ability to fly, in the service of good.

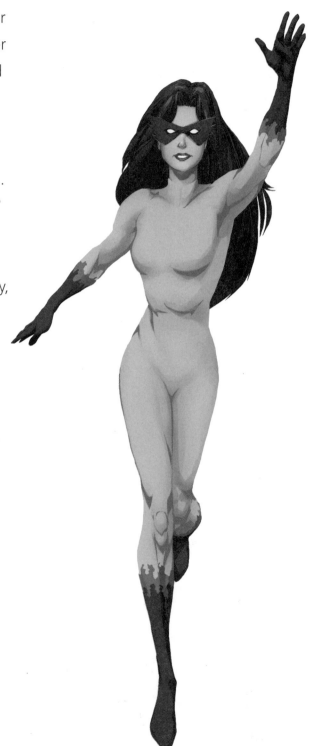

GAMBIT

FEW OF THE X-MEN trusted Gambit at first—maybe because New Orleans native Remy LeBeau had been a professional thief from the time he was just a little kid. After saving the life of an injured Storm, Remy was brought to the X-Men and slowly earned their trust. Gambit can take the little bit of energy in anything and make it much larger—and more dangerous. He can also make playing cards—his favorite weapon—as sharp as a **RAZOR BLADE AND EXPLODE LIKE A GRENADE.** His Bo staff is powerful enough to take down a house.

GAMORA

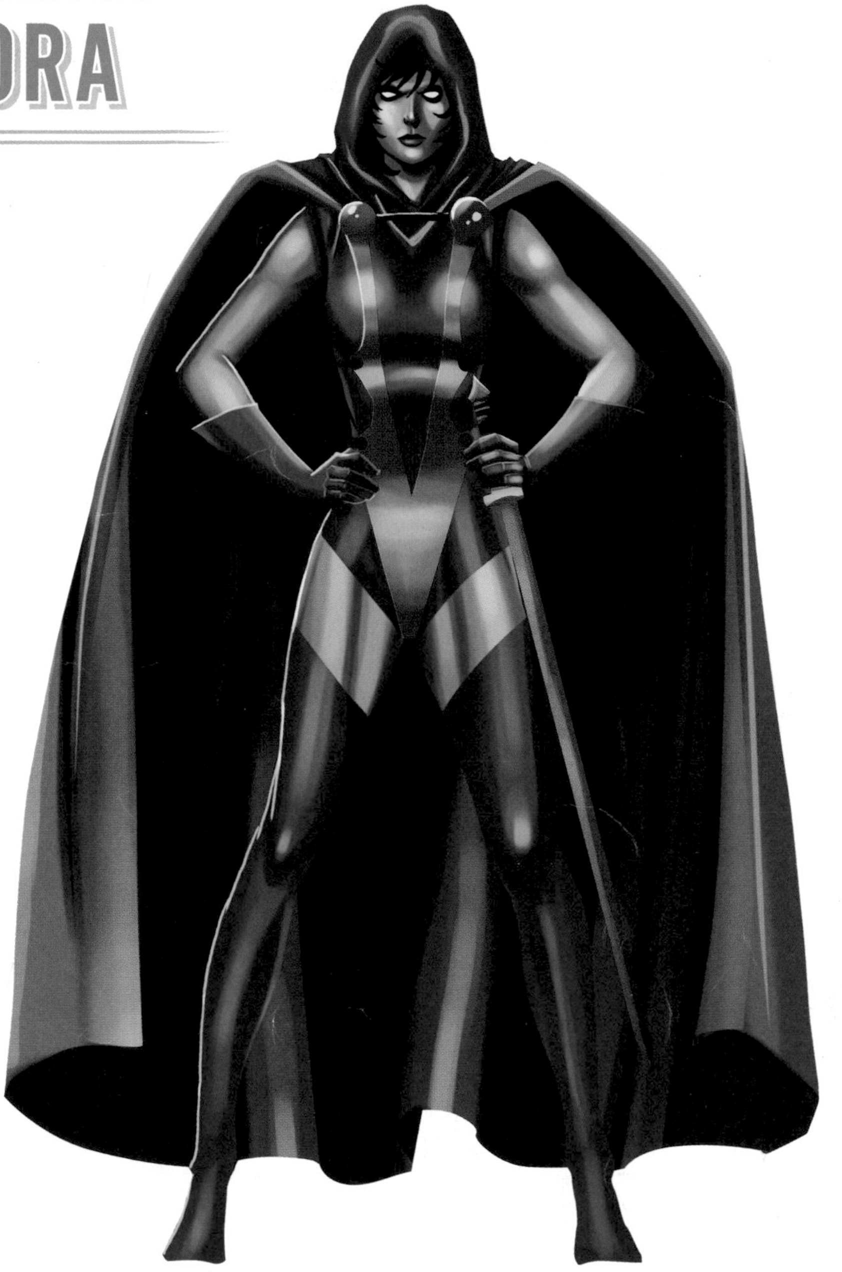

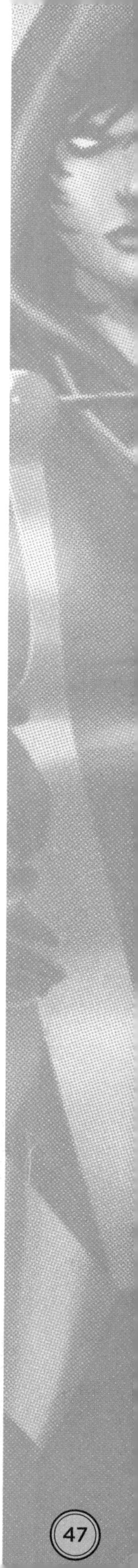

THE ADOPTED DAUGHTER of the intergalactic Super Villain Thanos, Gamora is the last survivor of the alien race known as the Zen Whoberis. Superstrong and incredibly tough, she earned the nickname ***"THE MOST DANGEROUS WOMAN IN THE UNIVERSE".*** Realizing her father's true nature, Gamora teamed up with Captain Mar-Vell and the Avengers to defeat him. In an effort to make up for her father's evil ways, Gamora joined the Guardians of the Galaxy. It's a start.

GHOST RIDER

HERE'S A RULE OF THUMB: selling your soul to a demon is a bad idea. Johnny Blaze can attest to that. He sold his soul to protect his stepfather. Now he's the Ghost Rider, **A FIERY BIKER** who does what good he can. Ghost Rider is superstrong and nearly impossible to hurt. Even his motorcycle is amazing: it has flaming tires, is much faster than normal bikes and it can jump incredible distances and even drive straight up walls.

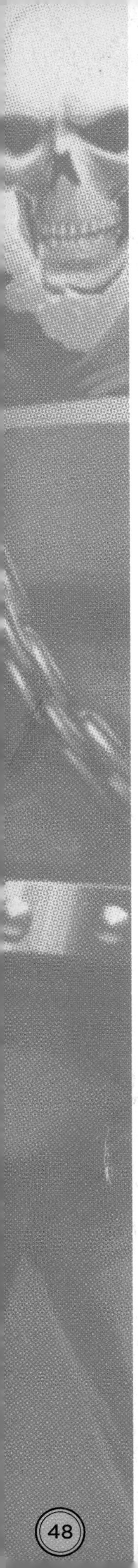

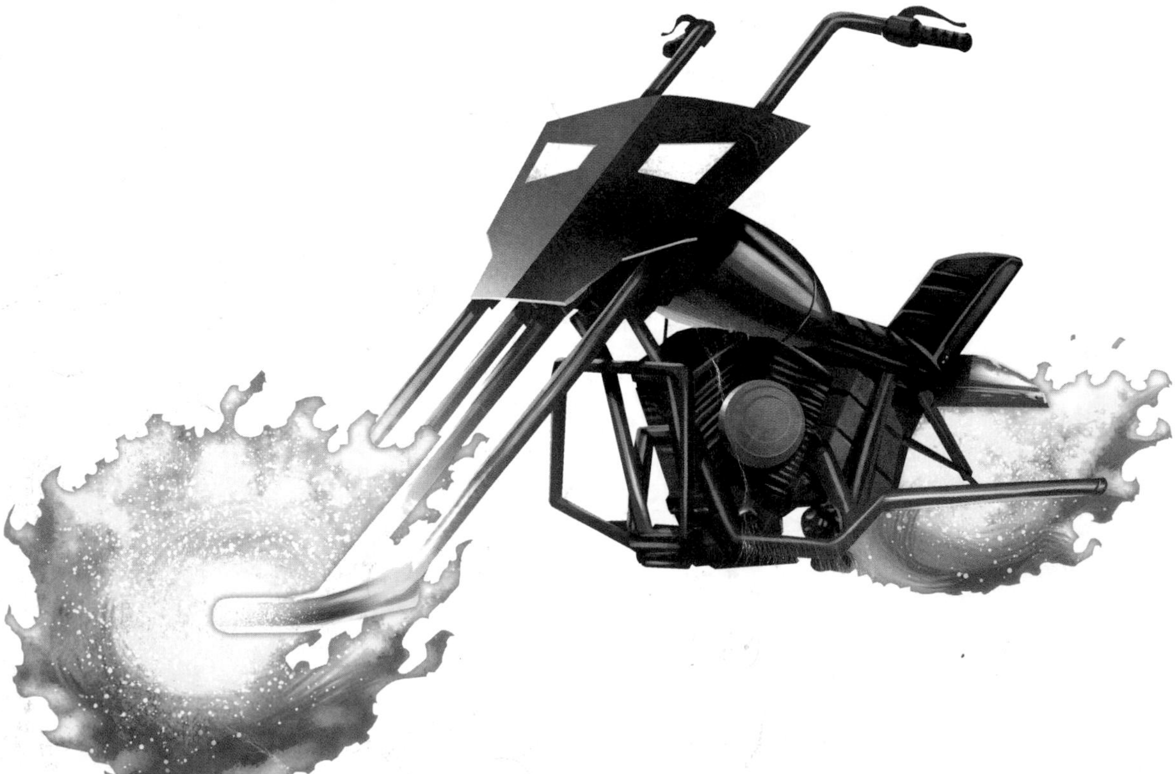

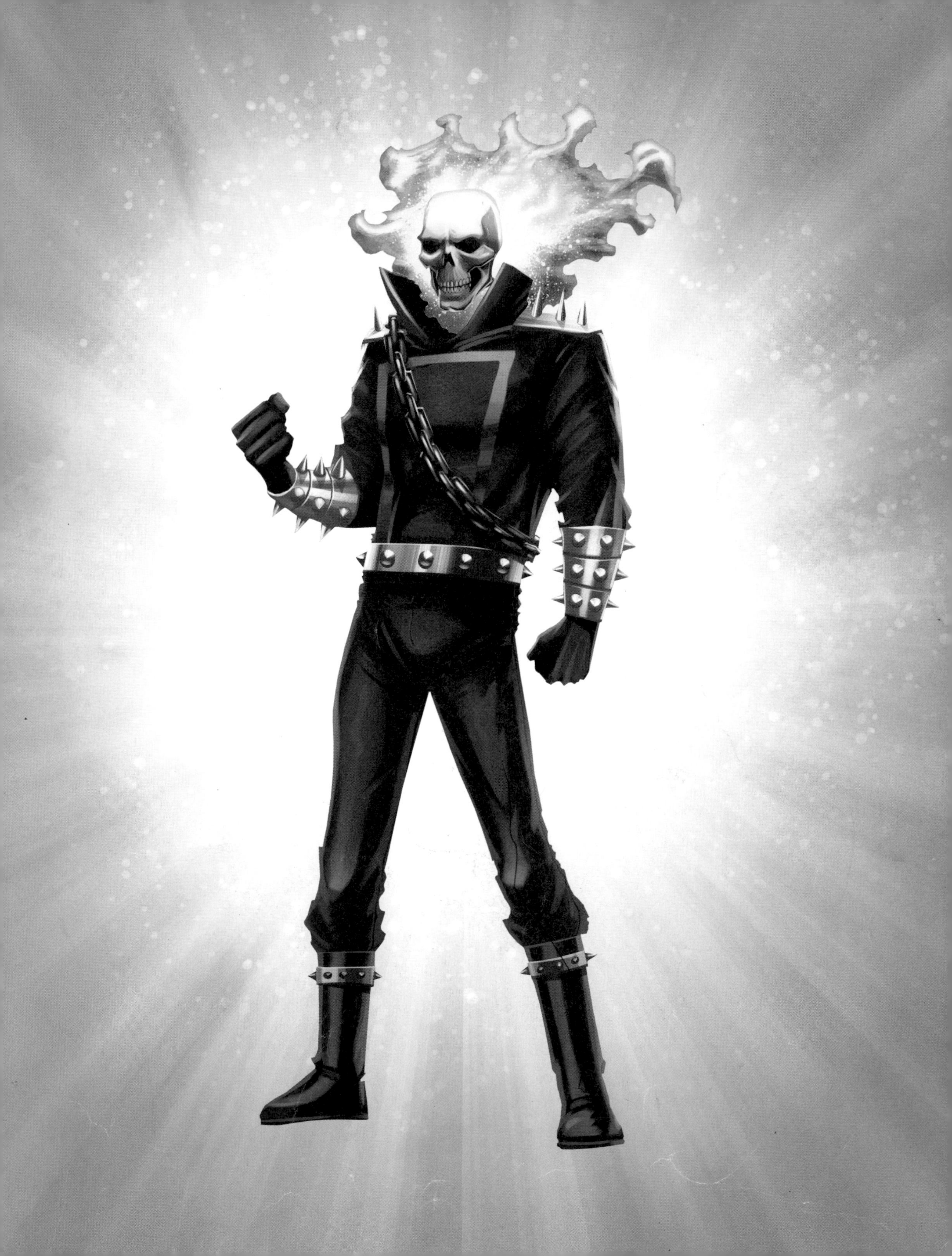

GROOT

GROOT'S an extraterrestrial plant creature who first came to Earth because he wanted to capture humans to study them. But what else would you expect from the monarch of Planet X? He's not as frightening as he looks.

Groot suddenly had a change of heart and decided not to study humans, but protect them. Groot uses his power **OVER TREES**—he is able to absorb them and grow stronger and larger, or even "command" them to become the scariest army ever—to help the Guardians of the Galaxy patrol space.

HAVOK

BEING A LITTLE BROTHER is often hard. But when your big brother is the leader of the X-Men . . . that's a lot more to live up to. Alex Summers knows. As the younger brother of Cyclops, Alex can create incredibly **POWERFUL ENERGY BLASTS.** Unfortunately, he can't control them very well—which is how he got the codename Havok.

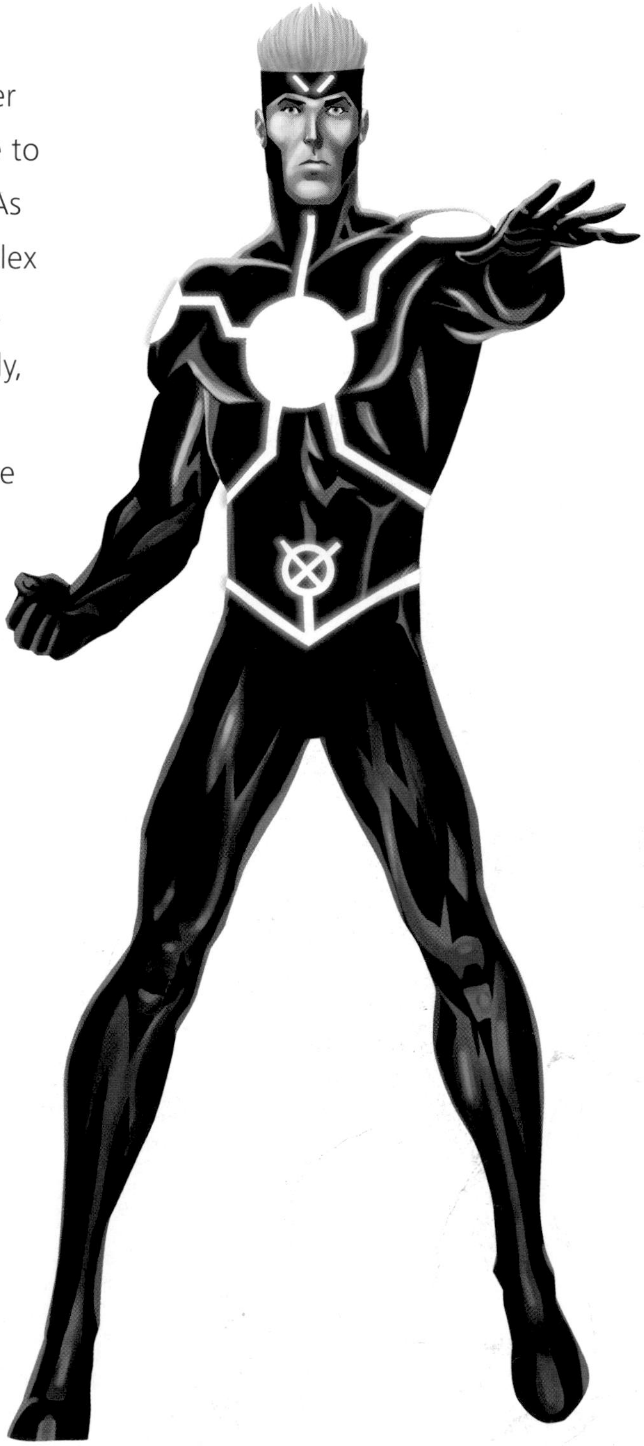

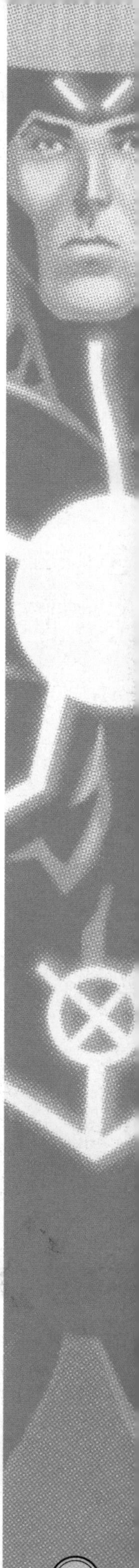

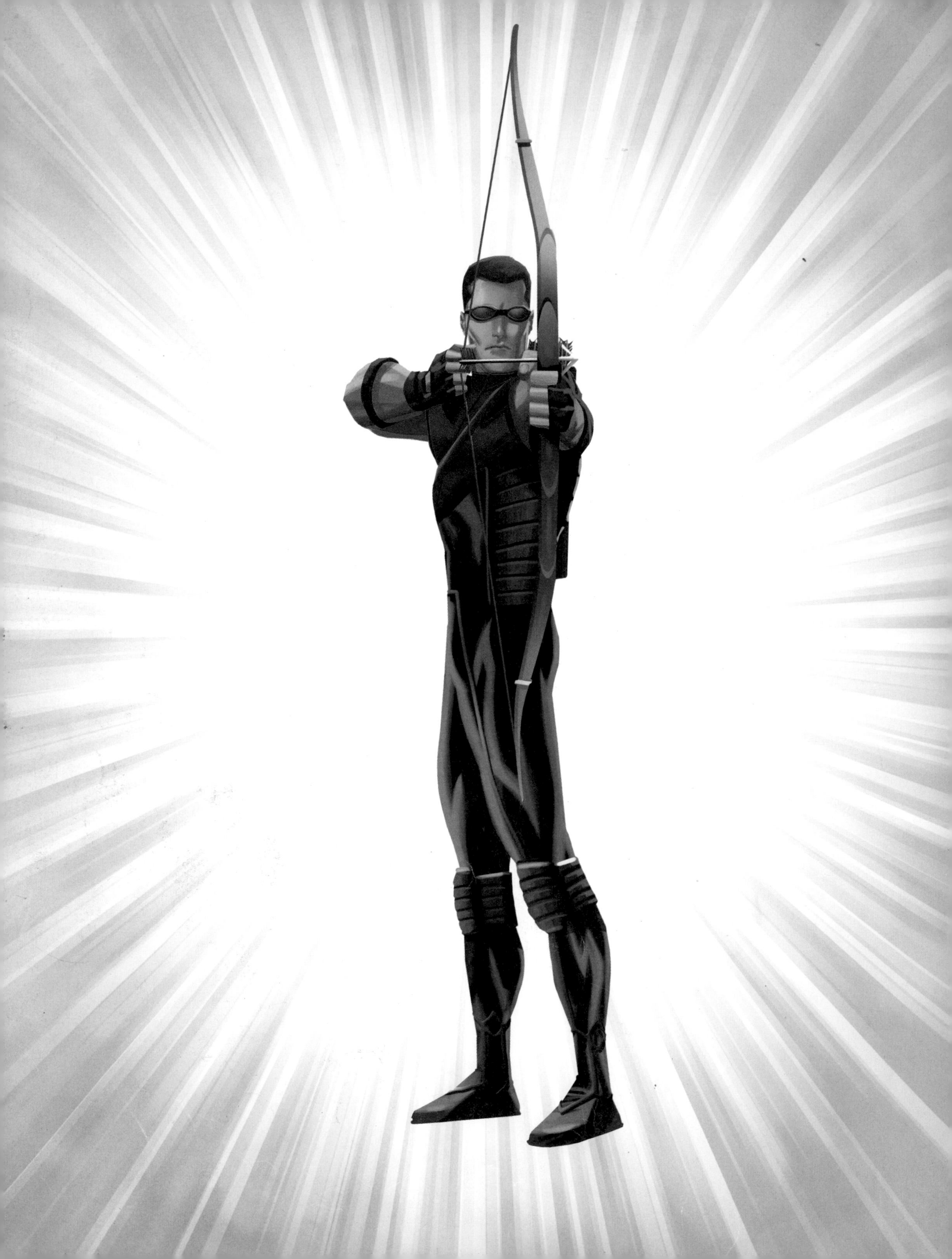

HAWKEYE

WHEN CLINT BARTON and his little brother lost their parents, they were sent to a home for orphans. Unhappy, they ran off and joined the circus. That's where Clint learned how to **SHOOT A BOW AND ARROW** better than anyone else. When he saw Iron Man in action, Clint decided he wanted to be a Super Hero too—and **HAWKEYE** was born. Although he was first mistaken for a villain, Clint was later able to join the Avengers thanks to Iron Man's help.

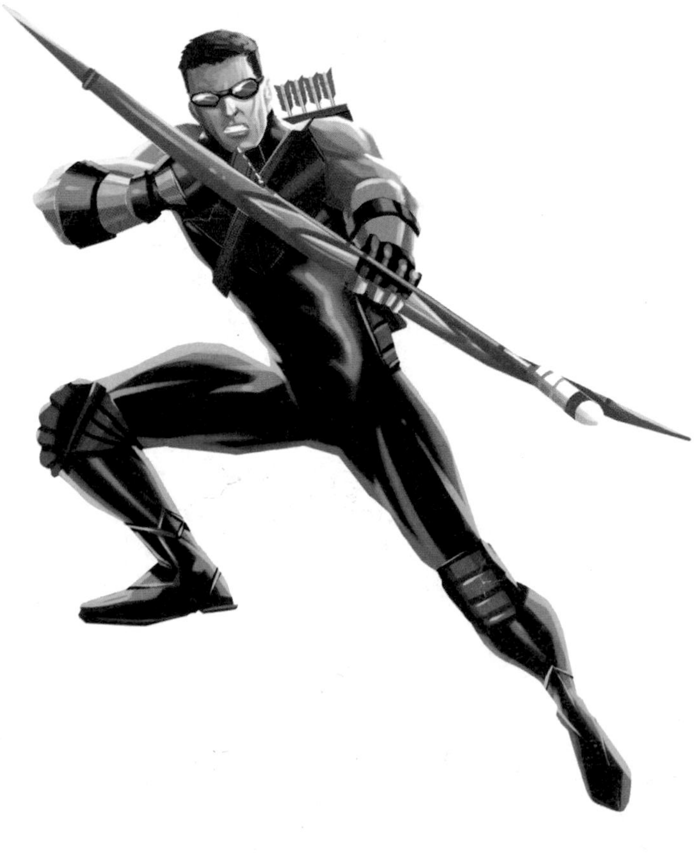

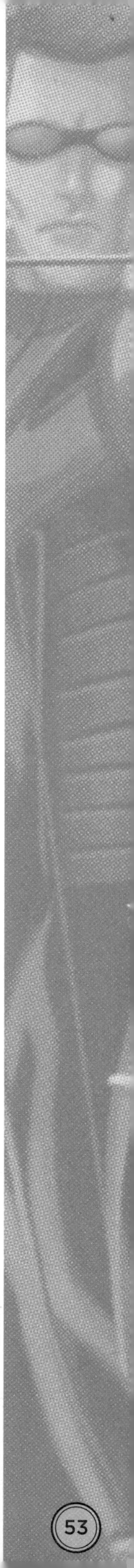

HEIMDALL

THE GUARDIAN of the Rainbow Bridge that connects Thor's world with other realms, Heimdall is Asgard's first defense against attack. Like all Asgardians, he's got superstrength and superspeed.

With his superdense body, he's also even harder to injure than most Asgardians. As watcher of the Rainbow Bridge, Heimdall wields the **GJALLERHORN,** (guh-yar-er-horn) which he blows to warn Asgard of danger. What would Thor do without Heimdall and his sister, the Lady Sif? The God of Thunder hopes he never finds out.

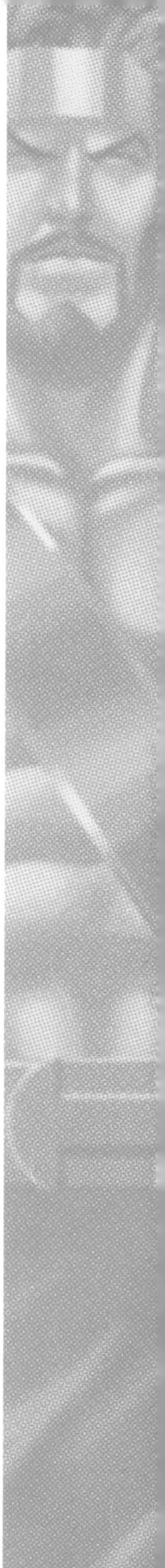

HERCULES

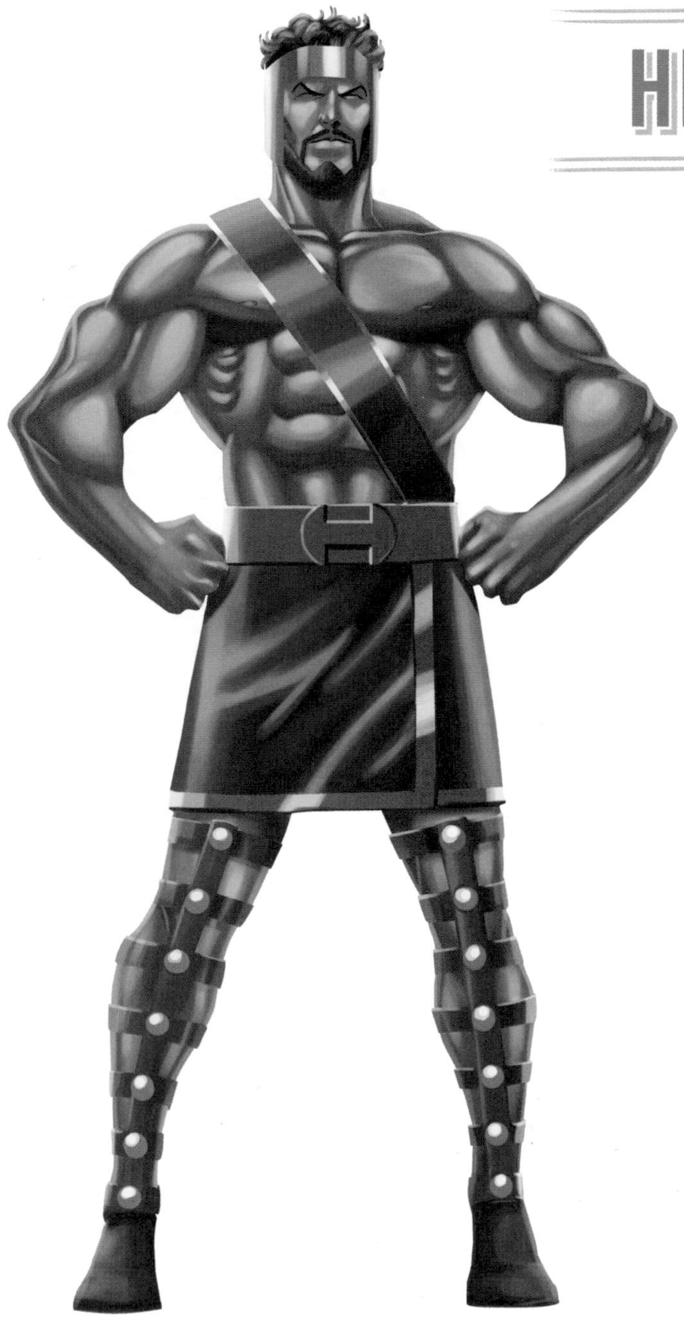

HERCULES IS THE SON OF ZEUS, king of the gods. His superstrength was first discovered when he strangled a deadly snake as a baby. As he grew, he went on amazing adventures. At the end of his Earthly life, Zeus brought him to **OLYMPUS,** home of the gods. But he was eventually drawn back to Earth by the Enchantress, an evil sorceress from the realm of Asgard. She sent Hercules to attack the Avengers, but Hawkeye broke the spell. After defeating the Enchantress, Hercules decided to stay on Earth as an Avenger.

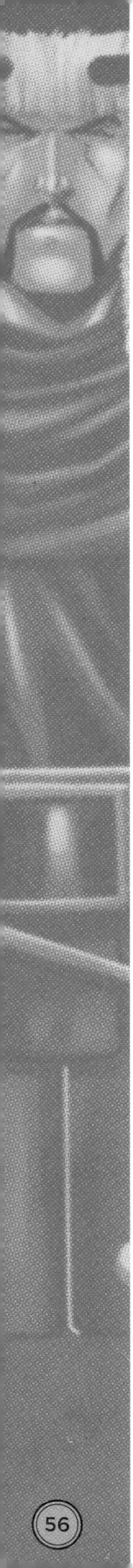

HOGUN

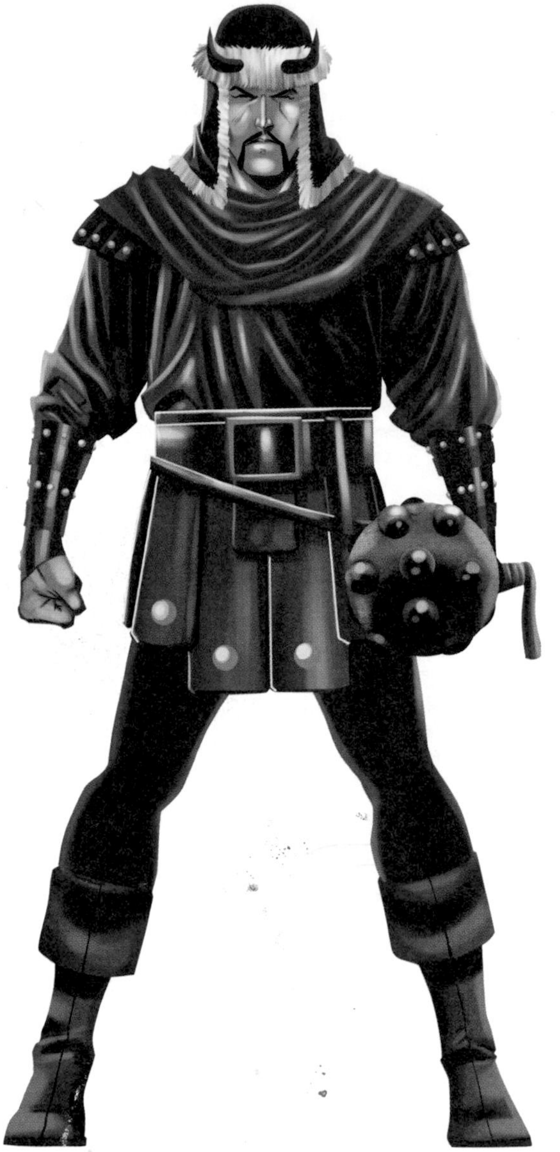

A CHAMPION of Asgard and one of the key members of the Warriors Three, Hogun the Grim is also one of Thor's closest friends.

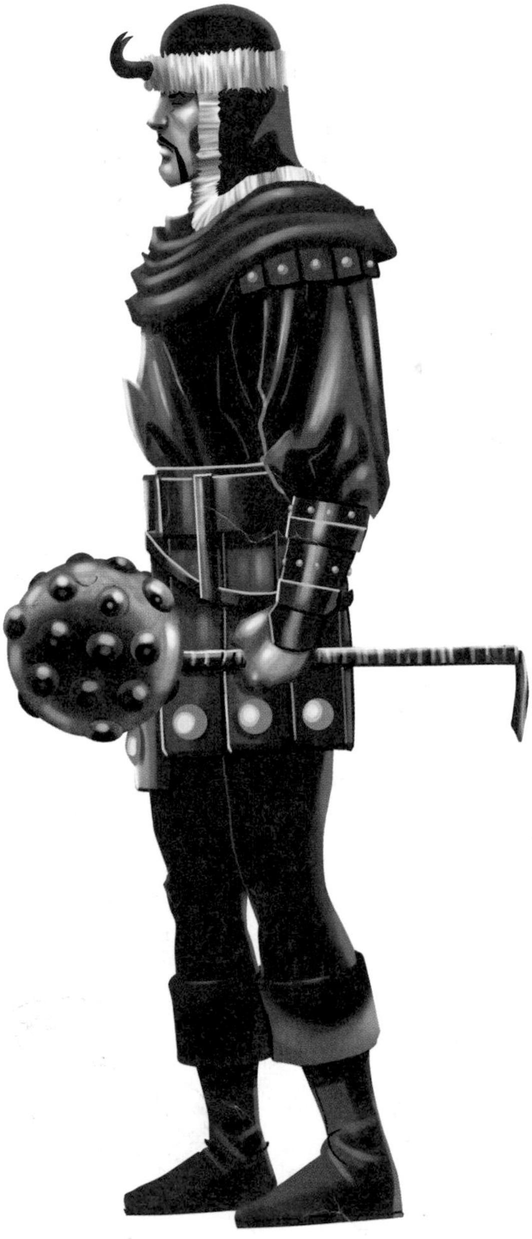

Wielding a mace when in battle, Hogun also possesses **ENHANCED STRENGTH, SUPERIOR HAND-TO-HAND COMBAT, AND FIGHTING SKILLS** that no mortal can measure up to. Though he is short tempered and silent, Hogun is always ready to jump into battle with his fellow Asgardians: Thor, Lady Sif, and the other Warriors Three.

HULK

BRUCE BANNER was one of the world's greatest scientists. While he was working on a new weapon—a gamma bomb—he realized someone had mistakenly driven into the testing area. Bruce rushed out and saved the person . . . but got caught in the blast himself. Radiation from the bomb shot through Bruce's body. Amazingly, he seemed just fine . . . until he got upset. Now whenever Bruce gets mad, he turns into **AN ANGRY GREEN GIANT.** Gone is the brilliant scientist: enter the Incredible Hulk. Strong enough to rip a tank apart but no smarter than a very young child, the Hulk is an unpredictable and destructive force. When the Hulk calms down he turns back into Bruce—but there's no way of knowing when something will anger Bruce enough to trigger the Hulk's return.

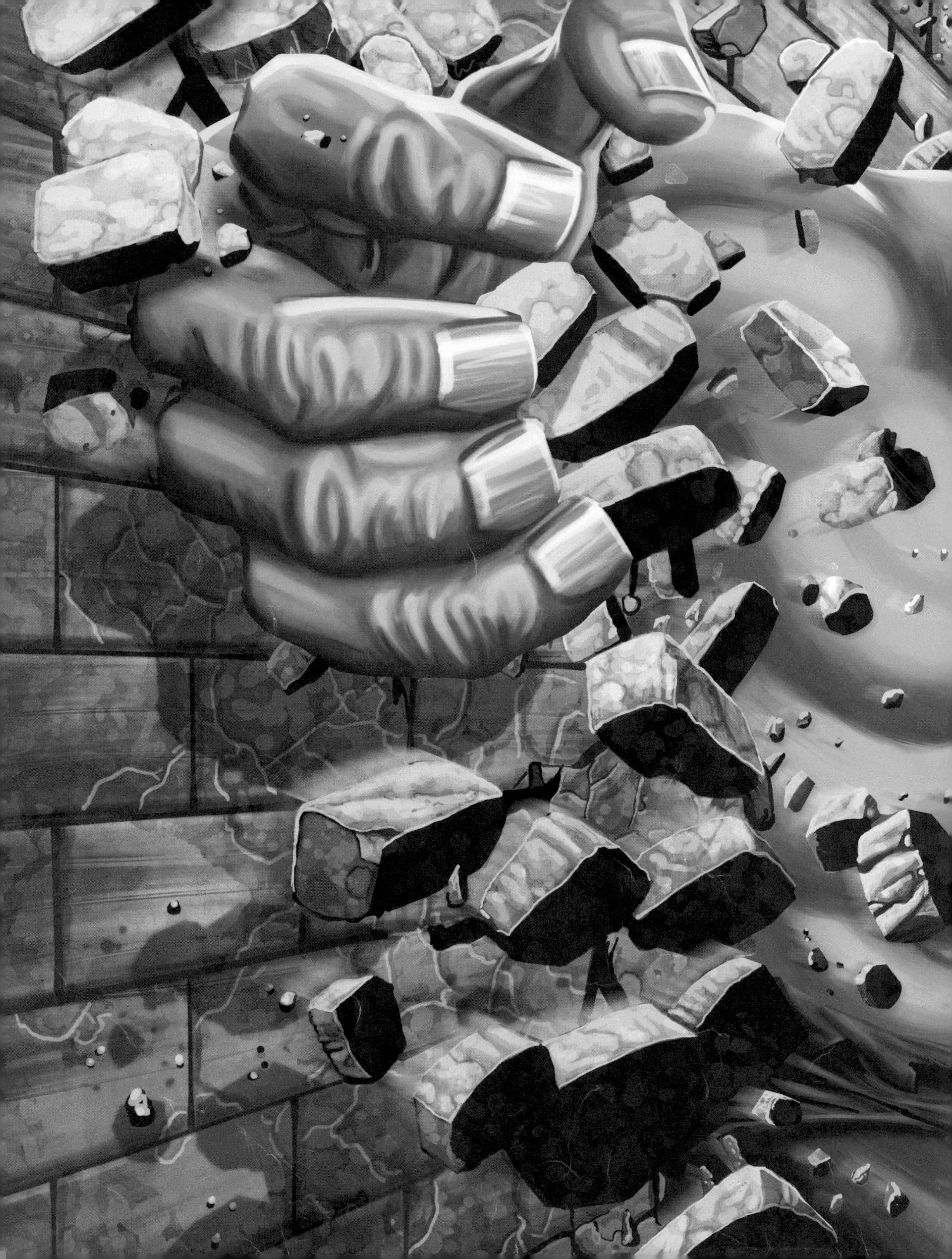

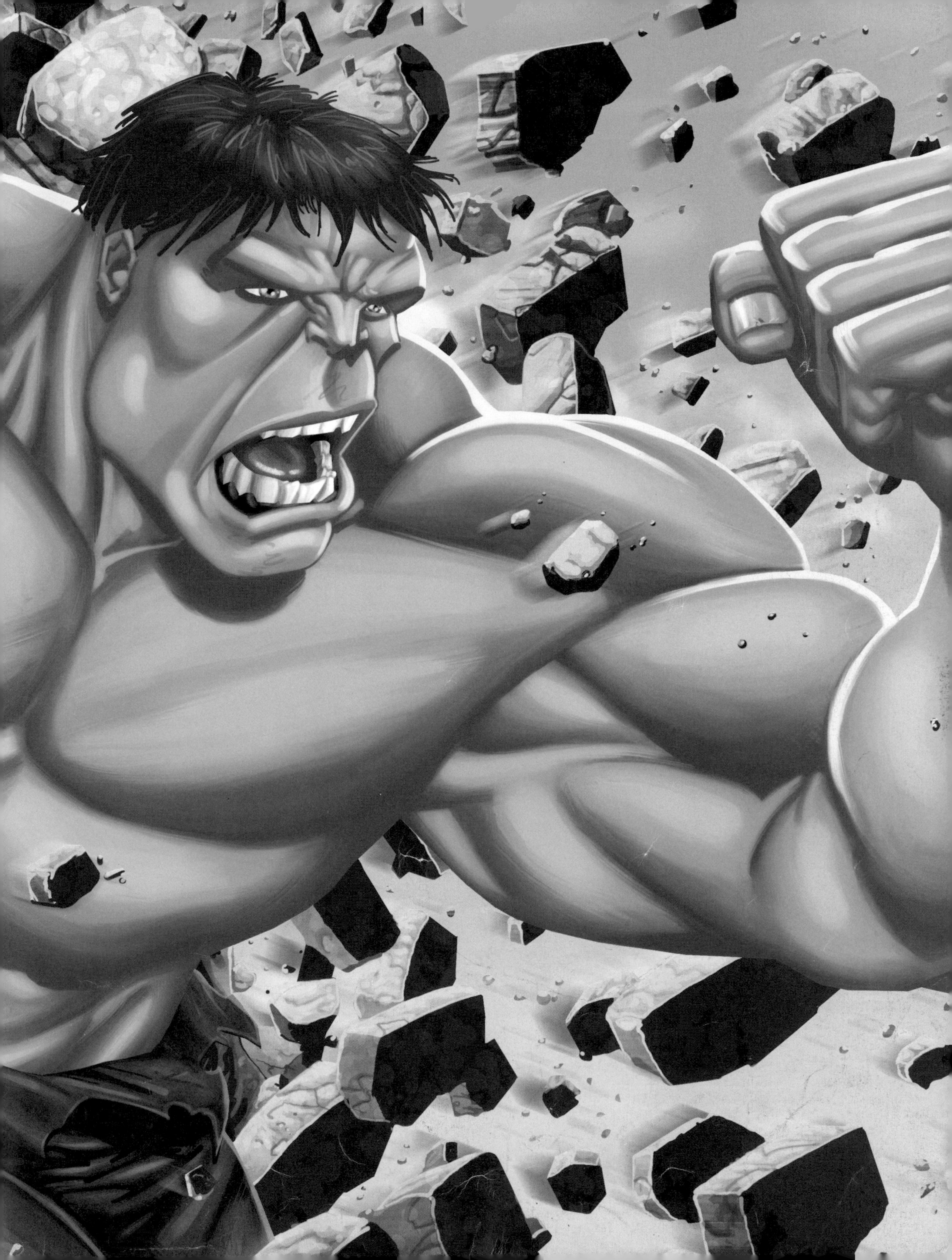

HUMAN TORCH

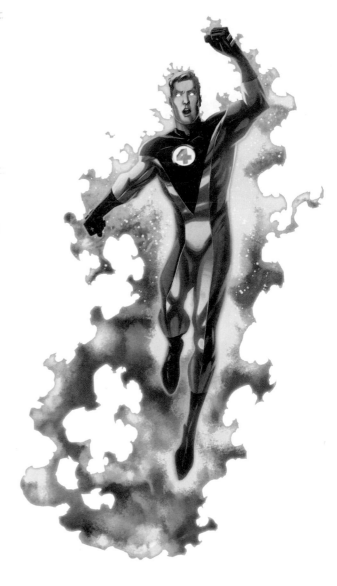

JOHNNY STORM was always tagging along with his sister, Sue. When he was older, he even tagged along on Sue's secret trip to space with her boyfriend, Reed Richards, and Reed's best friend, Ben Grimm.

The trip didn't go as planned, however, and they were all exposed to cosmic radiation. The radiation affected them all, but each reacted differently. Johnny found he could turn his entire body into a **LIVING FLAME.** He could throw fireballs and even fly leaving behind a streak of fire. Teaming up with the others known as the Fantastic Four, Johnny is now known as the Human Torch.

ICEMAN

BOBBY DRAKE discovered his was a mutant when he was on a date. A bully tried to grab his girlfriend, so Bobby pointed his finger. The next thing any of them knew, the bully was trapped in a **SOLID BLOCK OF ICE** and Bobby was sitting in jail. Until that is the jail wall exploded and Cyclops invited Bobby to join the X-Men! One of the founding members of the X-Men, there is no end to the amazing things Iceman can do with water and ice. He could even freeze the entire planet if he wanted. Fortunately, he doesn't. He's a good guy.

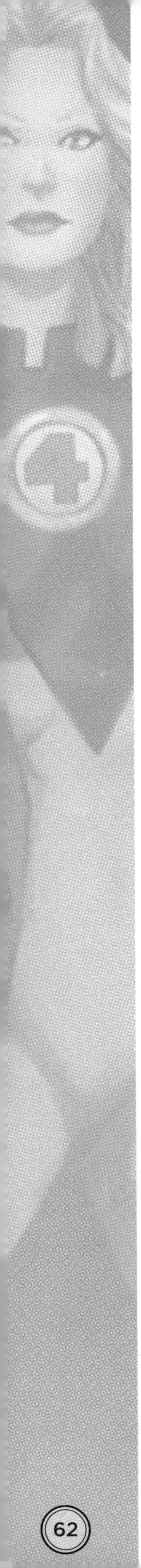

INVISIBLE WOMAN

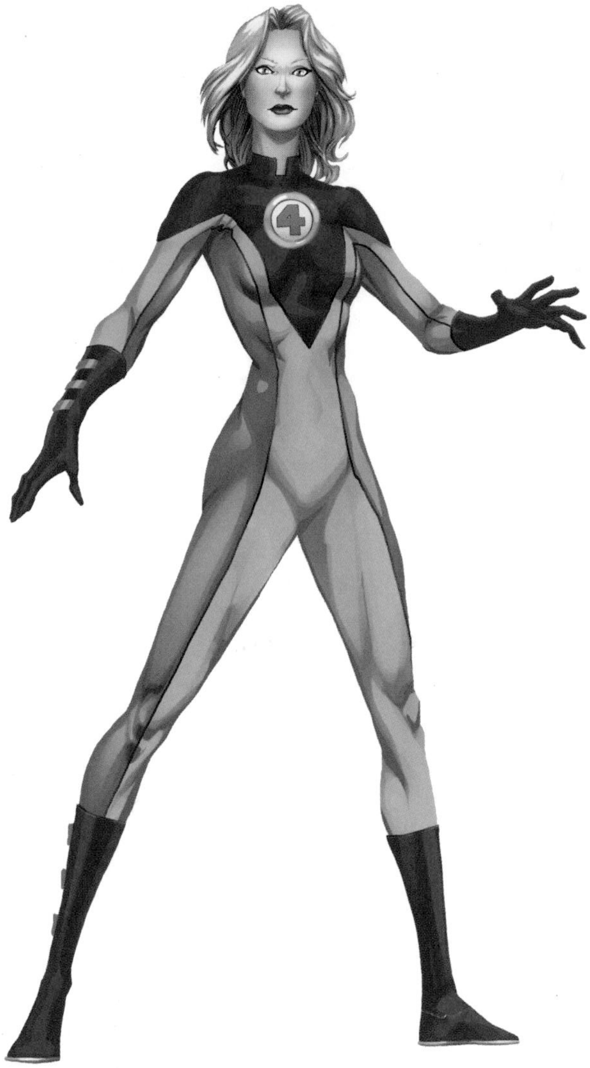

WHEN THEIR PARENTS DIED, Sue Storm had to take care of her little brother Johnny. She even took him along on a secret space flight with her boyfriend, Reed Richards, and Reed's best friend, Ben Grimm.

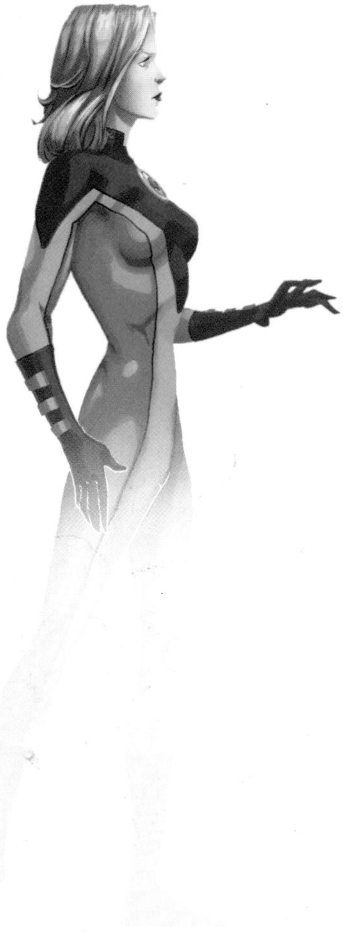

When the spaceship was exposed to cosmic radiation, they all developed superpowers. Sue discovered she could turn herself or even other things **INVISIBLE,** as well as produce protective force fields. Now married to Reed, Sue is the Invisible Woman, and the soul of the Fantastic Four.

IRON FIST

DANNY RAND'S father wanted to show Danny the mystical city of K'un-Lun he had discovered. Unfortunately, he fell off a mountain on the way there. The city's people took Danny in and trained him in their martial arts until he was even good enough to defeat a dragon known as Shou-Lao the Undying.

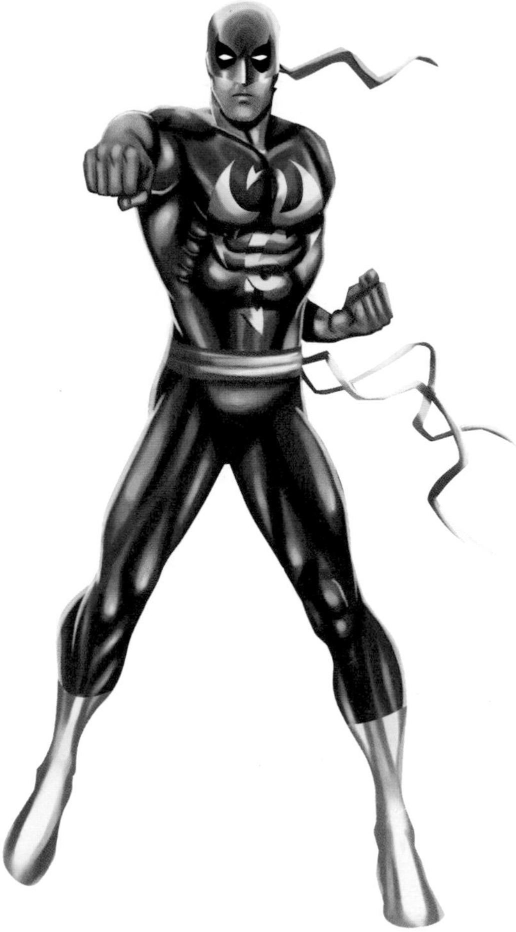

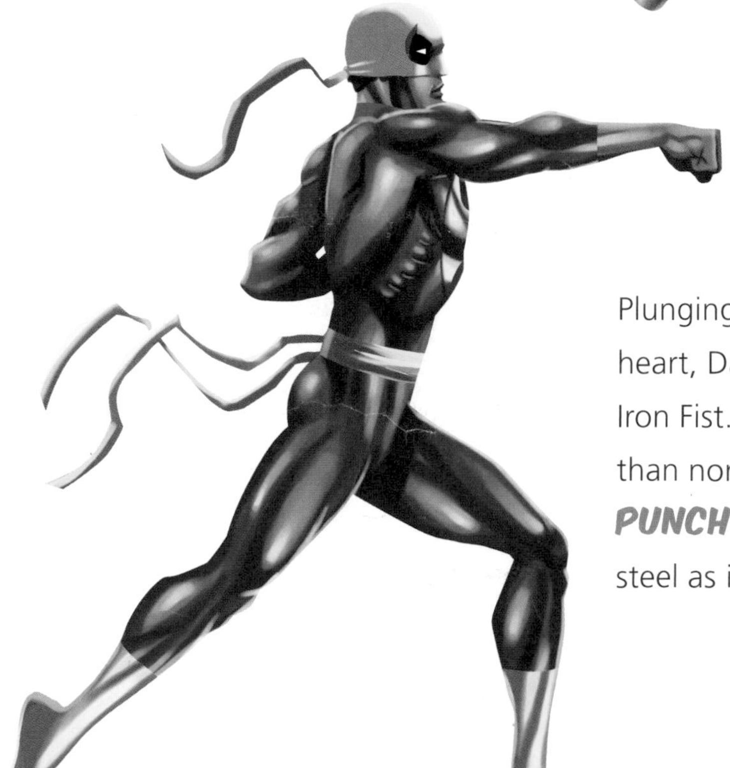

Plunging his hands into its molten heart, Danny became owner of the Iron Fist. Much stronger and faster than normal humans, Iron Fist's **PUNCHES** can go through rock or steel as if they were made of paper.

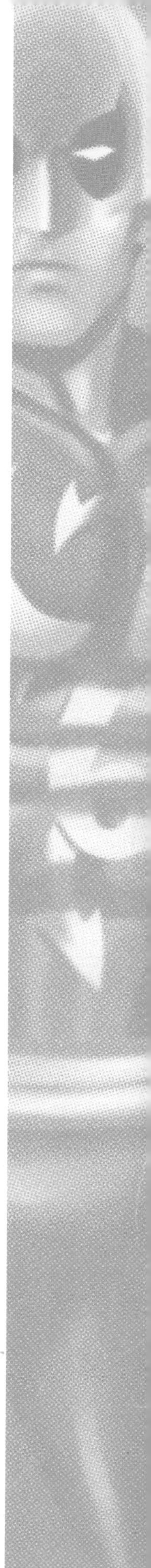

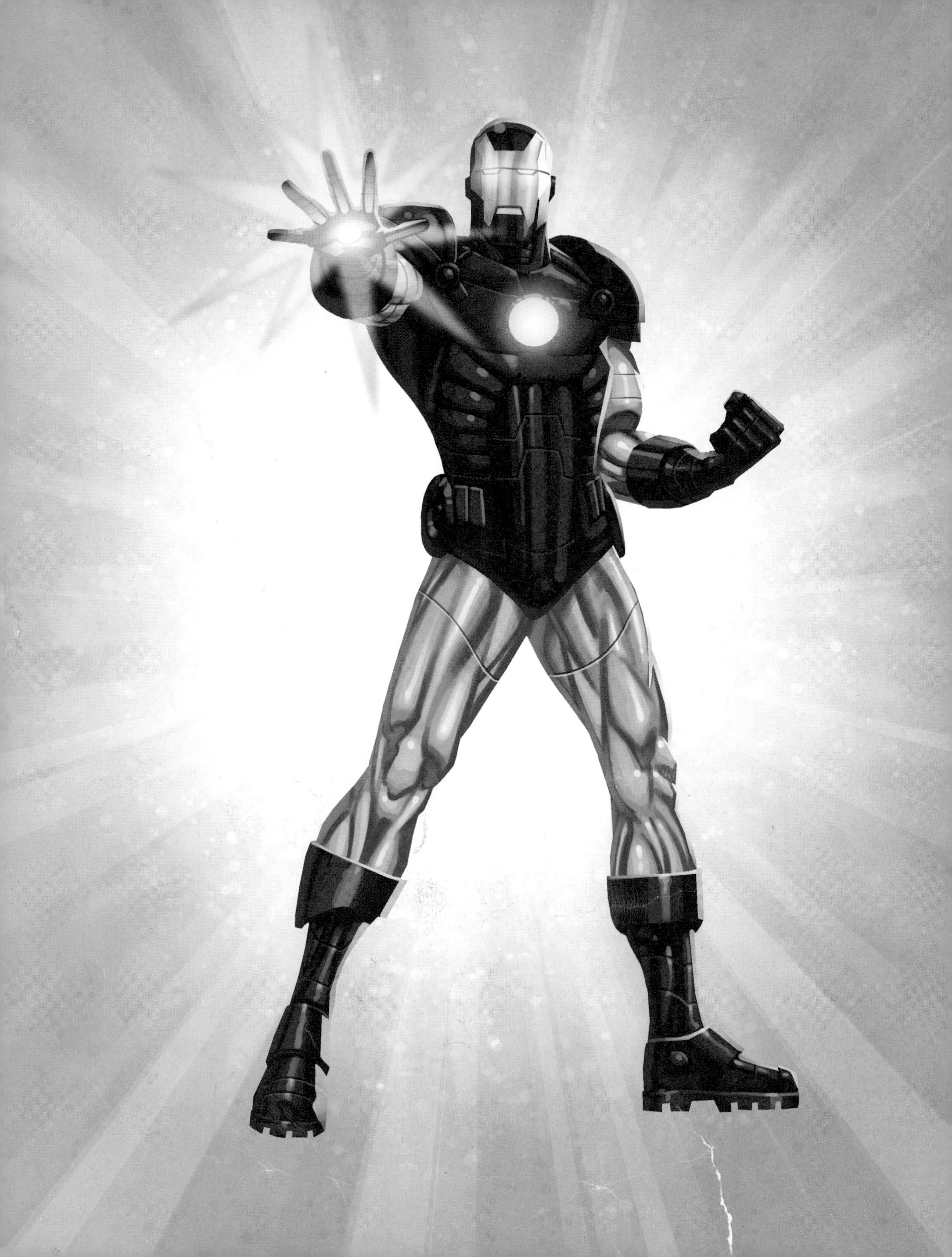

IRON MAN

TONY STARK seemed to have everything in life. He was young, rich, brilliant, and handsome. Then came the day when an explosion in a war-torn country drove a piece of metal into Tony's heart. Despite being injured, Tony used his amazing design skills to create the Iron Man suit. The Iron Man armor not only protects Tony's heart, it is bulletproof and also gives Tony the ability to fly. He can even fire **REPULSOR BLASTS** strong enough to knock out a tank. Now, as the Invincible Iron Man, he really does have everything—and he's determined to make the most of his second chance.

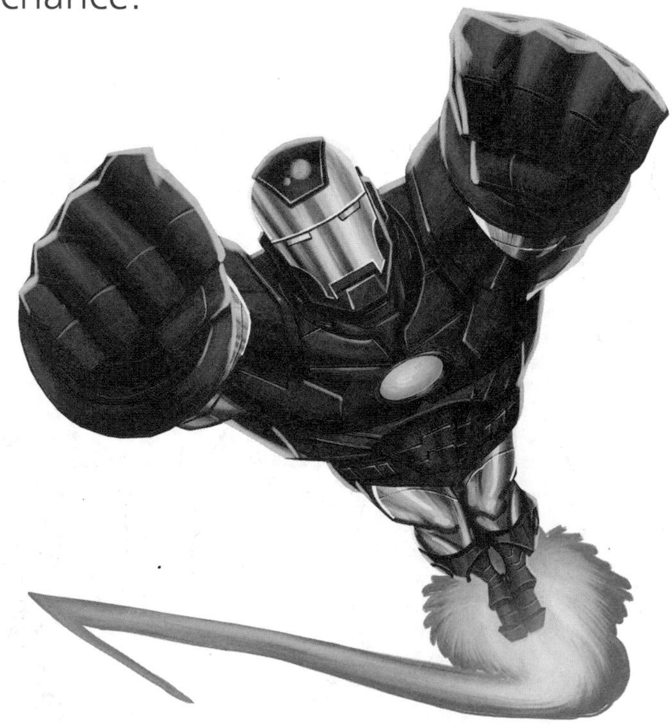

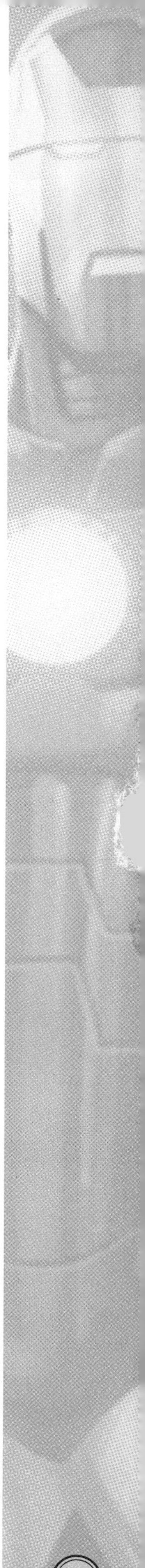

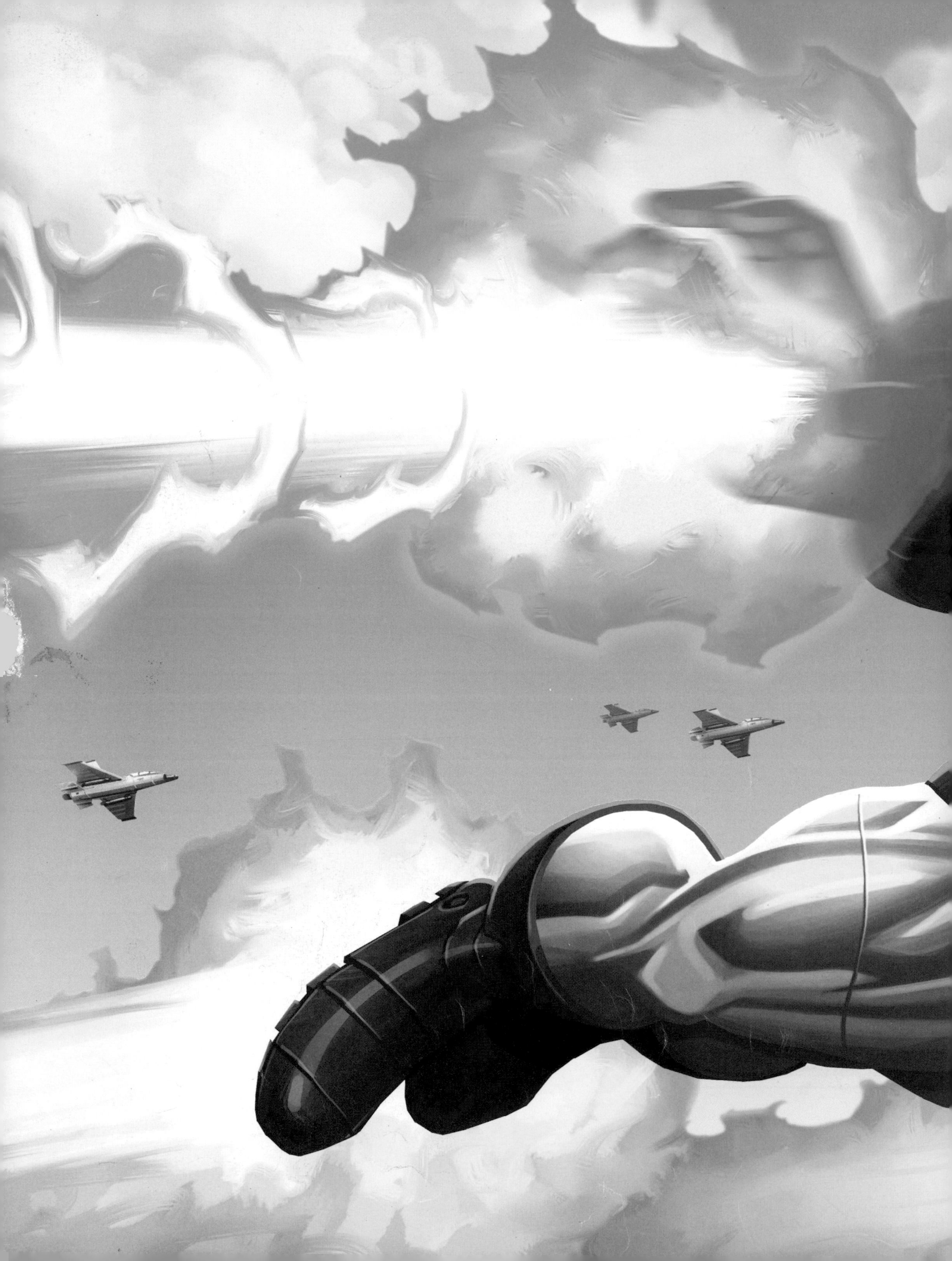

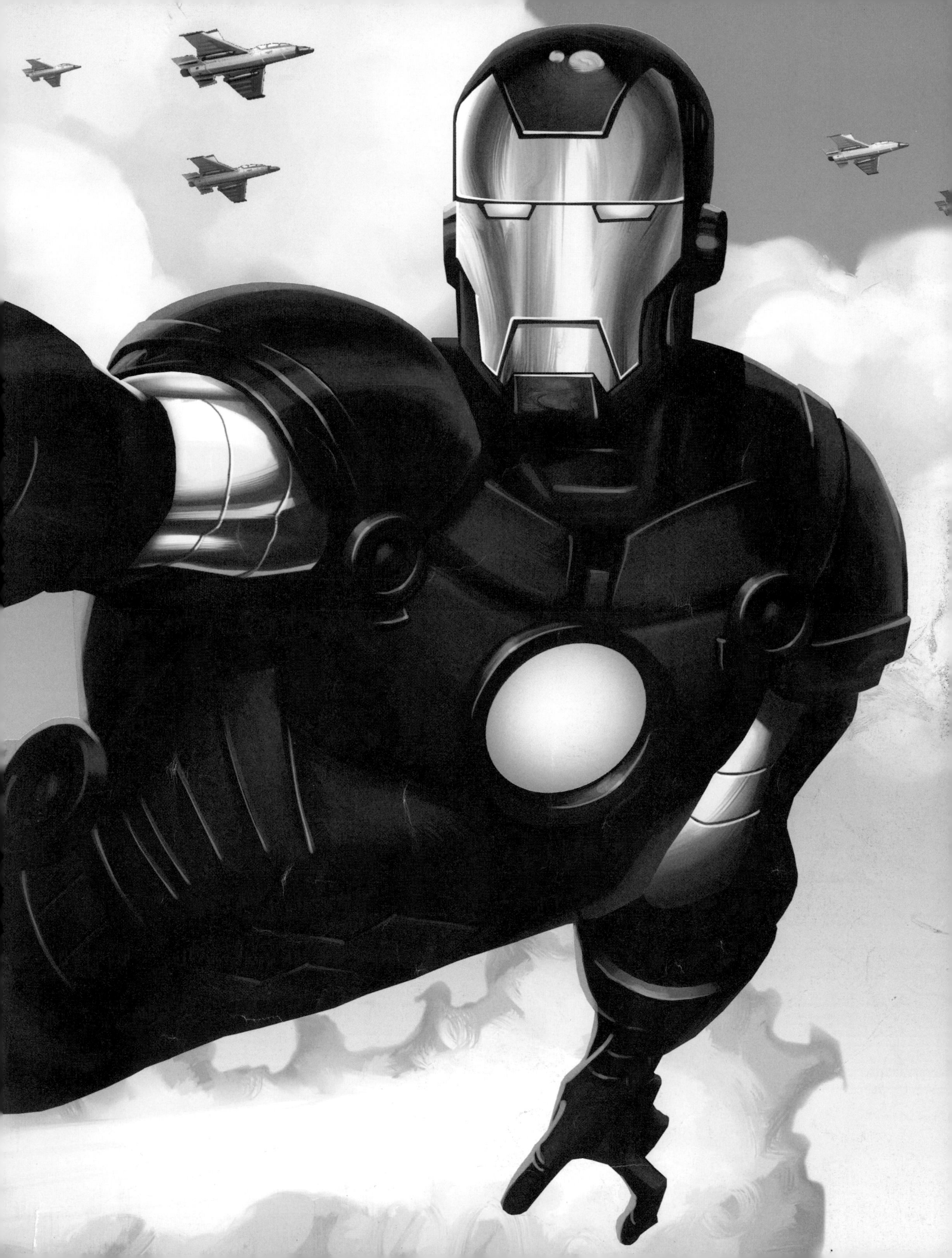

JUBILEE

JUBILATION LEE was a young gymnast who qualified for the Olympics. When her parents died, however, that dream vanished. After running away from an orphanage, she lived in a mall. One day she was saved from mall security by X-Men Storm and Rogue. Fascinated, she secretly followed them through a portal and ended up hiding in one of their secret headquarters—where her mutant abilities manifested. Having seen her prove herself, Professor X was overjoyed to take her in. Jubilee can create what she calls **"FIREWORKS":** colorful bursts of energy which can range from small and beautiful to huge and destructive. She's also able to guard her mind from telepaths.

KARMA

XI'AN COY MANH had a tough life. Having to take care of her younger siblings from an early age all by herself in New York City, she had to learn how to convince reluctant kids to do what she needed them to do.

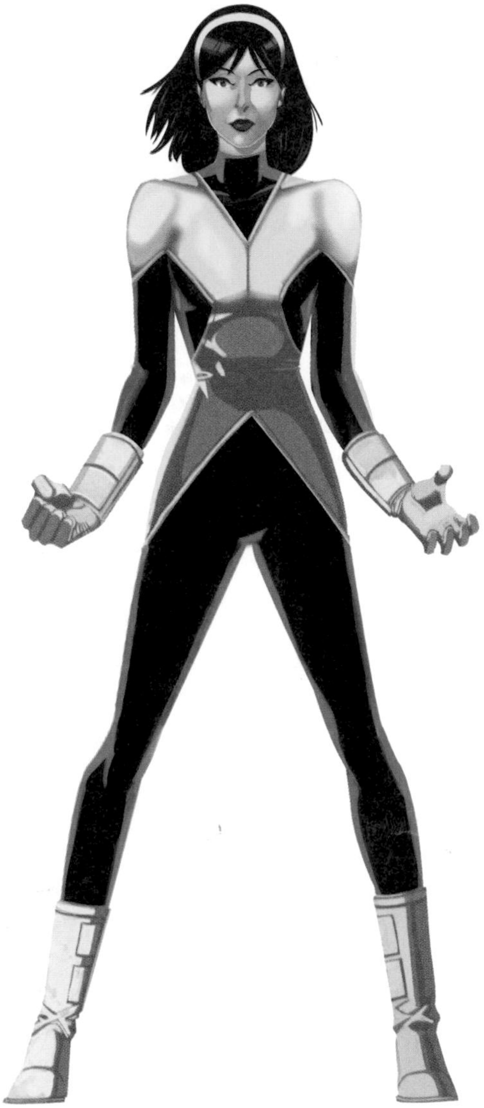

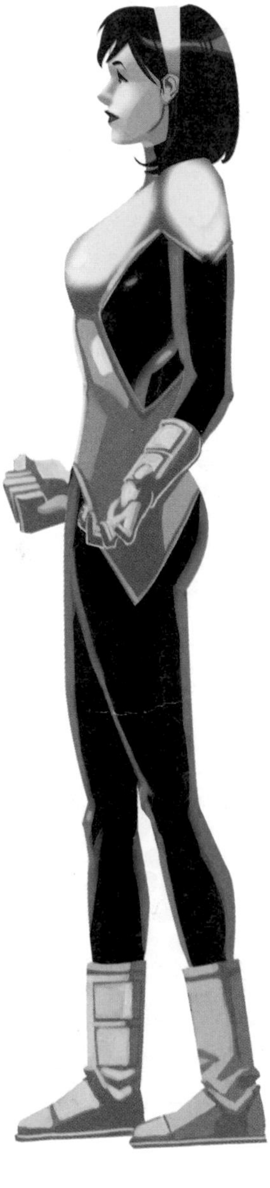

These lessons served her well, even after her mutant abilities kicked in. Since she's able to **TAKE OVER A PERSON'S MIND** and control their body, it's no surprise Professor X wanted Karma to be one of the first members of the New Mutants. She has to be careful, though: if she stays in someone's mind too long, she can lose herself and get stuck there . . . forever.

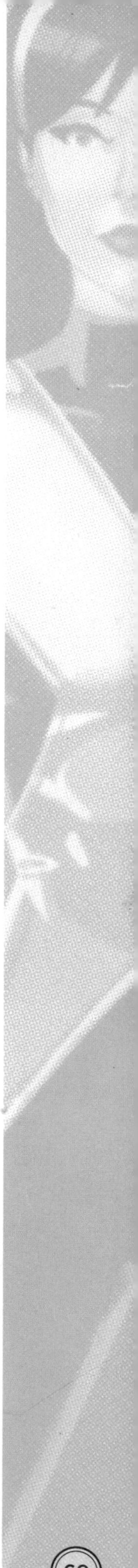

KA-ZAR

THERE IS A LAND below Antarctica, created by aliens and populated by Atlanteans, where dinosaurs still roam and fish people live. This is the Savage Land, and Ka-Zar is its guardian. Although he sometimes seems like a brutal savage, in reality he is Lord Kevin Plunder, the son of an English nobleman. Raised by a saber-toothed tiger, Zabu, after his father died, Ka-Zar learned the ways of the beasts. He uses these skills to keep the **SAVAGE LANDS** safe from outsiders who want to profit from its rich resources. No one and nothing gets past Ka-Zar.

KITTY PRYDE

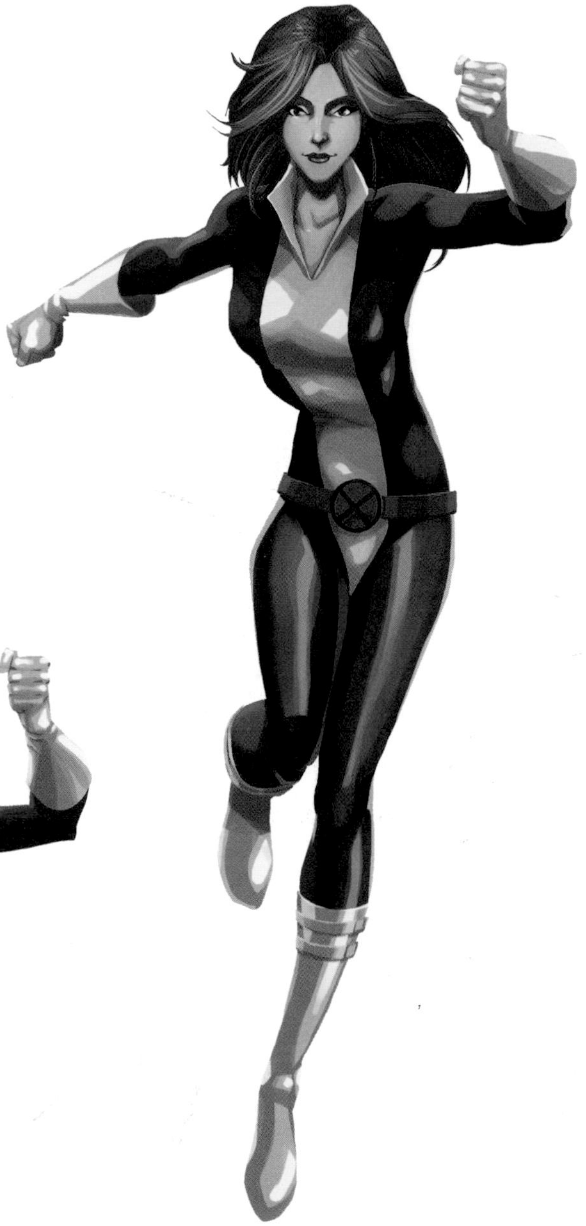

SPRITE. ARIEL. SHADOWCAT. Those are just some of the codenames used by the girl pretty much everyone just calls Kitty Pryde, a computer genius with the mutant ability to phase through solid objects, such as walls and floors.

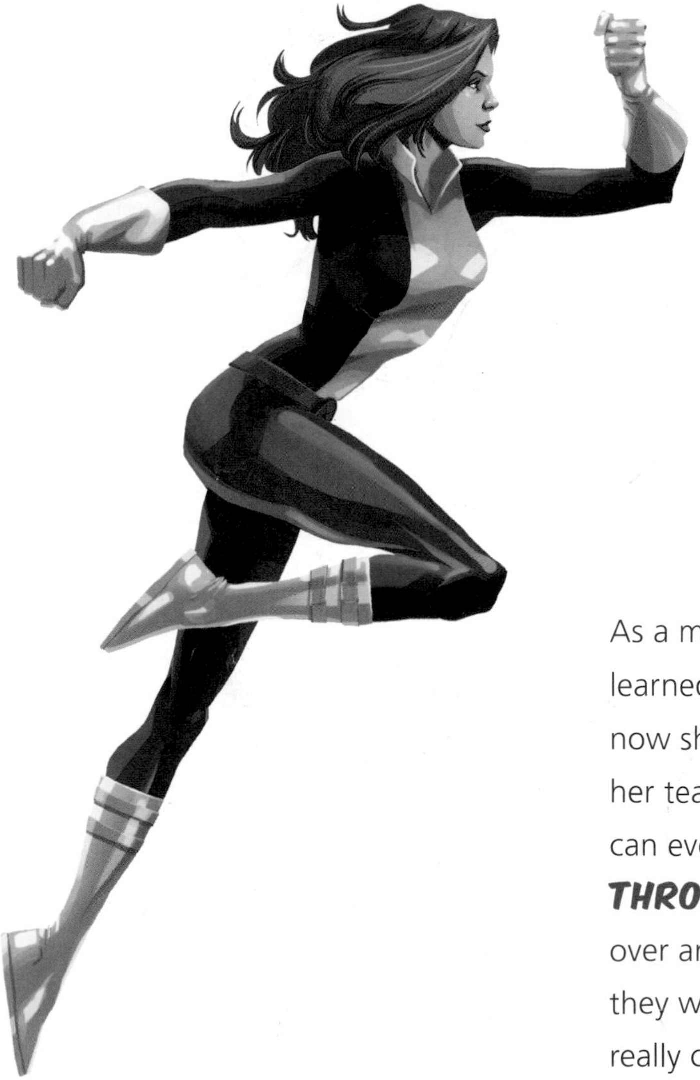

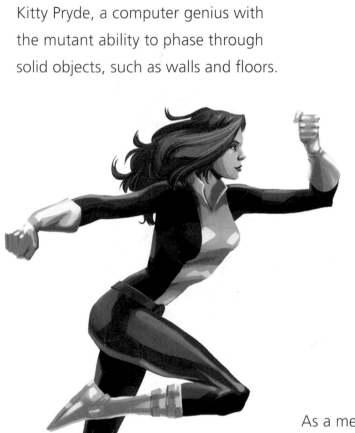

As a member of the X-Men, Kitty learned how to phase so well that now she's able to not only phase her teammates with her powers, but can even **LEVITATE, OR WALK THROUGH THE AIR,** by phasing over and over. Some folks only think they walk on air—here's one girl who really can.

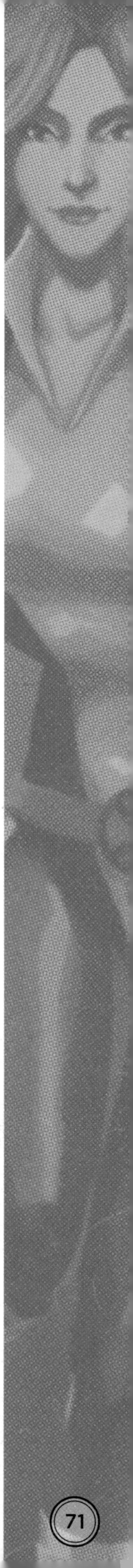

LADY SIF

ONE OF THOR'S oldest and closest friends, Lady Sif and Thor fell in love when they were young. Jealous, Thor's brother Loki cut off Sif's golden locks. When it grew back, Loki was furious that Thor found her new jet black hair even more beautiful.

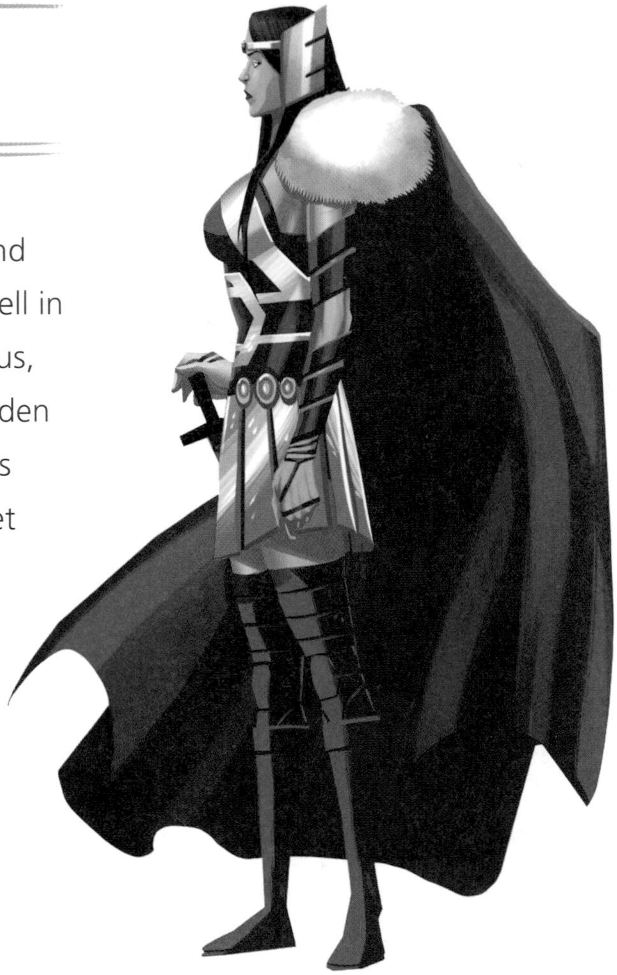

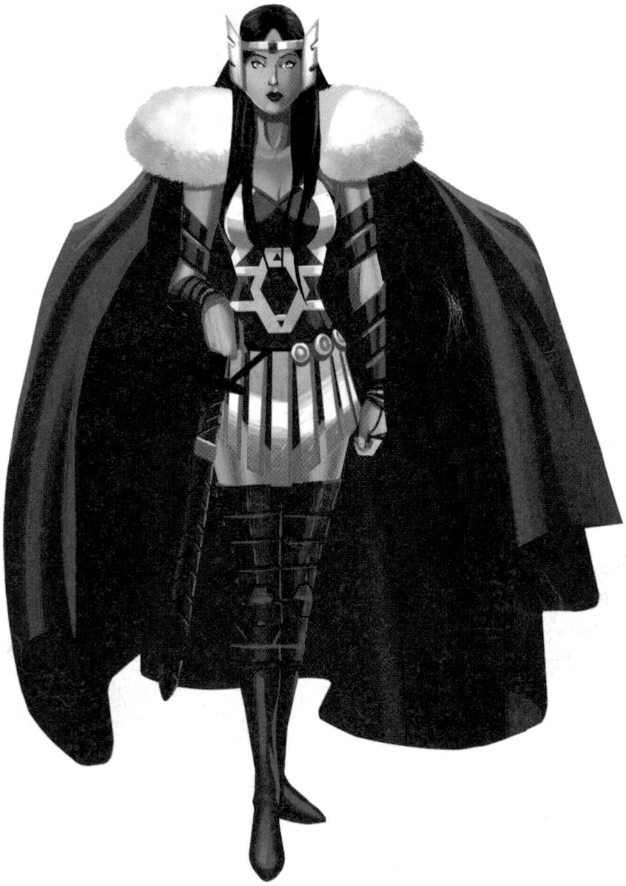

ONE OF THE FINEST AND FIERCEST WARRIORS in all Asgard, Sif has superspeed and superstrength like all Asgardians. She also has a special sword, given to her by Odin, which can cut open a pathway to other dimensions. Now that she's grown up, Loki thinks twice before attacking her—and then decides not to.

LILANDRA

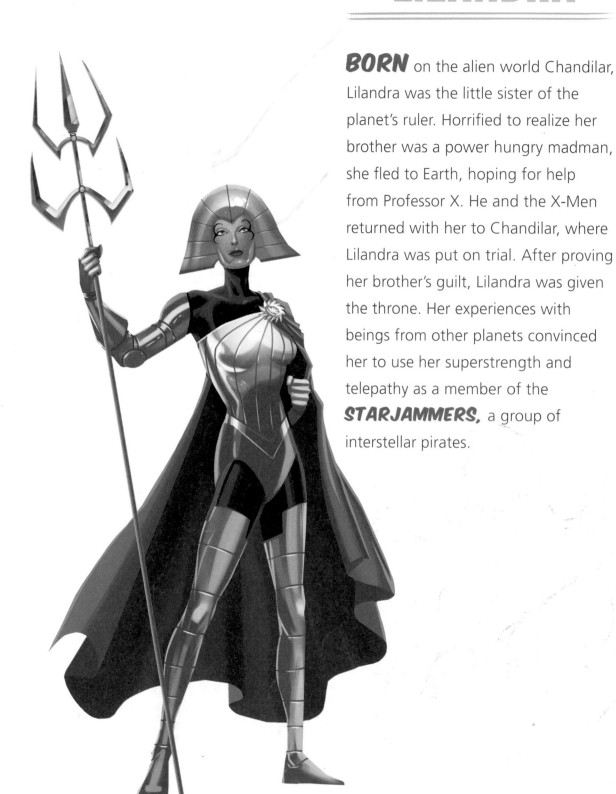

BORN on the alien world Chandilar, Lilandra was the little sister of the planet's ruler. Horrified to realize her brother was a power hungry madman, she fled to Earth, hoping for help from Professor X. He and the X-Men returned with her to Chandilar, where Lilandra was put on trial. After proving her brother's guilt, Lilandra was given the throne. Her experiences with beings from other planets convinced her to use her superstrength and telepathy as a member of the **STARJAMMERS,** a group of interstellar pirates.

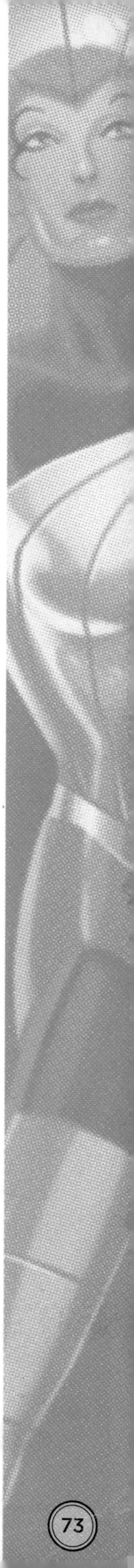

LUKE CAGE

LUKE CAGE, also known as Power Man, was sent to prison for a crime he didn't commit. In order to get out, Luke agreed to take part in a test. The experiment gave him **SUPERSTRENGTH AND ROCK-HARD SKIN** that can withstand bullets and explosions. Taking the name Power Man, he used his new abilities as a private detective, teaming up with Iron Fist to form Heroes for Hire and help those in need.

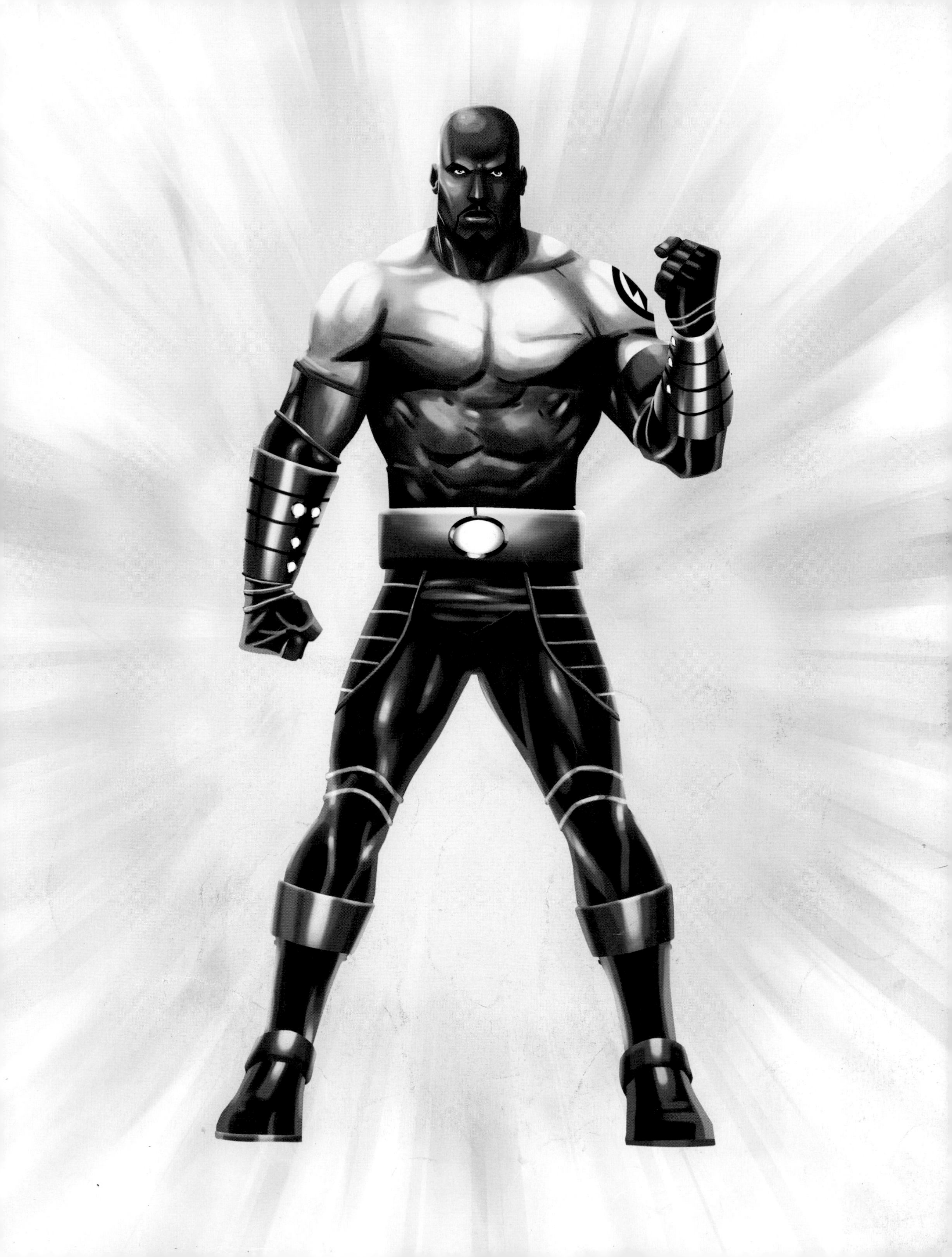

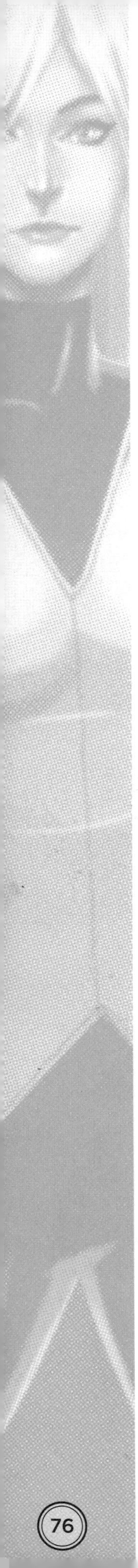

MAGIK

SOME YOUNGER siblings follow in their older brother's footsteps. Not Illyana Rasputina. Whereas her big brother is the X-Men's man made of steel, Colossus, she's the sorceress supreme of another dimension.

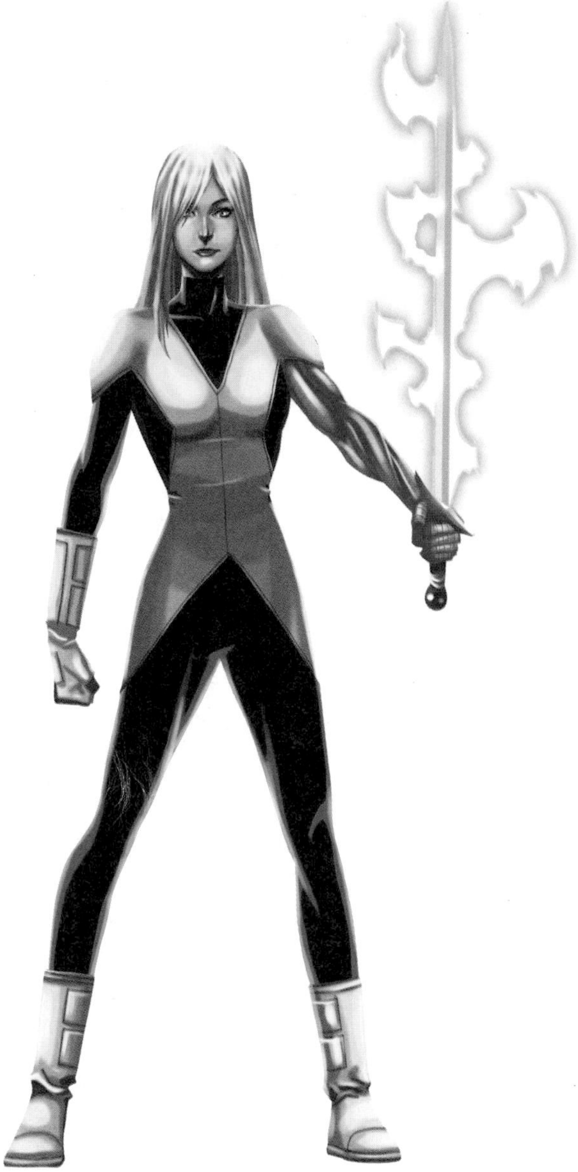

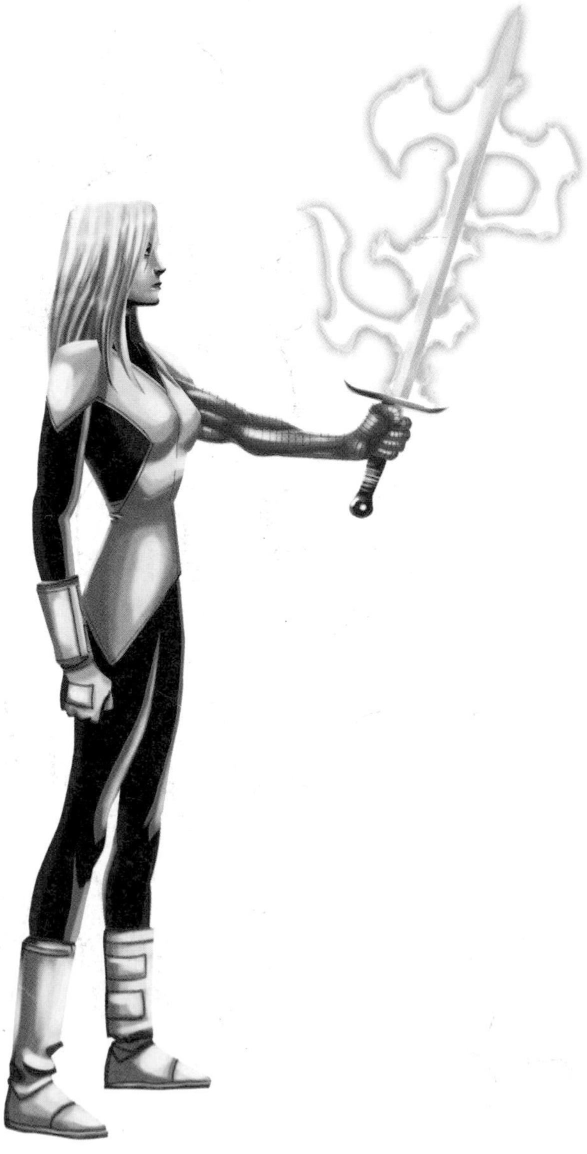

In our world, as Magik, she can use her magical **STEPPING DISKS** to teleport anywhere, instantly—even to another time. She can conjure magical armor to protect herself. She even has a soulsword, which destroys magical things, but passes right through ordinary humans without harm.

MAN-THING

DR. TED SALLIS was one of many scientists trying to reinvent the Super-Soldier Serum that created Captain America. Attacked by rivals at his laboratory in the Everglades, Dr. Ted destroyed his notes . . . but not before injecting himself with his serum. Crashing his car into the swamp, Ted Sallis perished—but from the ashes rose the Man-Thing. Superstrong and impossible to injure— its body being made of **A BUNCH OF PLANTS** which can regenerate themselves—Man-Thing isn't the smartest hero there is. But there's no one less likely to be tempted by evil.

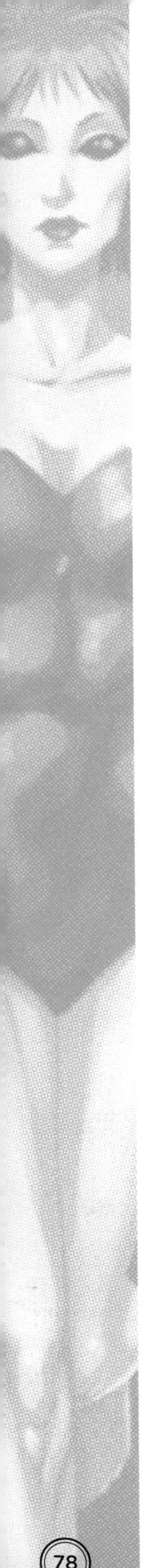

MARRINA

THE PLODEX is an alien race that sends its eggs to other worlds. When the eggs hatch, the baby Plodex take the form of the beings on the native planet. That's how Marrina Smallwood came to be part human, part alien.

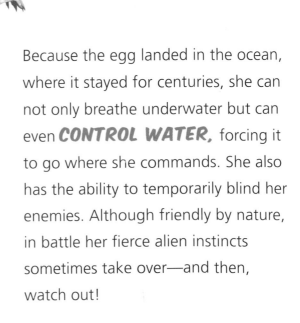

Because the egg landed in the ocean, where it stayed for centuries, she can not only breathe underwater but can even **CONTROL WATER,** forcing it to go where she commands. She also has the ability to temporarily blind her enemies. Although friendly by nature, in battle her fierce alien instincts sometimes take over—and then, watch out!

MARVEL GIRL

JEAN GREY is one of the strongest telepaths the world has ever known—so powerful that when she was young, Professor X had to block off part of her mind, so she wouldn't go crazy from reading everyone's thoughts all the time. Later, as she gained control of her powers, Jean joined the X-Men as Marvel Girl. While she can control objects with her mind—including herself, enabling her to fly—her greatest power is the ability to read and control other **PEOPLE'S MINDS.** She can make them do whatever she wants, and even erase their memories. With a mutant ability that powerful, it's a good thing she's a hero.

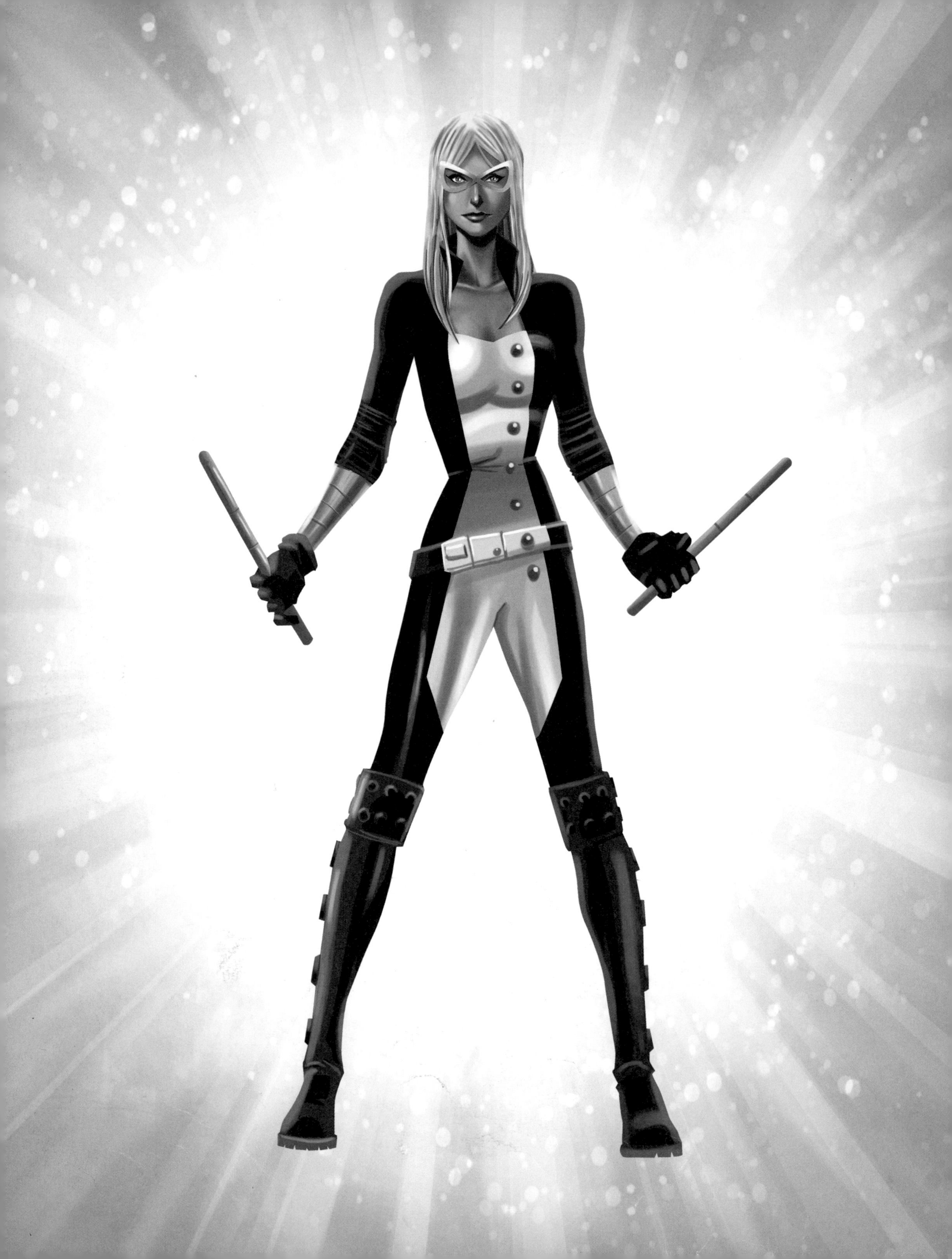

MOCKINGBIRD

TRAINED AS A BIOCHEMIST, Barbara Morse didn't do the expected. Rather than go to work as a scientist, she became a secret agent for S.H.I.E.L.D. before finally ending up as a member of the Mighty Avengers. One of the most powerful **MARTIAL ARTISTS** in the world, her secret weapon is her superior intellect, which allows her to outthink her opponents. Most of them lose the fight before it even begins—they just don't know it.

MOON KNIGHT

MARC SPECTOR was not a good person. So no one, including Marc himself, was surprised when he came to a bad and early end. But he was surprised when the Egyptian god Khonshu appeared and gave him a second chance. Taking him up on the offer, Marc was reborn as Moon Knight. Already an expert at fighting and using weapons, as Moon Knight he's superstrong—although his level of **STRENGTH DEPENDS UPON HOW FULL THE MOON IS**. His cloak, which acts as a parachute, allows him to jump from great heights safely.

MOONSTAR

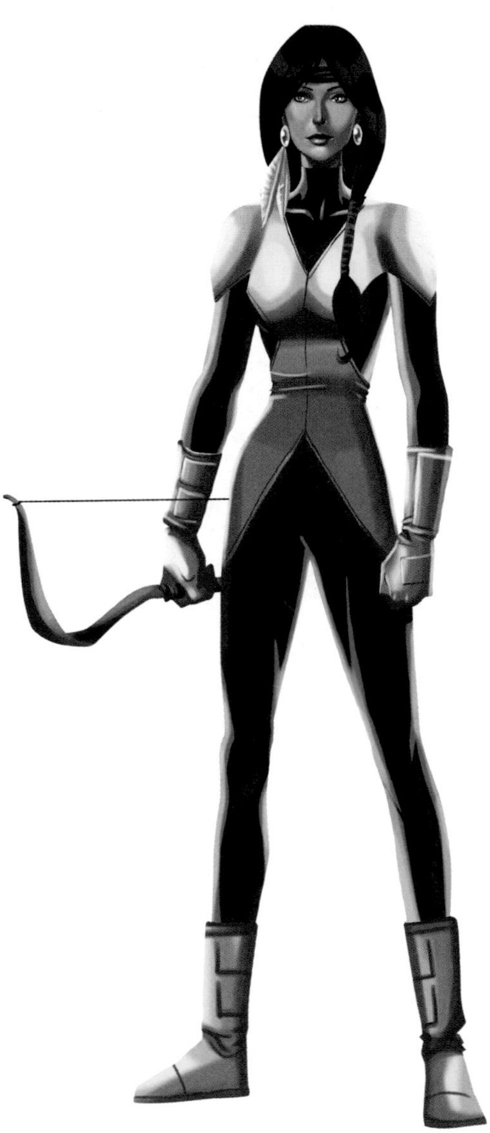

WHEN DANIELLE MOONSTAR'S parents were killed, their good friend Professor X saved the day and brought her in to join the New Mutants.

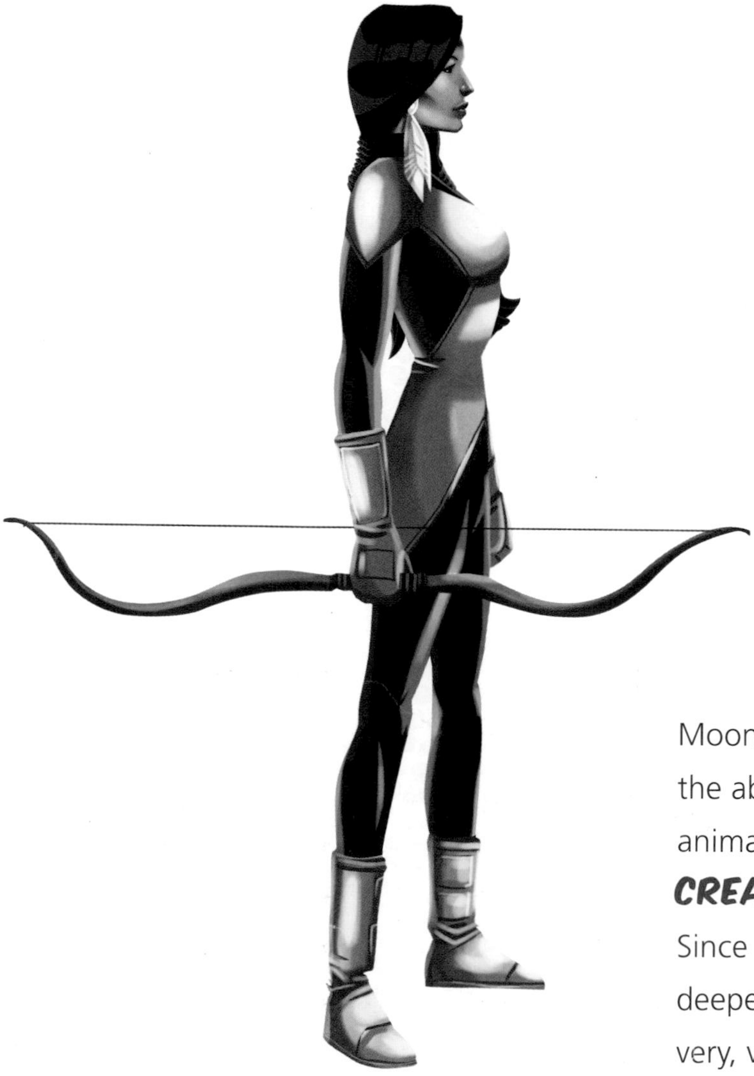

Moonstar's mutant powers include the ability to communicate with animals, as well as ***THE POWER TO CREATE REALISTIC ILLUSIONS.*** Since she can also sense people's deepest fears, her illusions are often very, very powerful.

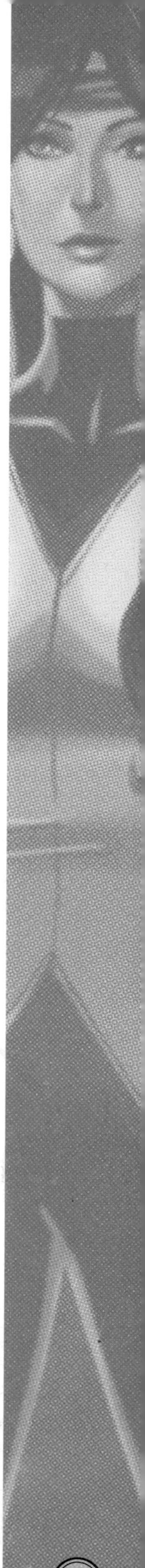

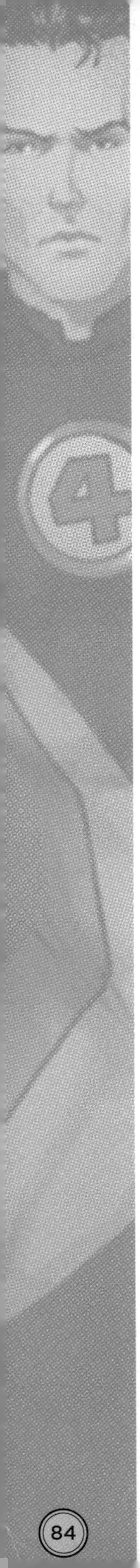

MISTER FANTASTIC

BY THE TIME REED RICHARDS was a teenager, it was obvious to everyone that he was a genius. Already a college student when most kids were still in junior high, Reed met Ben Grimm, who would become his lifelong best friend. He also met Victor von Doom . . . who would not. Ben was the pilot on the spaceship Reed designed, the spaceship which got hit with cosmic radiation. The radiation gave Reed the ability to **STRETCH HIS BODY TO AMAZING LENGTHS,** and even use it to contain explosions or stop bullets—powers which come in handy as the brilliant leader of the Fantastic Four.

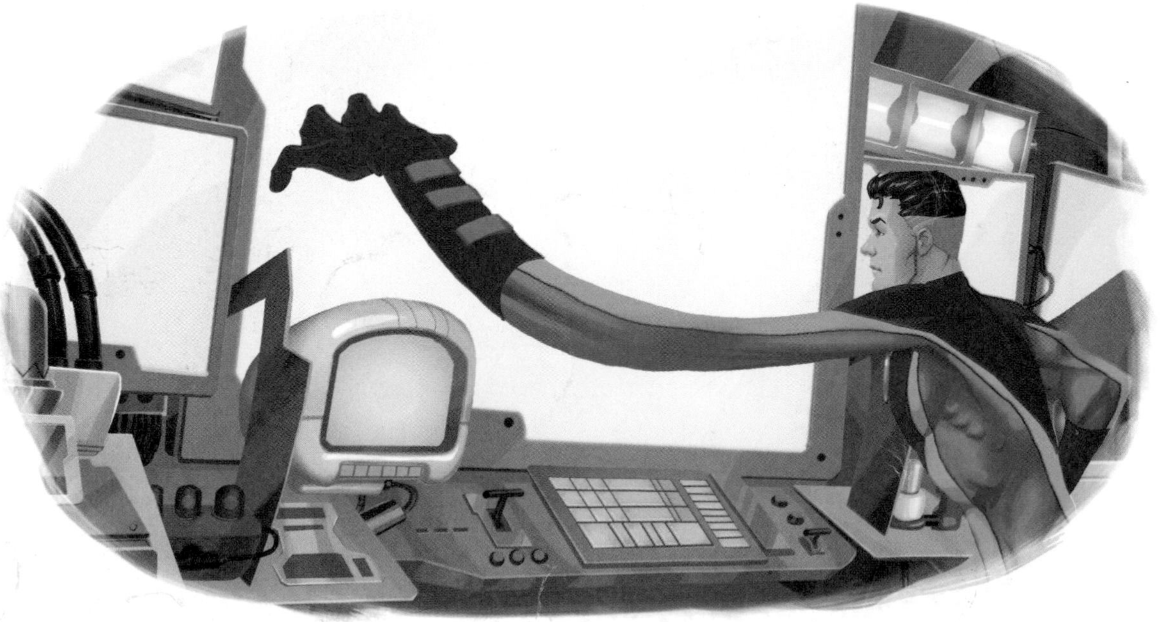

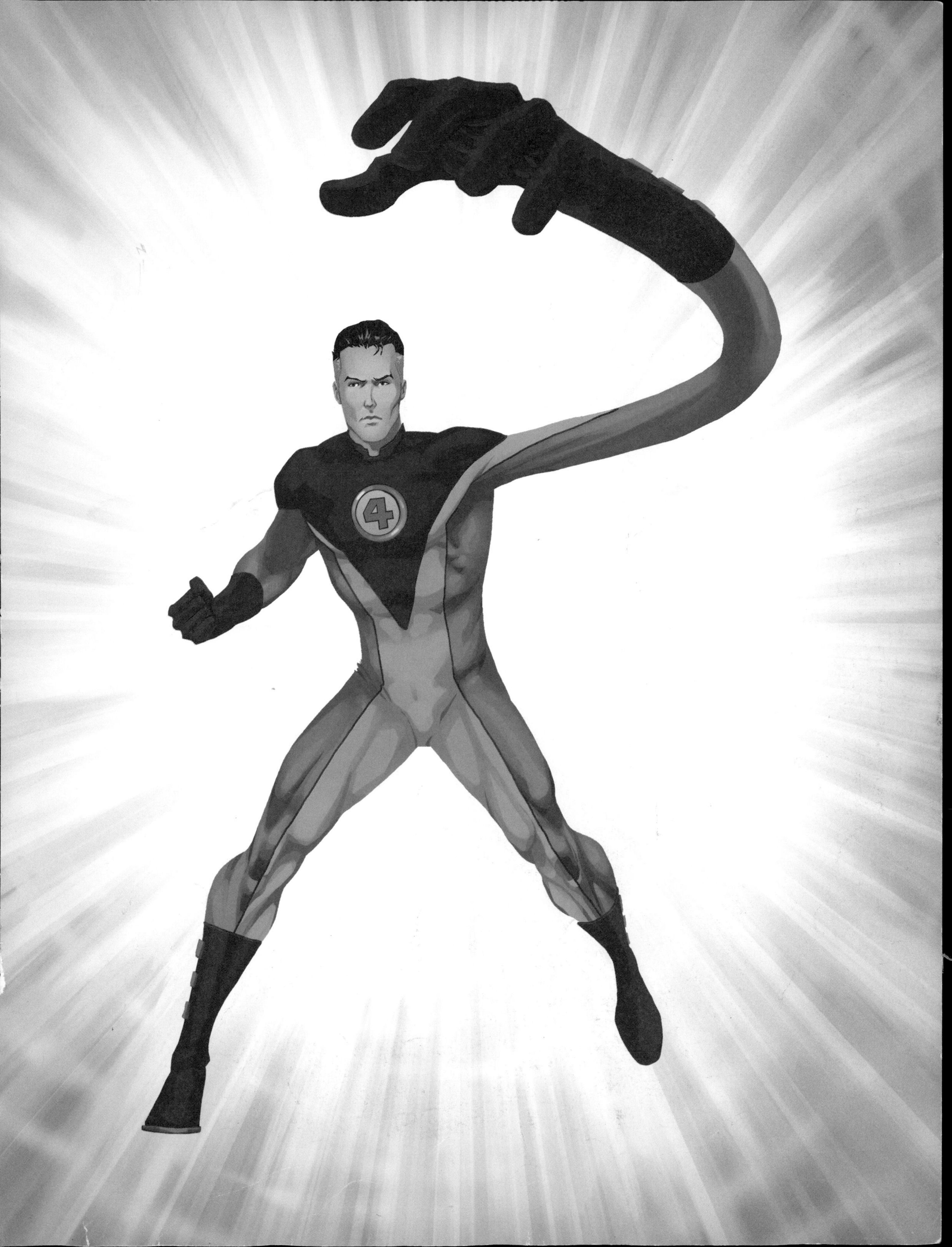

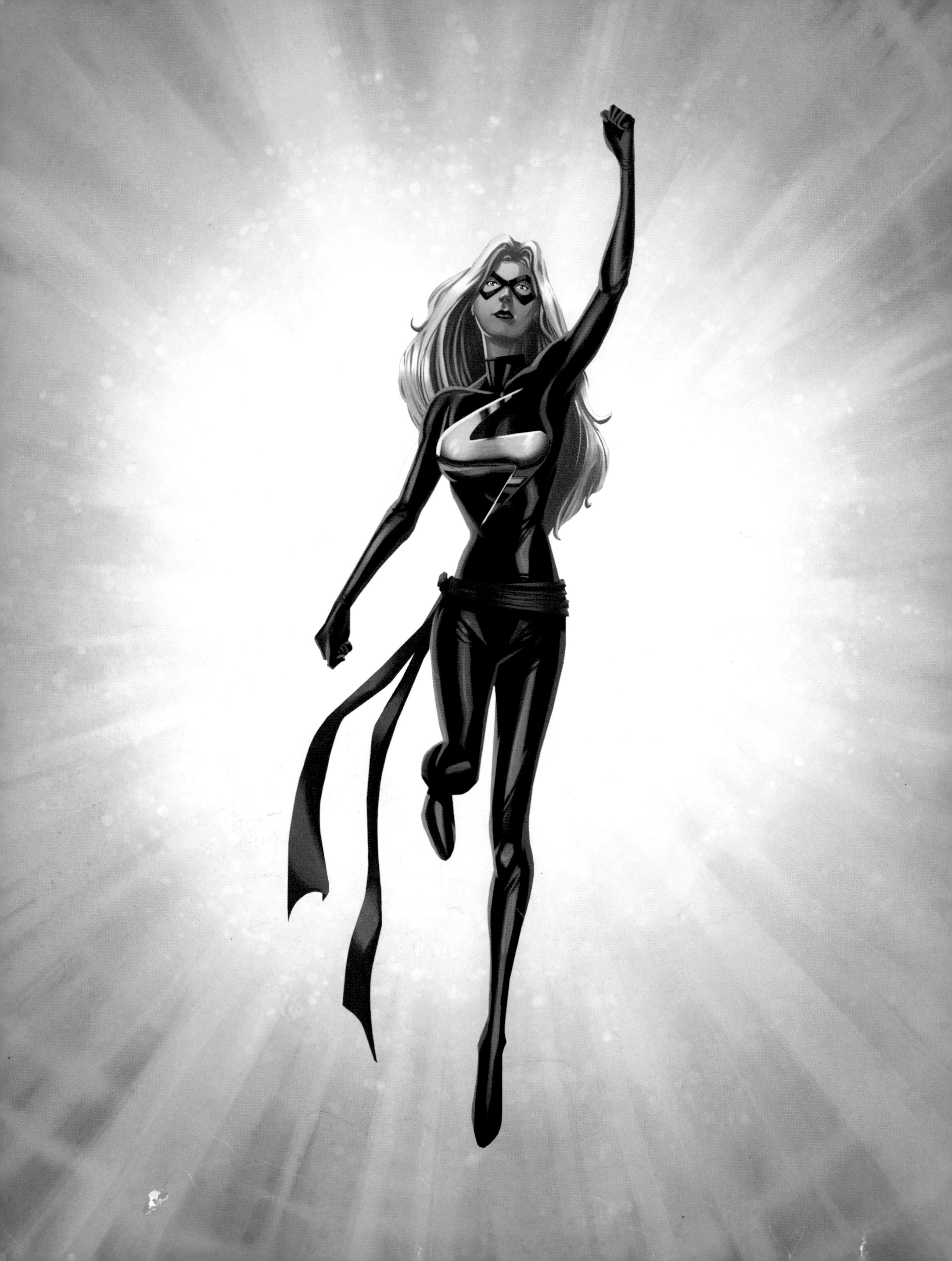

MS. MARVEL

CAROL DANVERS always dreamed big. Determined to be the best she could be, she worked as hard as possible. She became an Air Force officer and the chief of security at a top secret base. She was kidnapped by the alien villains known as the Kree, and tossed into a Kree machine. But instead of killing her—as intended—it gave her superpowers. Superstrong and supertough, she can also **FLY, FIRE ENERGY BLASTS, AND ABSORB ENERGY.** She uses these powers as a member of the Avengers and the Starjammers.

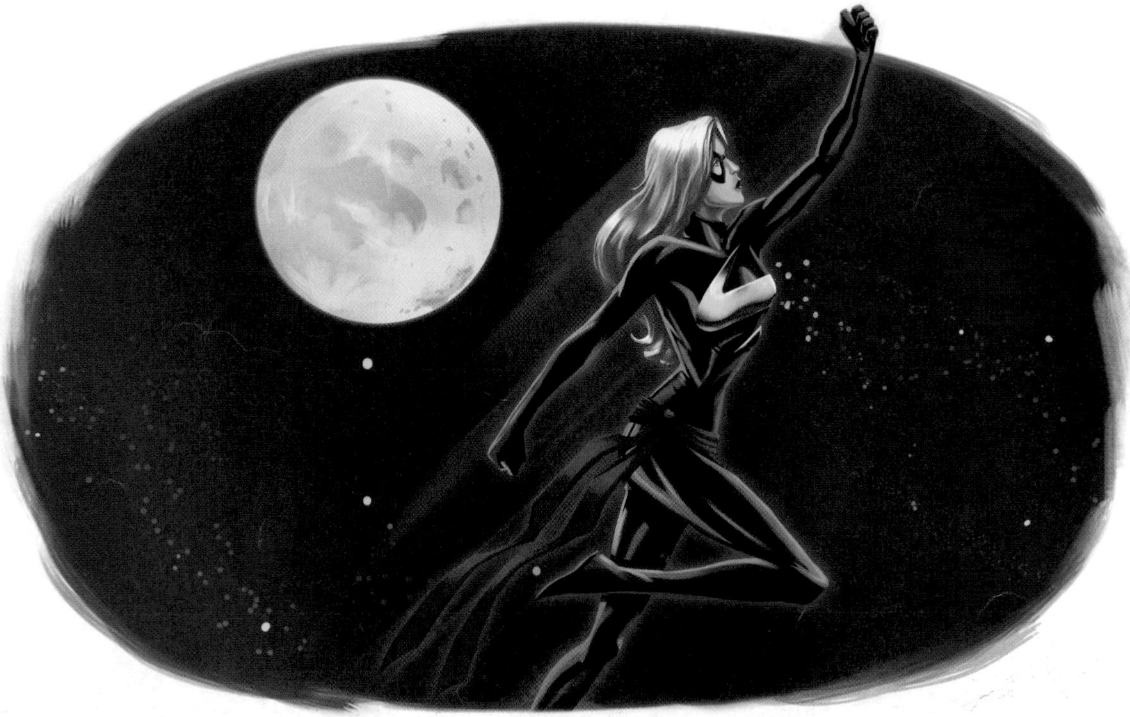

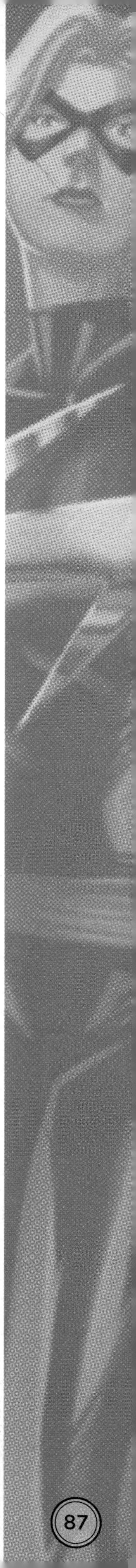

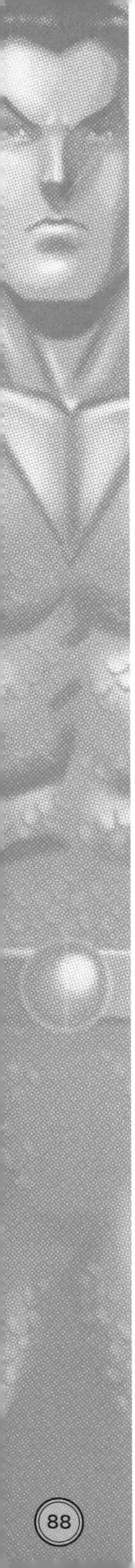

NAMOR

THE MUTANT SON of a human sailor and a princess from Atlantis, Prince Namor the Sub-Mariner can breath underwater, is superstrong and unusually fast, and can even fly.

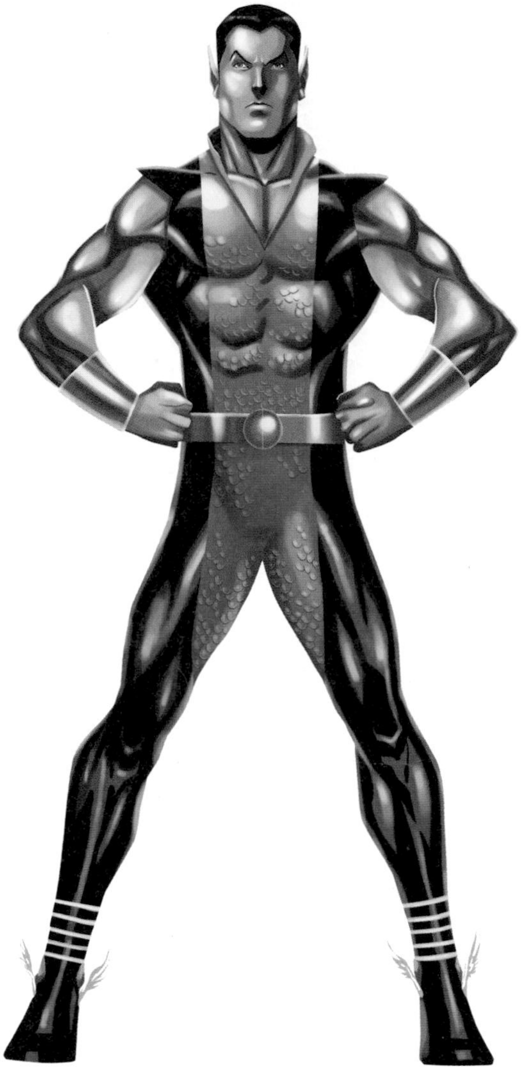

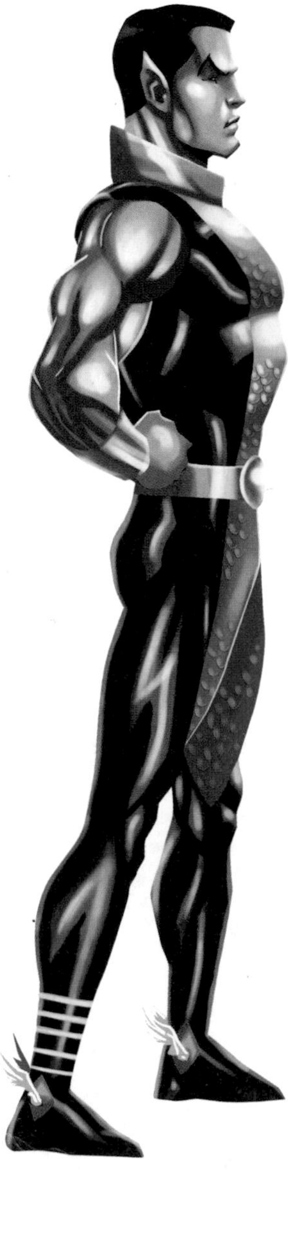

Namor has always been different from other Atlanteans, because he doesn't have blue skin the way they do. But he doesn't fit in with humans either, who insist upon polluting his oceans. After teaming up with the likes of Doctor Doom and Magneto, Namor quickly realized that while humans do make a lot of dumb choices, they're still good at heart. **SO WHILE HE STILL GETS MAD EASILY,** Namor always stays on the right side of things.

NAMORITA

PRINCE NAMOR'S cousin, Namora, couldn't have children. An Atlantean scientist cloned her—and the result was Namorita. Like her cousin Namor, Namorita is superstrong and can breathe underwater, and also fly. She can also **RELEASE ACID FROM HER HANDS** and camouflage herself so well that she seems to turn invisible. A member of the New Warriors, Namorita was one of the rulers of Atlantis, as part of the Council of Three. This is one fish that's never out of water.

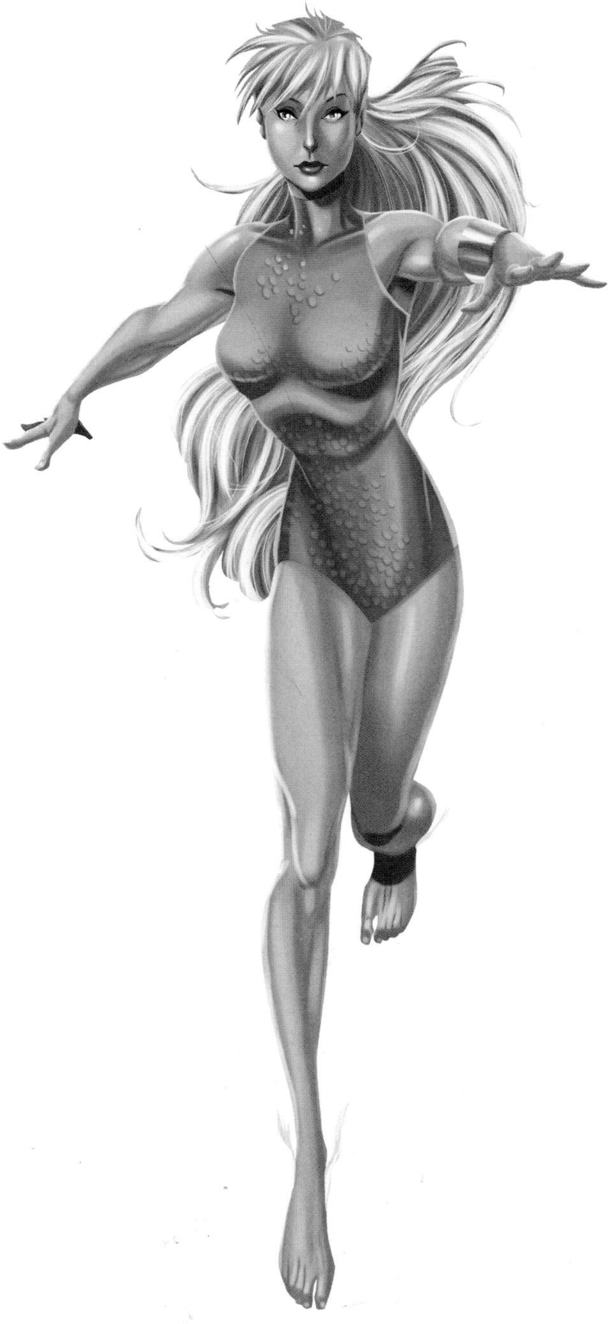

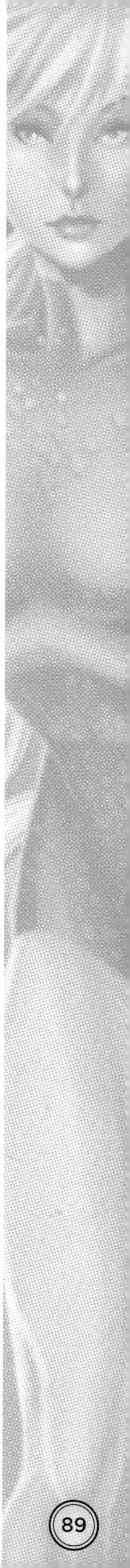

NICK FURY

GROWING UP in New York City's rough Hell's Kitchen neighborhood, Nick Fury learned to be tough at a young age. A boxer, he enlisted in the Army, where he quickly came to command a group of rangers known as the Howling Commandos. Nick joined the CIA before being recruited by Tony Stark to become the Director of S.H.I.E.L.D. As a young man, he was injected with **A SERUM WHICH SLOWED HIS AGING,** so he looks much, much younger than he really is. Turns out youth isn't always wasted on the young.

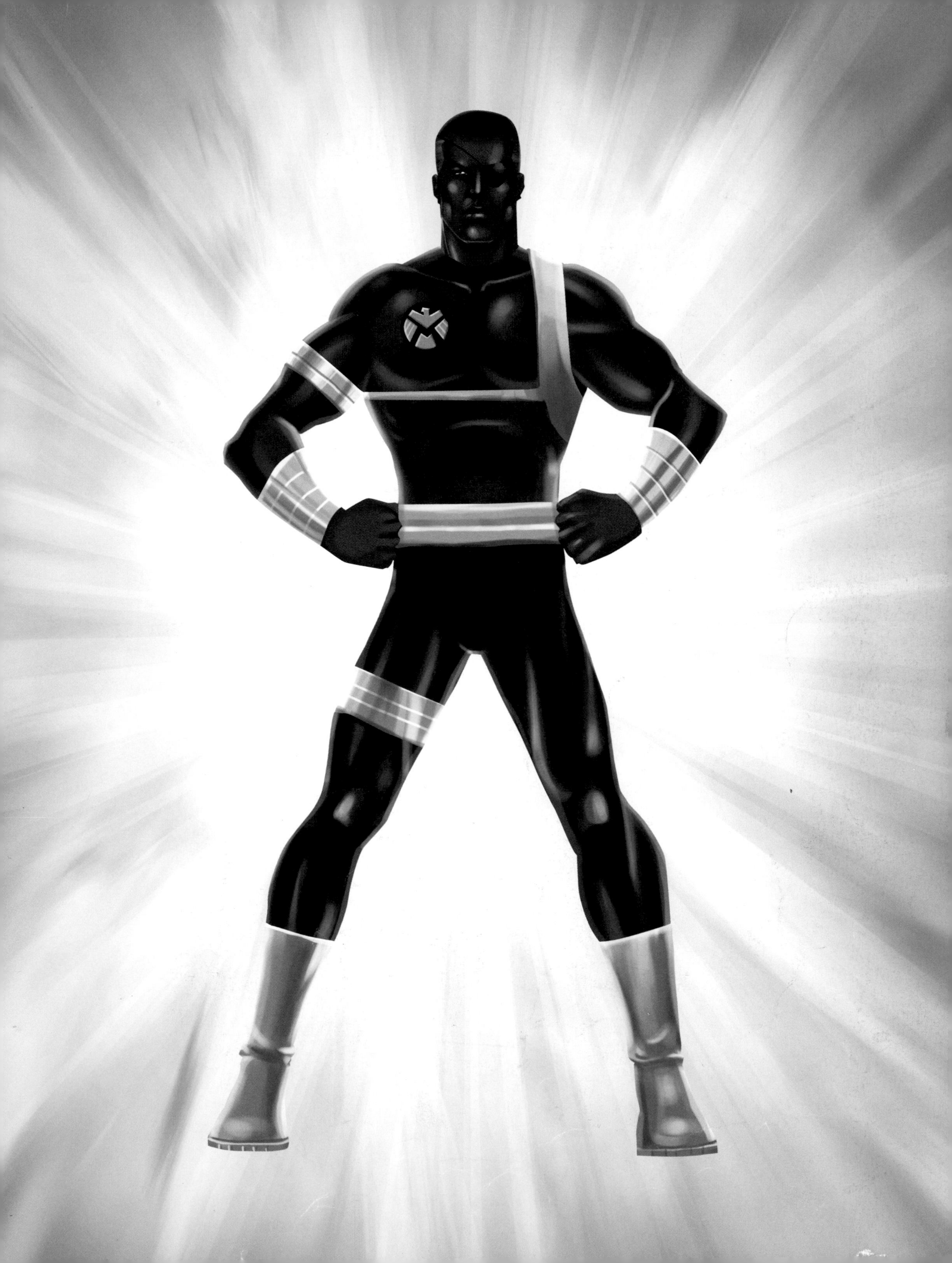

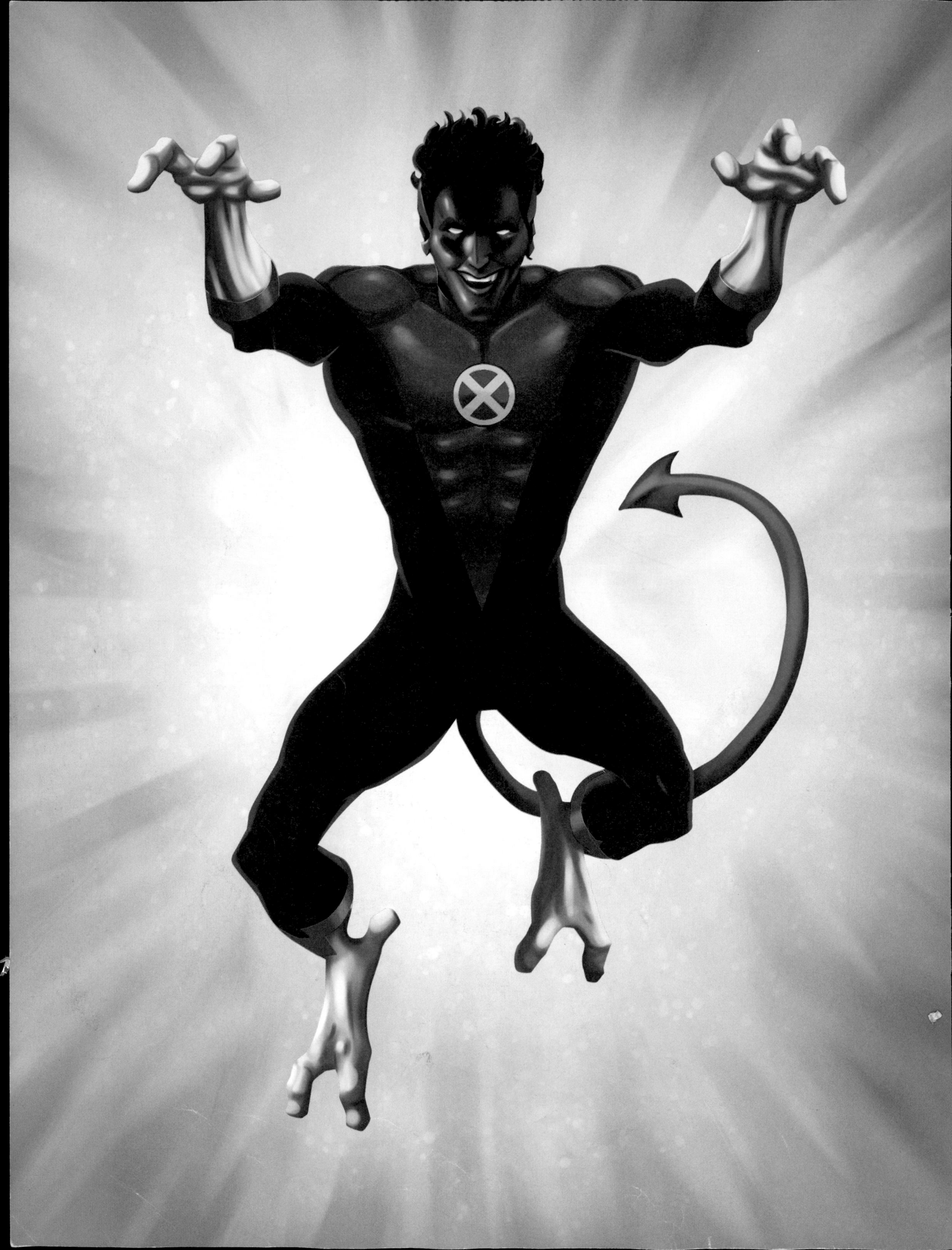

NIGHTCRAWLER

A LOT OF MUTANTS can pass for human. And then there's Nightcrawler. A lot of people would love Kurt Wagner's mutant abilities: he's incredibly agile, putting Olympic gymnasts and circus acrobats to shame, and can teleport. Unfortunately, he also looks like a **BLUE DEMON,** which takes a lot of the fun out of it. Most people recoil in terror when they see him, even though he's as noble a hero as there is. Fortunately, his teammates in the X-Men realize that looks don't matter. They know just how lucky they are to have him around.

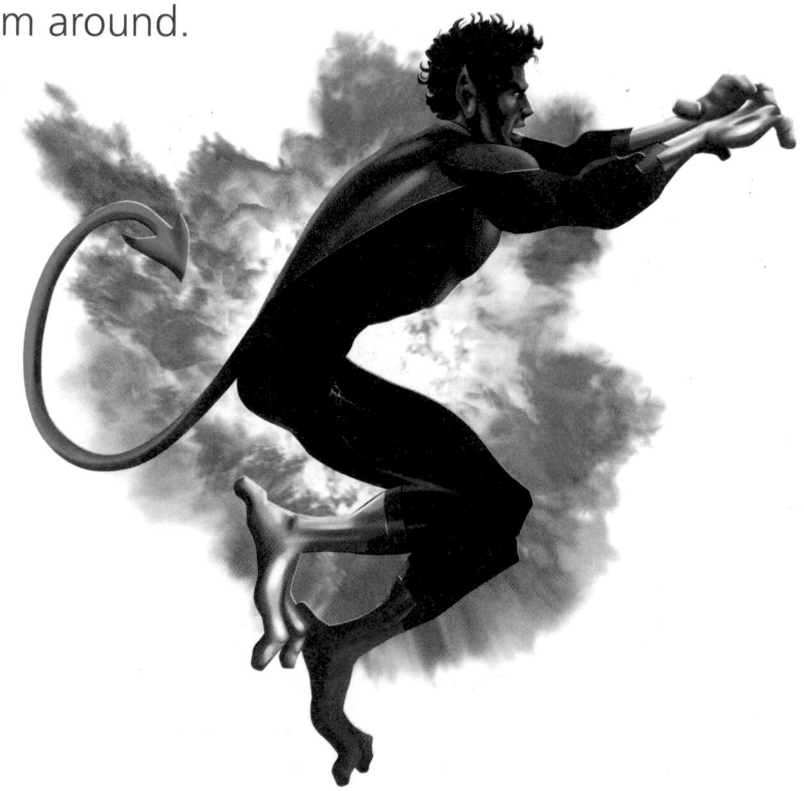

NIGHTHAWK

KYLE RICHMOND was a troubled young man. Rich and spoiled, he was stunned to discover he had a heart murmur. Determined to cure it, he found himself tricked by a mysterious alien known as the Grandmaster into drinking a secret potion. Kyle gained superstrength and his senses become superpowerful. **ARMED WITH RAZOR-SHARP TITANIUM GLOVES** and a jet pack, Nighthawk first joined the supervillain team Squadron Sinister. But he soon realized the error of his ways and switched sides to become a valued member of the Defenders, alongside other heroes heroes like Dr. Strange, the Hulk and Namor.

NORTHSTAR

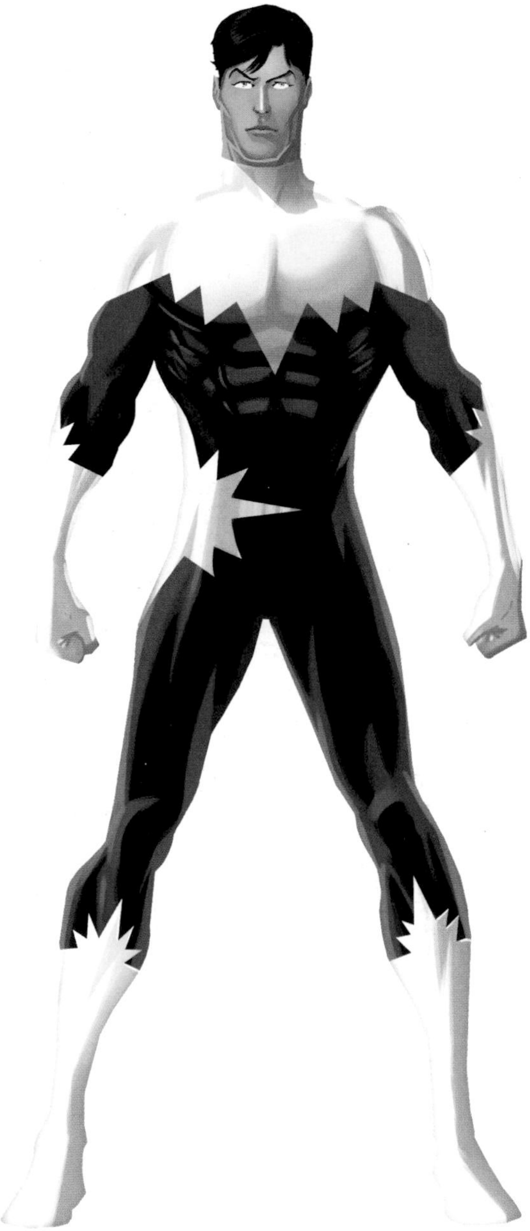

JEAN-PAUL BEAUBIER was a champion skier in Canada until his mutant ability kicked in—after that, skiing became so easy that he grew bored and quit.

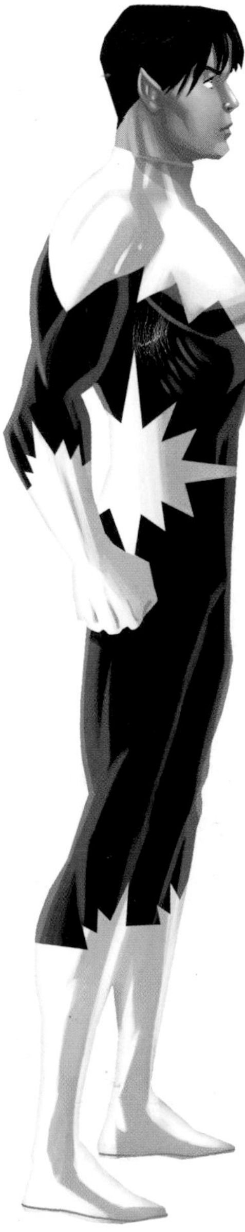

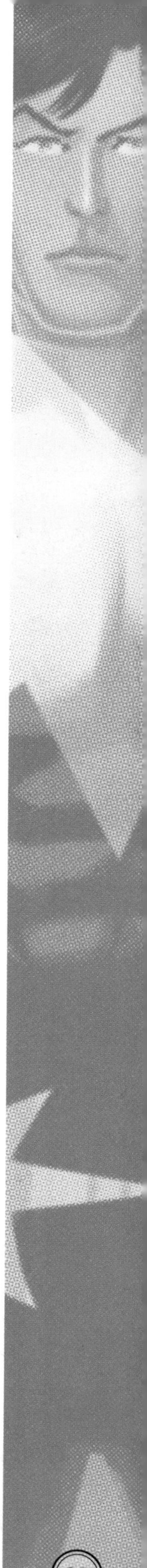

His government was forming a Super Hero team known as **ALPHA FLIGHT,** so he adopted the codename Northstar and signed on, reuniting with his long-lost sister Jeanne-Marie. Northstar has superspeed and can fly, as well as shoot light blasts.

NOVA

RICHARD RIDER was just an ordinary high school student until the alien Rhomann Dey, the last surviving Nova Centurion of the planet Xandar, chose him to be his heir. Suddenly, Richard found himself as the new Nova Prime, the highest rank in an **ELITE ALIEN MILITARY FORCE.** Richard discovered that he had superstrength, superspeed, and was indestructible—just about the most powerful being in the universe . . . but he had no idea how to use those powers. Also, he had homework due. Fortunately, Nova was a quick learner.

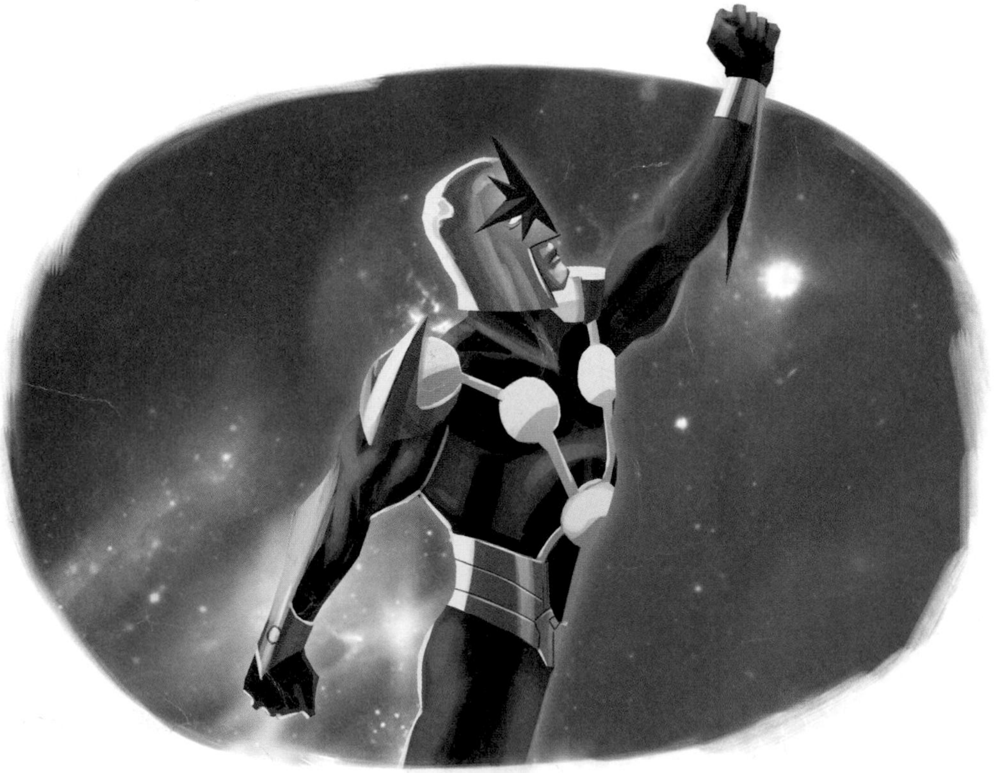

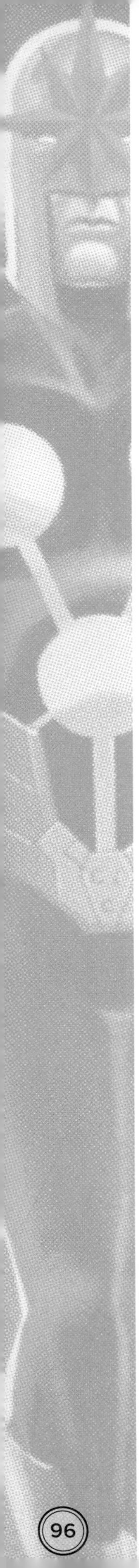

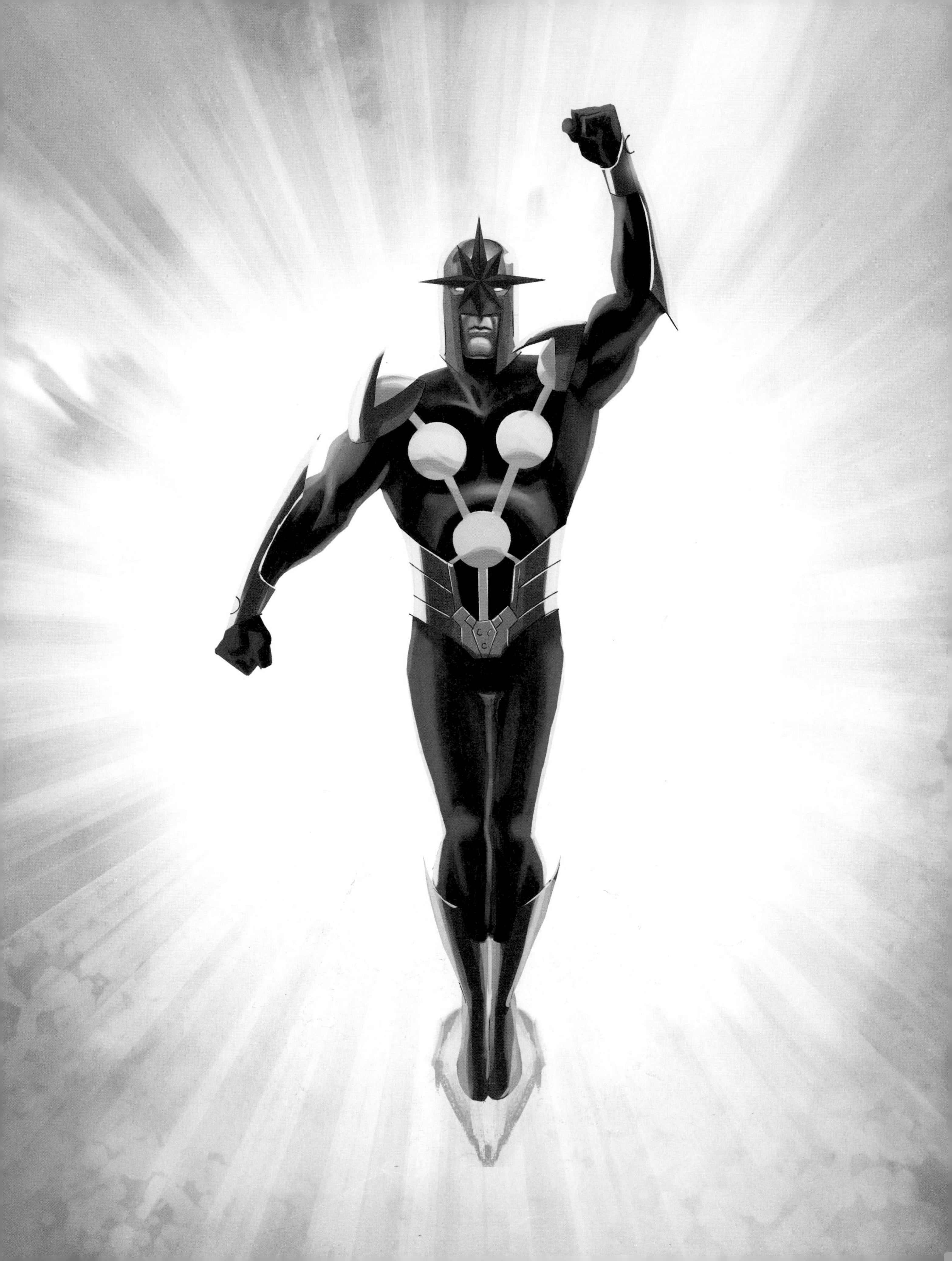

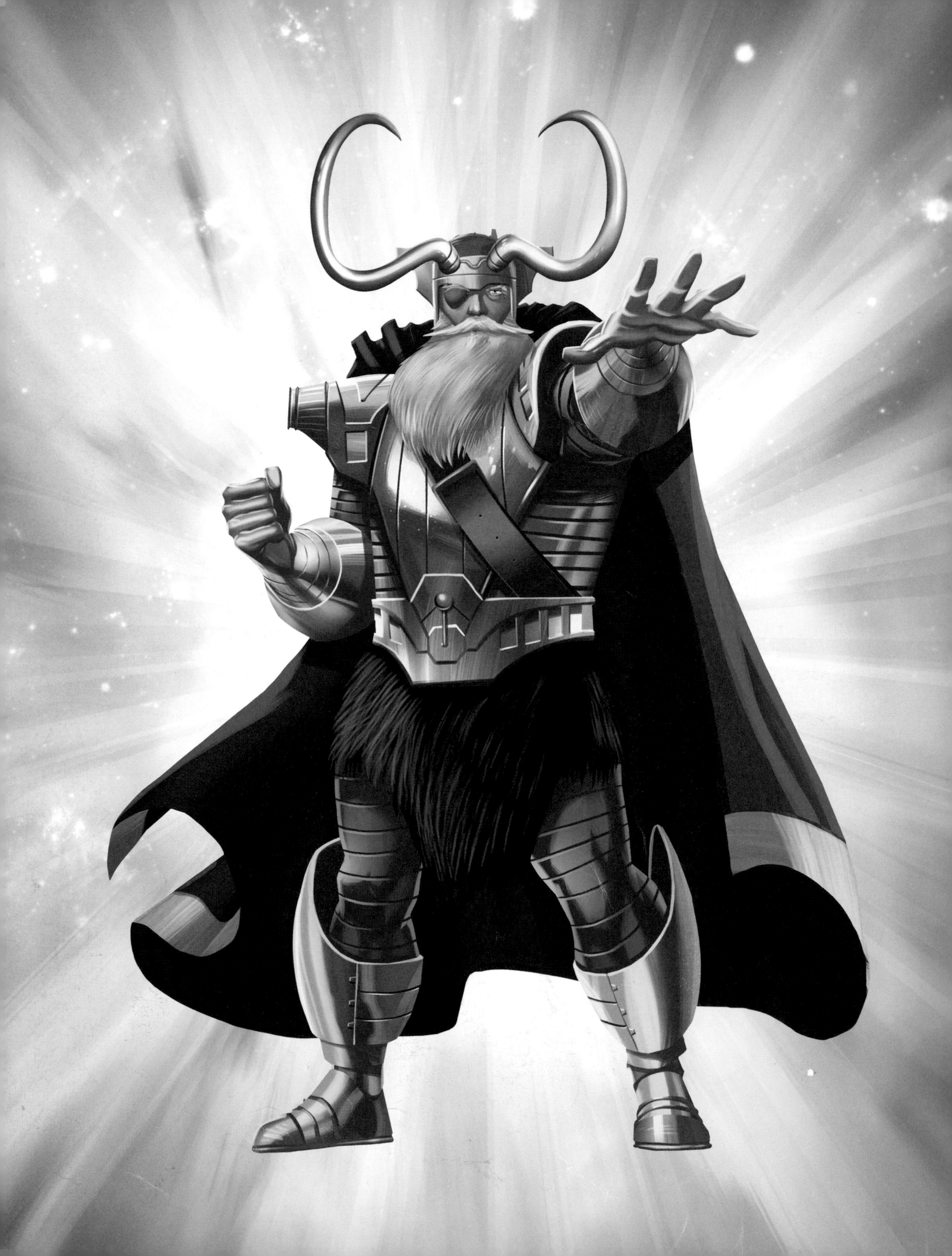

ODIN

IT CAN BE TOUGH living up to your parents' accomplishments. Just ask Thor. His father is Odin Allfather, the son of one of the first Asgardians and a Frost Giant. Young Odin was already powerful, but when his brothers died, he inherited their powers, too. Soon he was ruler of all Asgard. While Thor gets most of the headlines, Odin has ***SAVED ASGARD*** again and again, even dying three times. Fortunately, he returned to life by falling into Odinsleep. Superstrong and with an obviously amazing healing ability, he can also tap into the Odinforce, enabling him to project force fields, shoot energy blasts, shrink or grow, teleport huge numbers of people to other dimensions—just about anything, really.

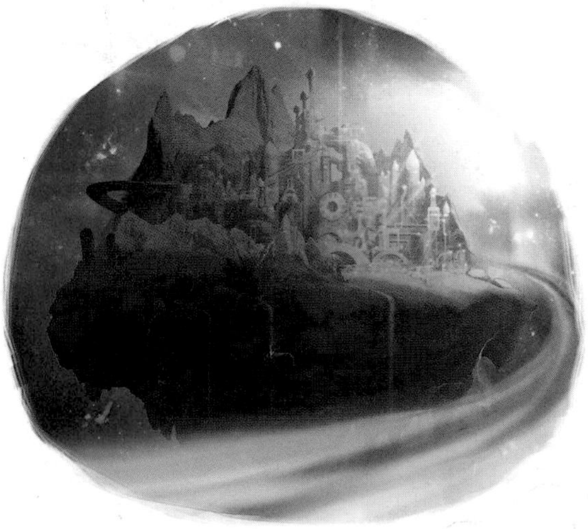

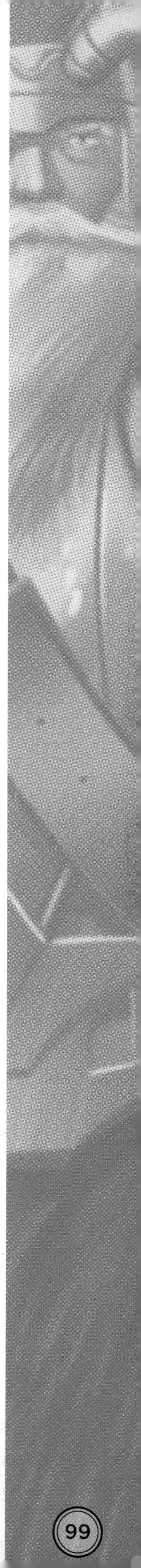

PHOTON

BORN IN NEW ORLEANS, LOUISIANA,

Monica Rambeau was the captain of a cargo ship and a lieutenant in the New Orleans Harbor Patrol. While on duty, she was investigating the creation of a very dangerous weapon when she was suddenly exposed to an energy not from this world. The contact gave Monica the ability to convert her body into pure energy.

Photon can also **ABSORB PURE STELLAR ENERGY**, giving her super-strength and the ability to fly. She can also shoot energy blasts. Plus, she has "cosmic awareness"—which means she knows everything that is happening, ever happened, or will happen. This is not as much fun as it sounds.

POLARIS

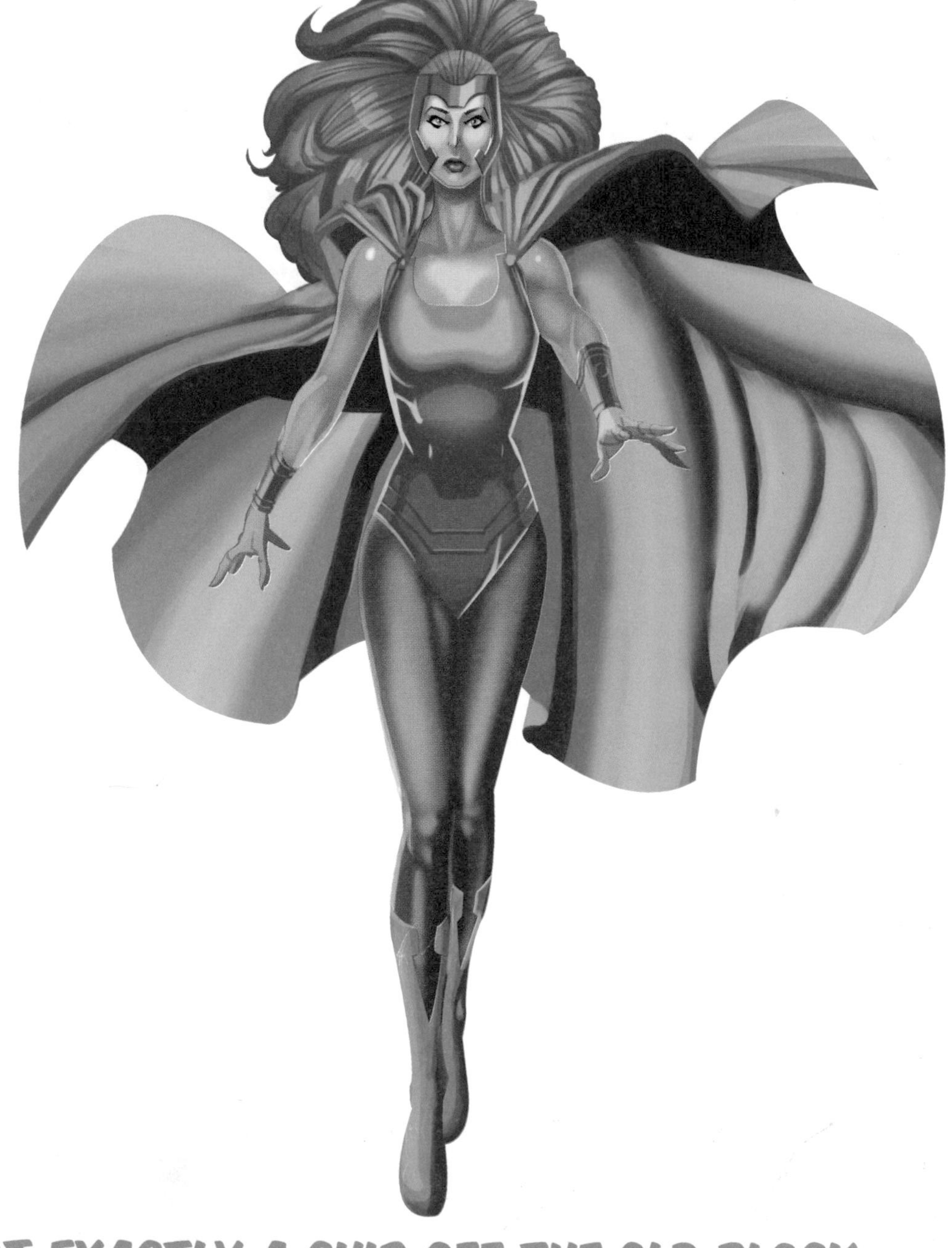

NOT EXACTLY A CHIP OFF THE OLD BLOCK, Lorna Dane inherited the mutant ability to **CONTROL METAL** from her father, Magneto. But whereas he uses his powers to try to wipe out humanity, Polaris uses hers to try to protect it as a member of the X-Men. Both Havok and Iceman have fallen madly in love with her, showing that her magnetism doesn't only work on metal.

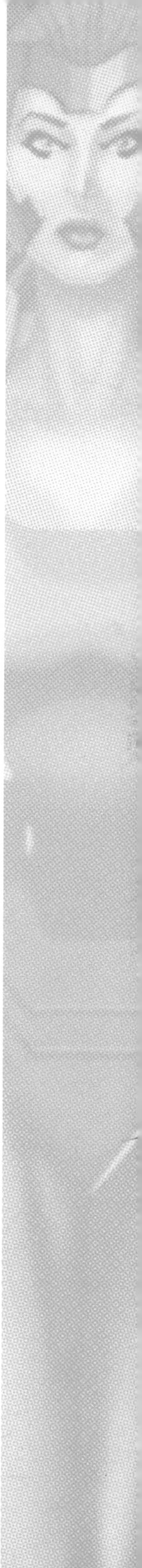

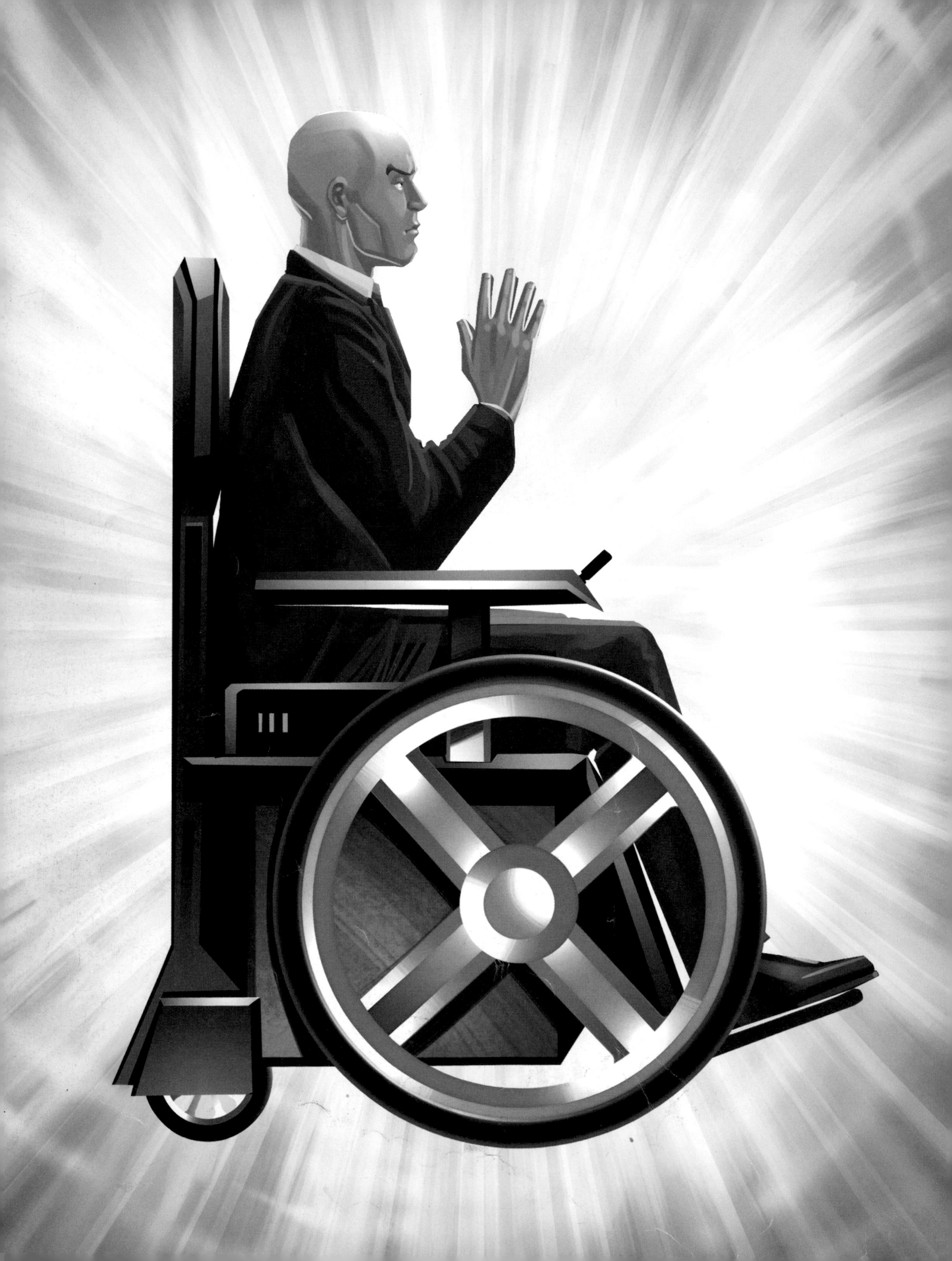

PROFESSOR XAVIER

CHARLES XAVIER REALIZED he could read people's minds when he was still a child. As he got older, his powers grew and grew until he could read the minds of people hundreds of miles away. Eventually Charles became the most **POWERFUL TELEPATH** in the world. After he lost the use of his legs defending the Earth from an alien invasion, Charles decided to open a school for young mutants, to help them learn to use their powers for good, as he had. Now the head of the School for Gifted Youngsters, Professor X trains and leads the amazing team of superpowered mutants known as the Uncanny X-Men and the junior X-team, The New Mutants.

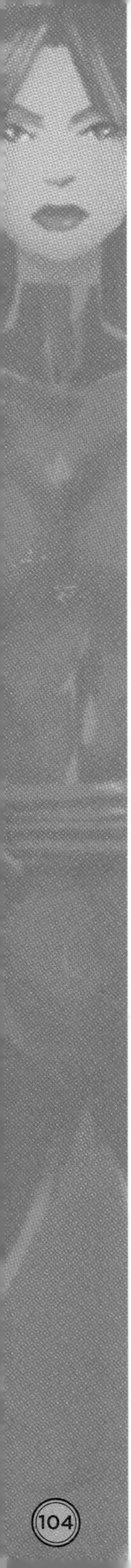

PSYLOCKE

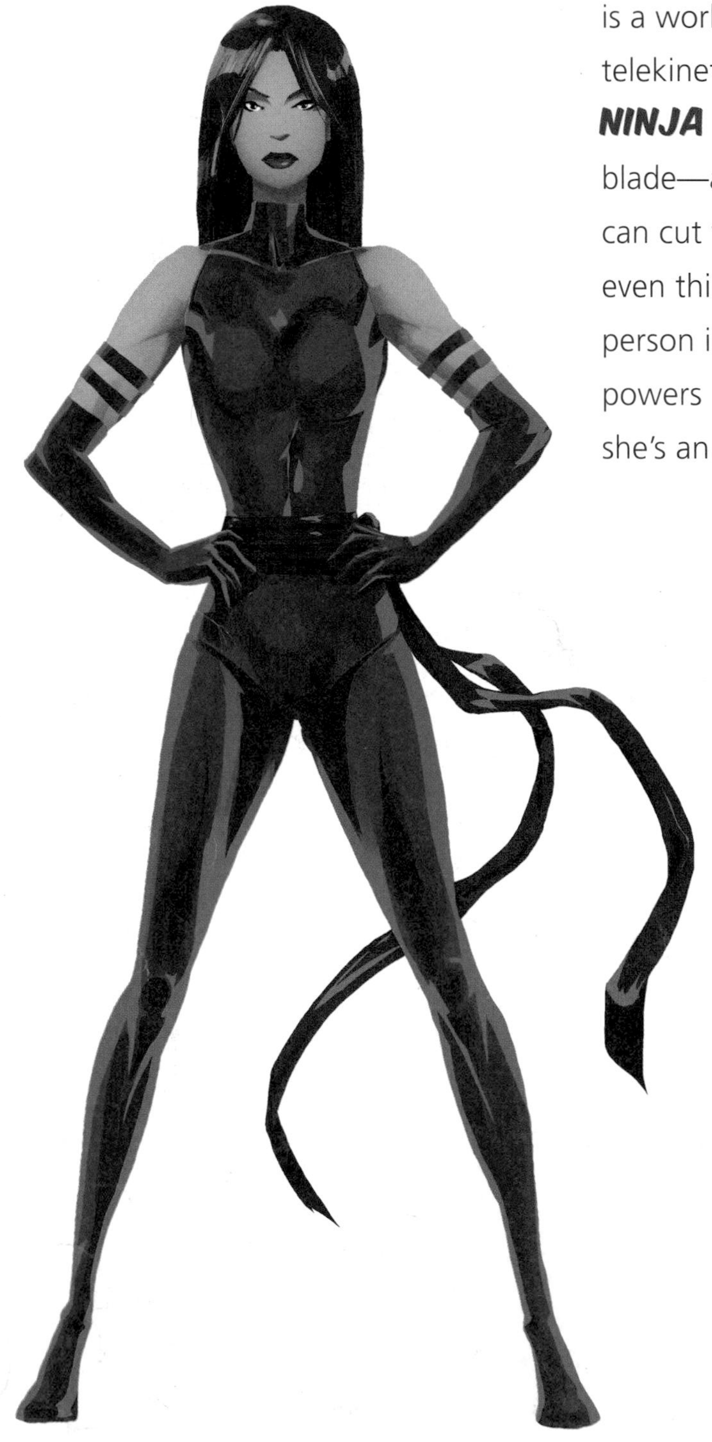

ELIZABETH BRADDOCK is a world-class telepath with telekinetic powers. She's also a ***NINJA*** with a telekinetic katana blade—a kind of mental sword—that can cut through pretty much anything, even thick armor . . . yet leave the person inside the armor. With mutant powers like these, it's a good thing she's an X-Man.

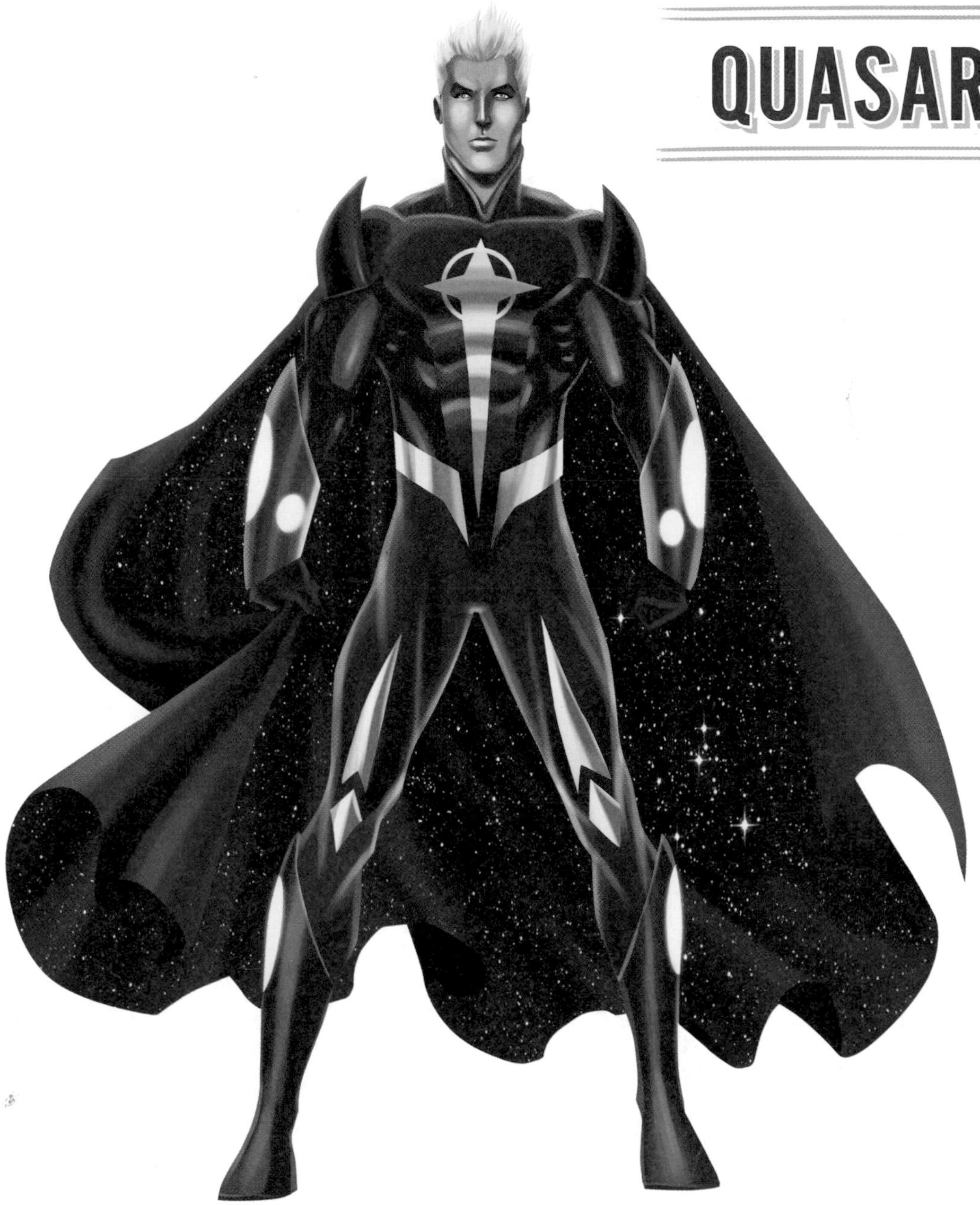

QUASAR

WENDELL VAUGHAN was a guard at Stark Industries the day scientists there were testing experimental devices called the **QUANTUM BANDS.** The Quantum Bands quickly proved very dangerous, when they killed one of the scientists. But when rivals attacked, hoping to steal the bands, Wendell did the only thing he could: he put on the Quantum Bands himself. His training as a security guard and his open, curious nature allowed him to quickly master the bands. Now, as Quasar, he is a being of pure and limitless energy, able to take any form he can imagine—all of them unbelievably powerful.

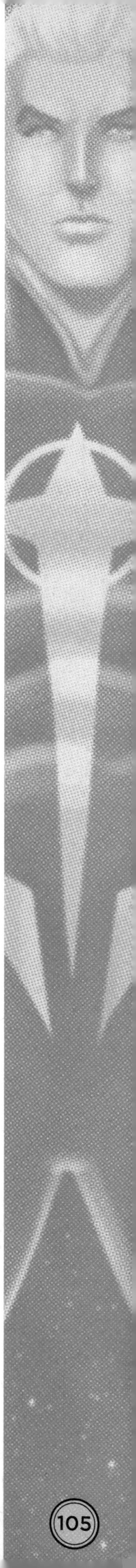

QUICKSILVER

AND YOU THOUGHT YOUR family was weird! Mutant Pietro Maximoff's dad is the Super Villain Magneto, his twin sister is the Scarlet Witch and Polaris is his half-sister. Then Pietro and his twin gave up the whole evil thing to become good, upstanding members of the X-Men and the Avengers. Pietro can run at **FOUR TIMES THE SPEED OF SOUND,** making his name pretty self-explanatory. He can also use his superspeed to destroy most things, by shaking them so quickly their molecular bonds fall apart. Not unlike his familial ones.

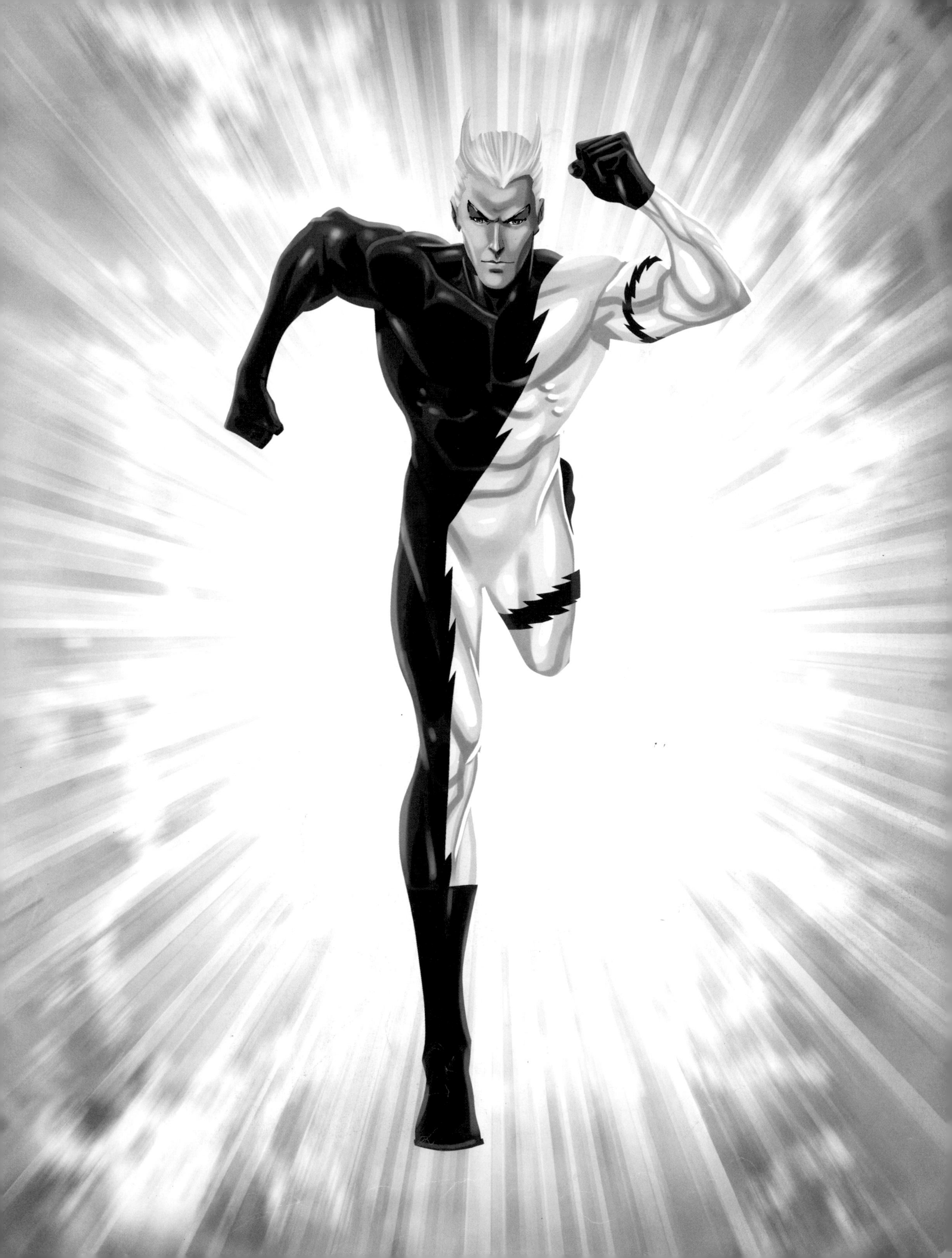

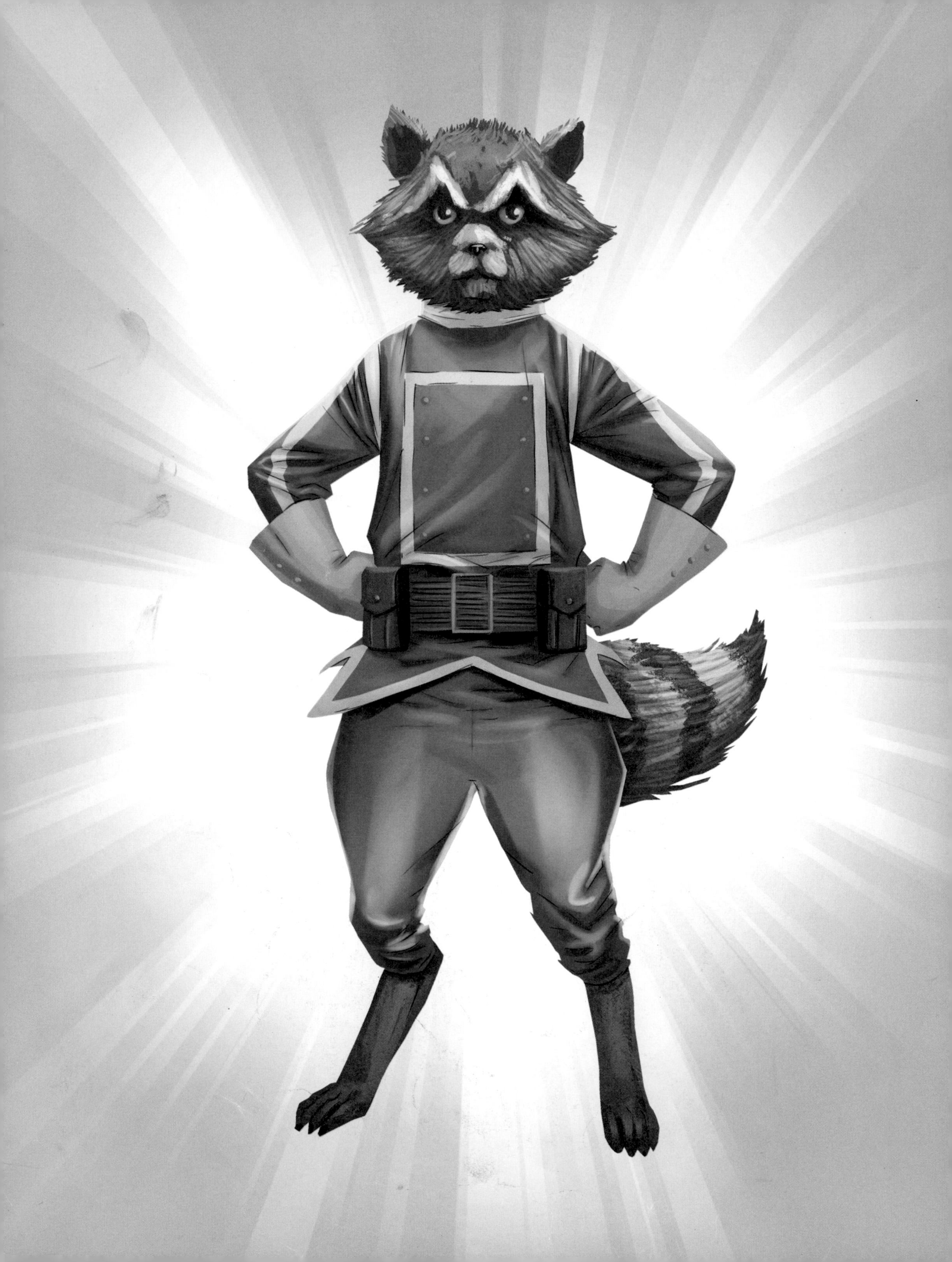

ROCKET RACCOON

THERE ARE HEROES and then there are **HEROES.** And then there's Rocket Raccoon. The super intelligent robots who ran the insane asylum on the planet Halfworld were tired of their jobs, so they genetically engineered the asylum's pets to become sentient . . . so they could take over the place. That's how Rocket Raccoon became the planet's chief law officer. Blessed with **AN ASSORTMENT OF HEAVY WEAPONRY,** Rocket later became a Guardian of the Galaxy. Because, really, what Super Hero team couldn't benefit from the addition of a raccoon?

ROGUE

MANY MUTANTS WISH THEY WEREN'T MUTANTS, even though their abilities are amazing. You can't blame the hero known as Rogue for feeling that way. Her power is to **DRAIN** the memories, emotions, and superpowers, out of anyone she touches—and if she doesn't break contact soon enough, she will even drain away their very life. She wears extra clothing at all times, to make sure she doesn't accidentally kill someone by brushing up against them. It's not easy being the most dangerous member of the X-Men.

SCARLET WITCH

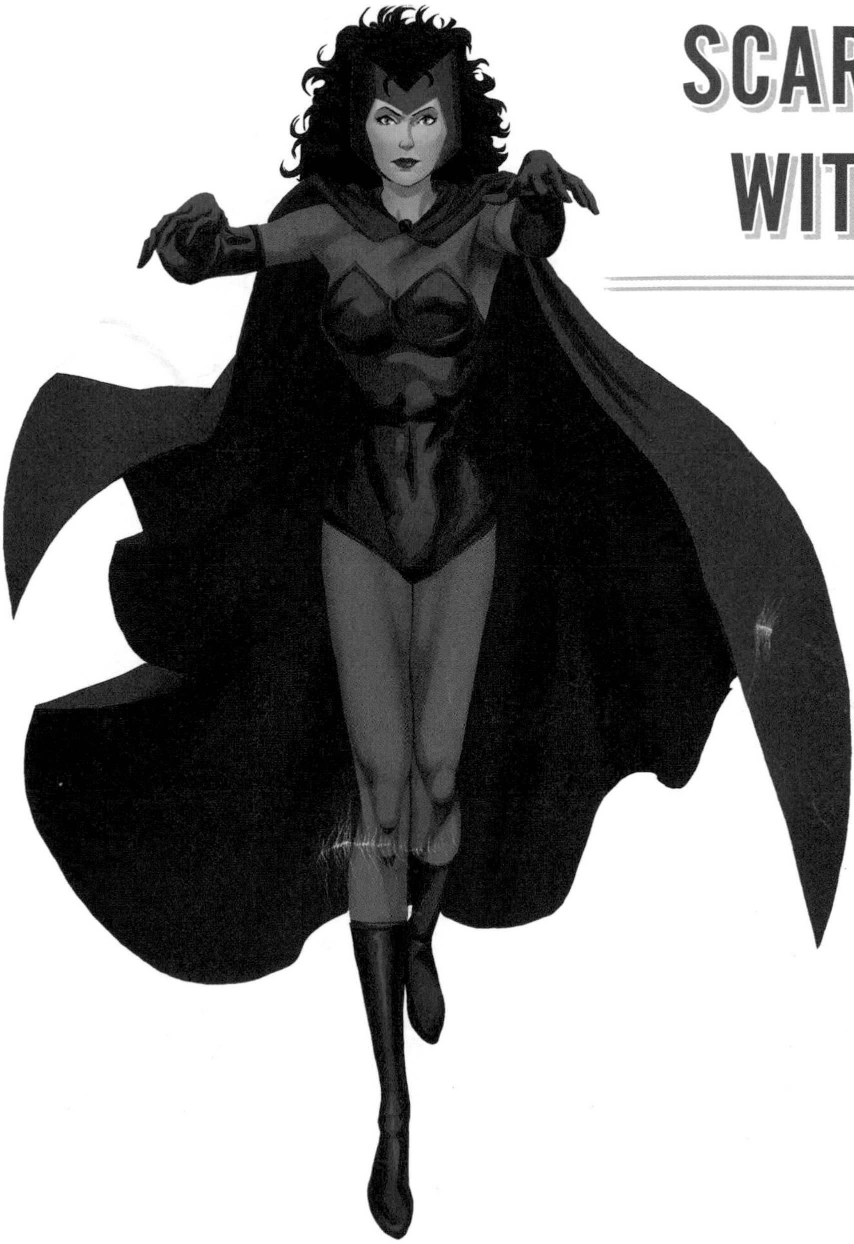

SEPARATED FROM HER FAMILY AS A CHILD, Wanda Maximoff didn't know her father was the Super Villain Magneto. She also didn't know that, as the Scarlet Witch, she was fighting alongside her twin brother Quicksilver in Magneto's Brotherhood of Evil—against her half-sister Polaris, a member of the X-Men. Ultimately, **SCARLET WITCH AND QUICKSILVER TURNED THEIR BACKS ON EVIL** and joined the Avengers. It's a hard time for any child when she realizes her dad is one of the most dangerous villains in the world.

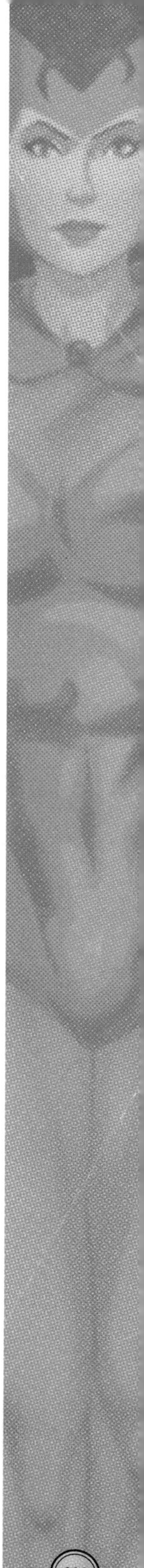

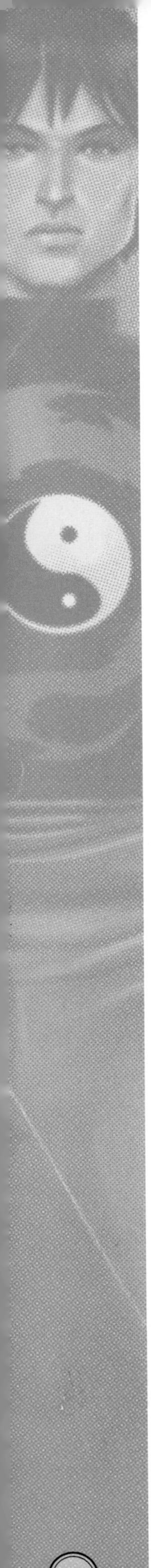

SHANG-CHI

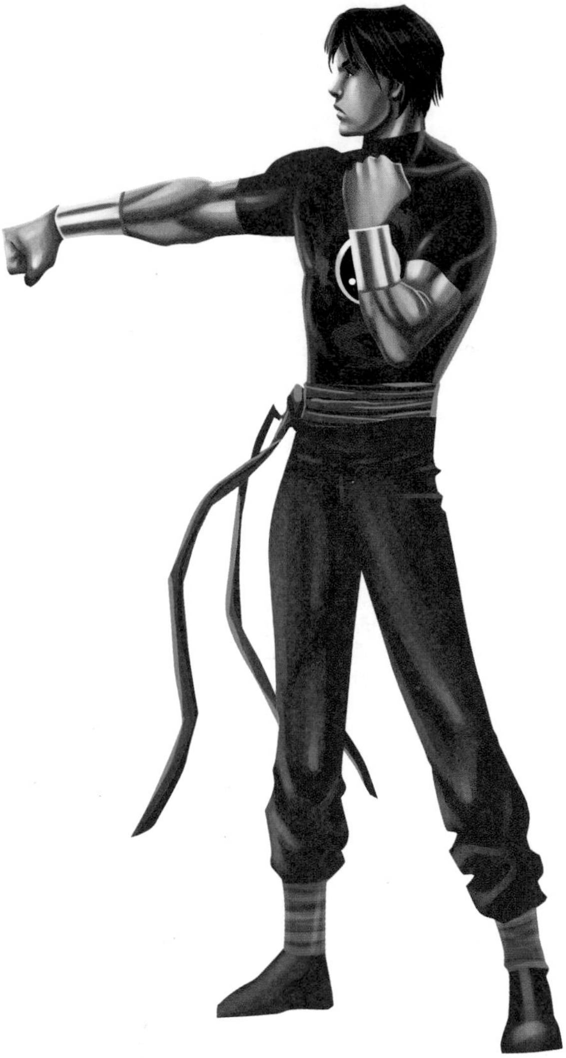

THERE IS ONE NAME that the finest fighters in history bow down before: Shang-Chi. Son of the legendary master criminal Fu Manchu, Shang-Chi's training in the martial arts began as a young child.

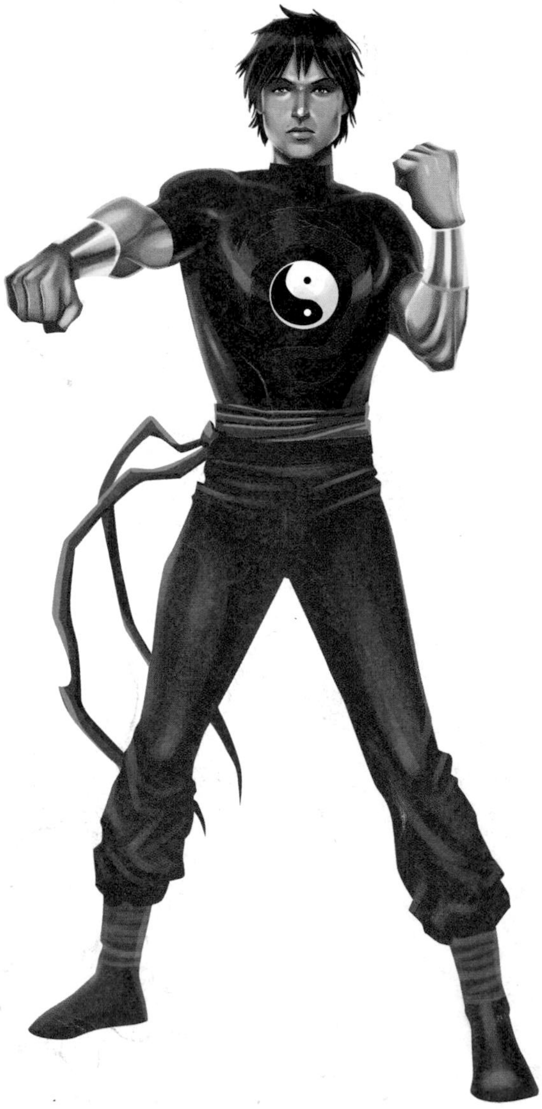

Although he has no superpowers, by the time he was an adult his skills were so well developed they were **PRACTICALLY SUPERHUMAN.** Learning the truth about his father, he devoted his life to fighting evil. After having gone up against him in the past, the likes of Spider-Man and the Thing are very, very happy to now have Shang-Chi on their side.

SHE-HULK

JENNIFER WALTERS is Bruce Banner's cousin. She is also a prosecutor. While Bruce was in town for a visit, Jennifer was attacked by a crook she was trying to convict. Naturally, Bruce donated his blood when she needed an emergency transfusion. One tiny problem: Bruce is the Hulk. And because they're cousins, his blood gave her powers similar to his as the Hulk. Fortunately, unlike her cousin, **SHE GENERALLY RETAINS HER INTELLECT** as She-Hulk. She is also usually able to change back and forth at will.

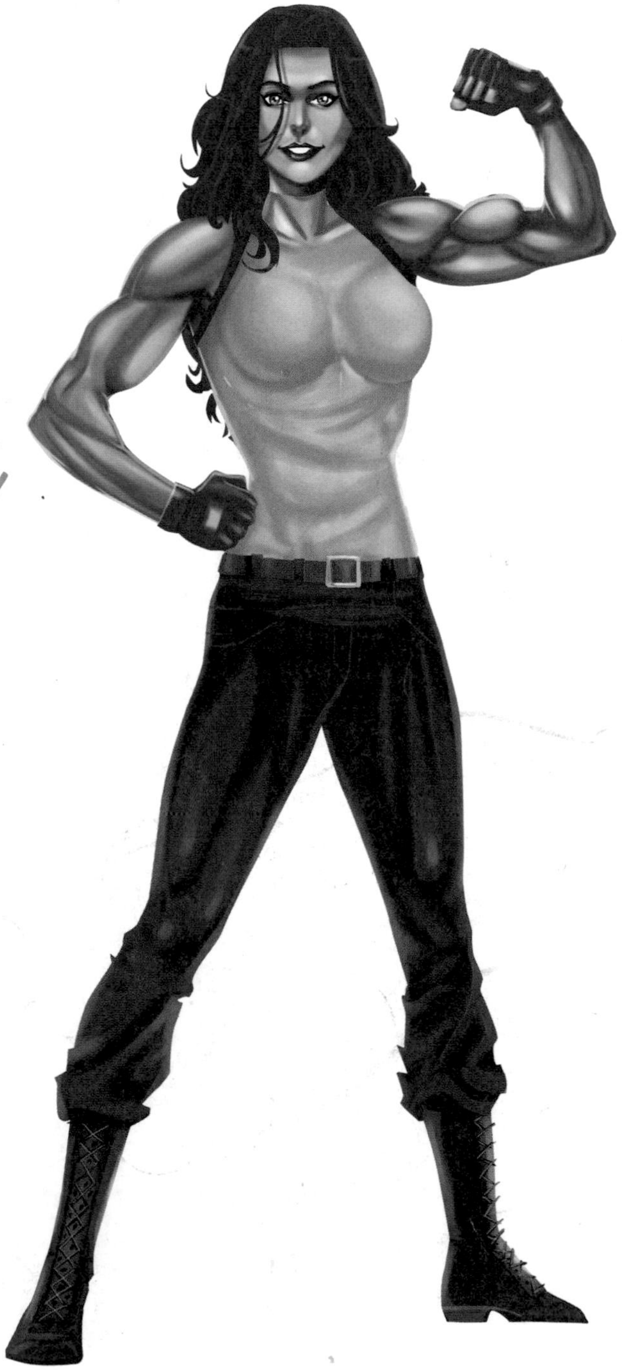

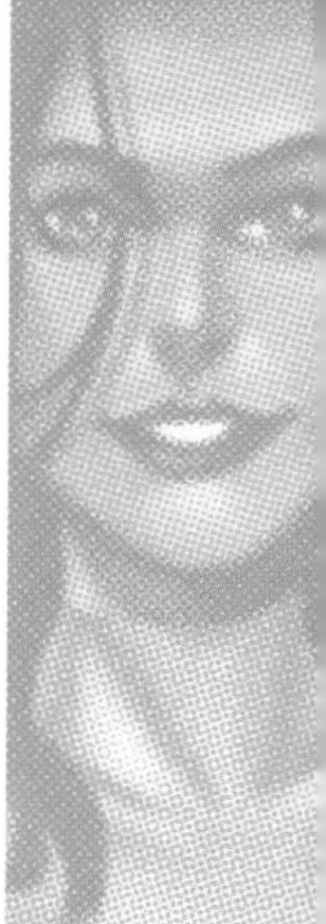

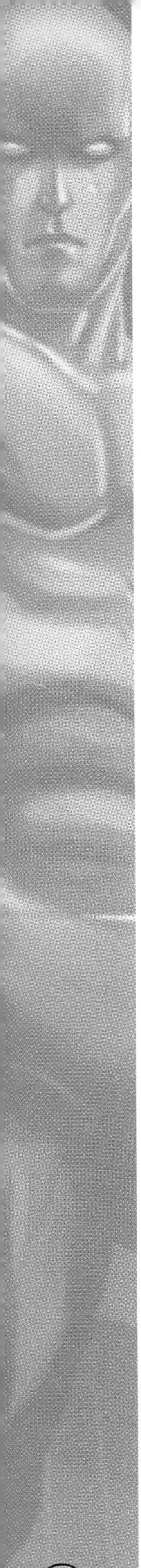

SILVER SURFER

POOR NORRIN RADD. His planet, Zenn-La, was a paradise, with no crime and plenty of food for everyone. So when Galactus, a being who eats entire worlds, approached, Norrin Radd offered to help him, if he would spare Norrin Radd's planet. That's how Norrin Radd wound up looking for planets for Galactus to eat, and how he landed on Earth. Realizing humans were worth saving, Norrin Radd fought back against **GALACTUS** alongside the Fantastic Four. He saved Earth, but was now stuck on our planet, never able to go home again. Now, as the Silver Surfer, he wanders the Earth, trying to make this strange new planet his home.

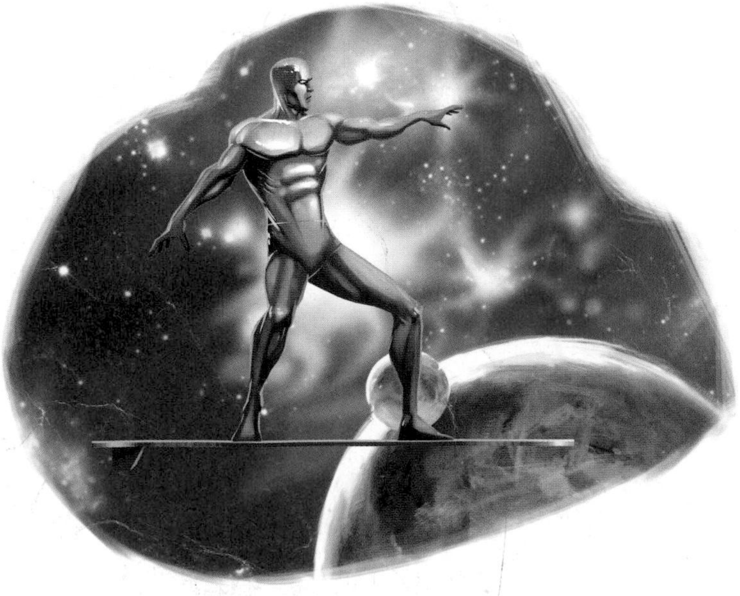

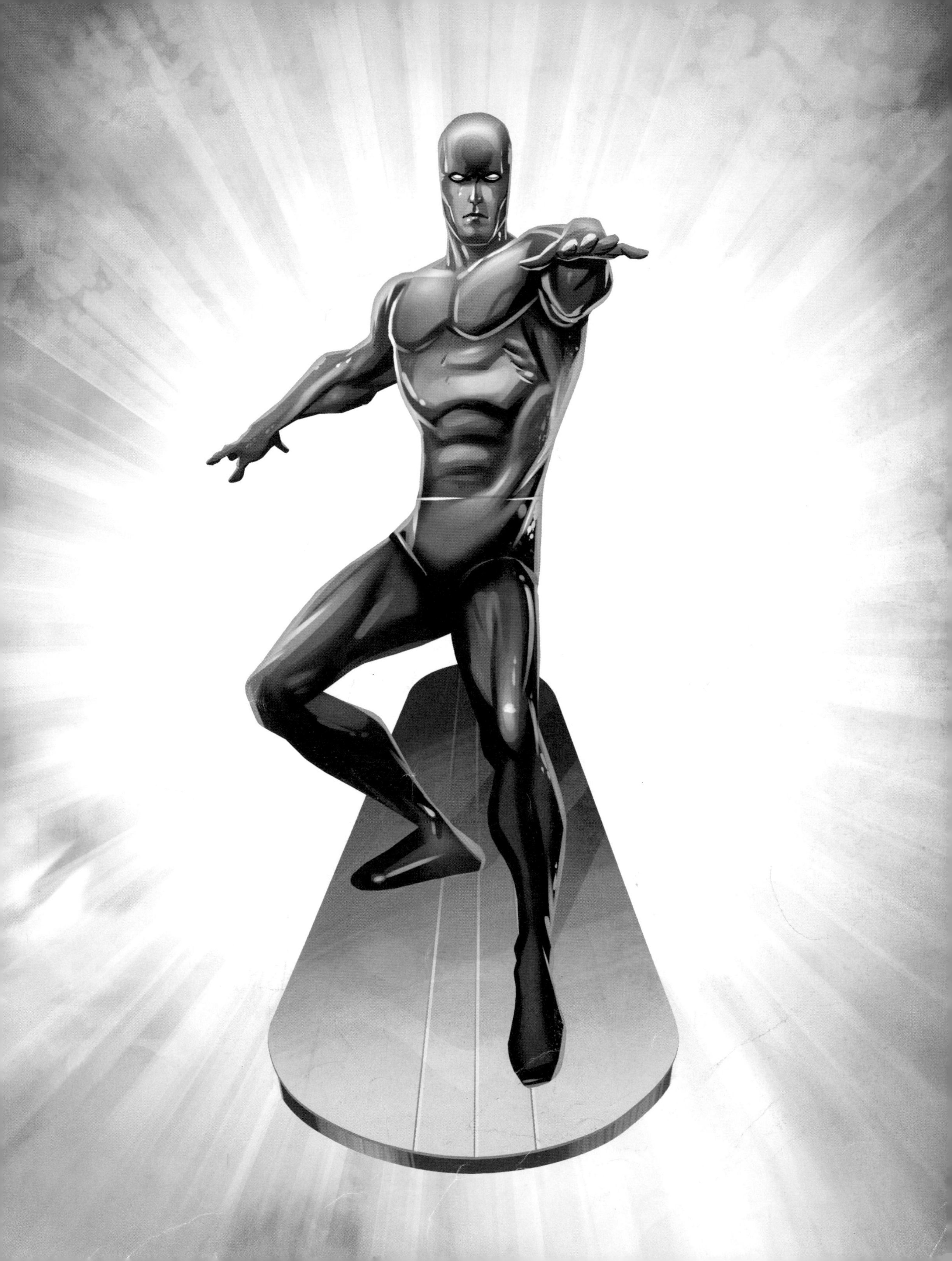

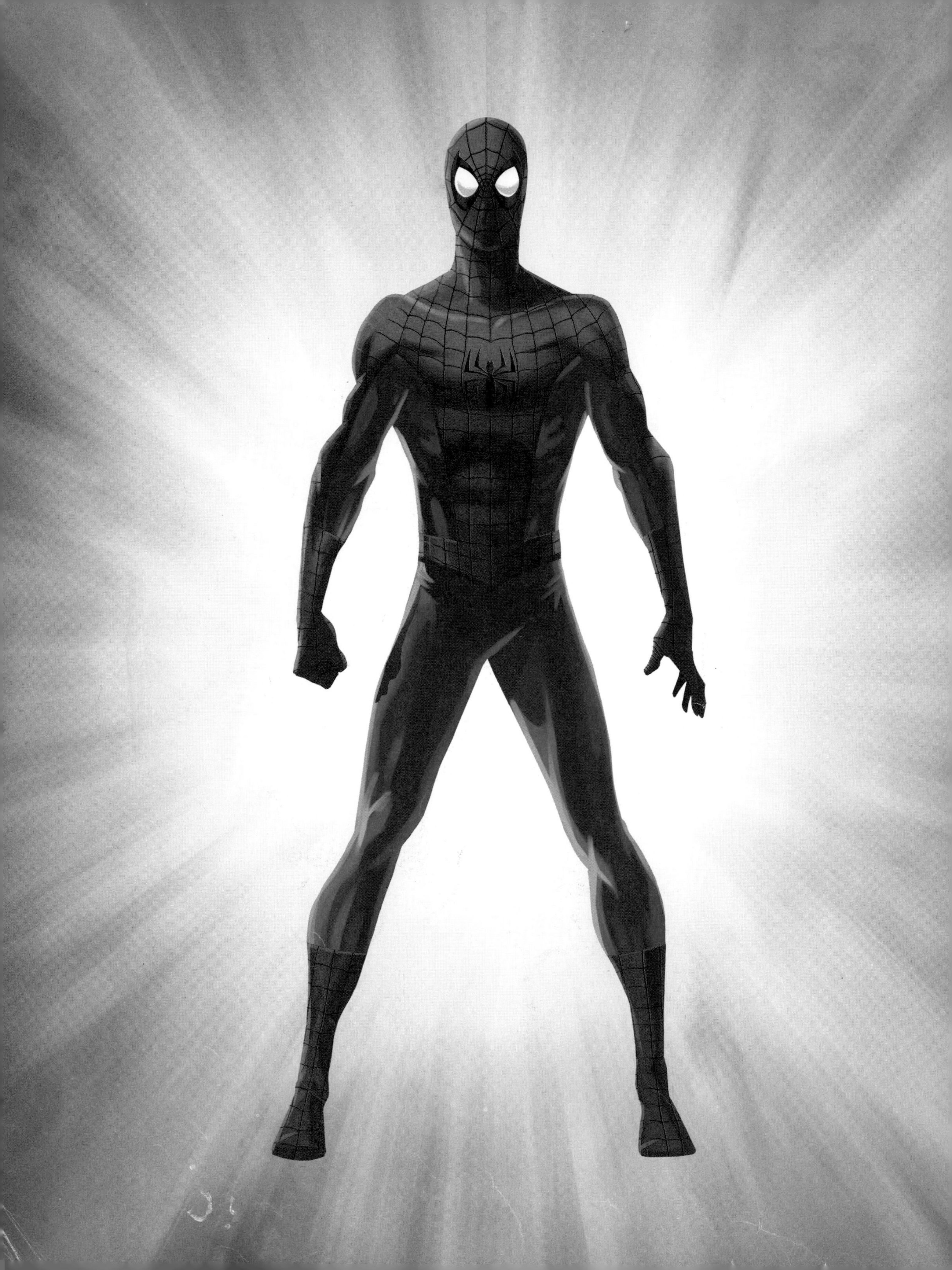

SPIDER-MAN

WHEN SHY HIGH SCHOOL STUDENT Peter Parker got bitten by a radioactive spider, he gained the powers of the arachnid. Suddenly as strong as a dozen men, he found he could climb straight up walls or stick to a ceiling. Using his training as a young scientist, Peter invented a way to shoot webs. He even has what he calls his spider-sense, which enables him to tell when danger is near. Peter remembered his beloved Uncle Ben's belief that **WITH GREAT POWER COMES GREAT RESPONSIBILITY.** Peter vowed to use his incredible new abilities to fight crime as the Amazing Spider-Man!

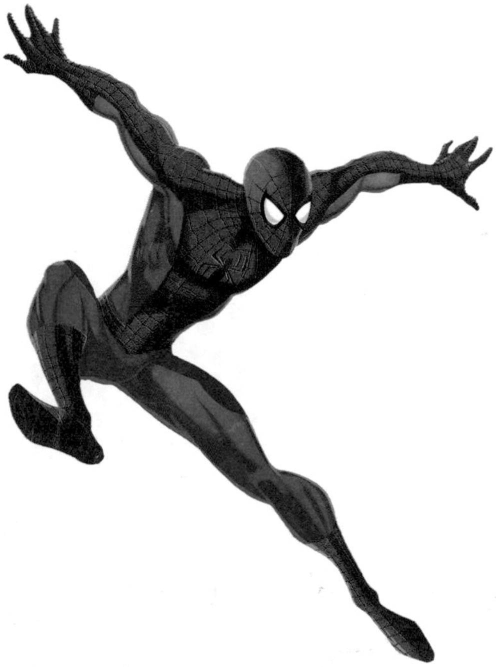

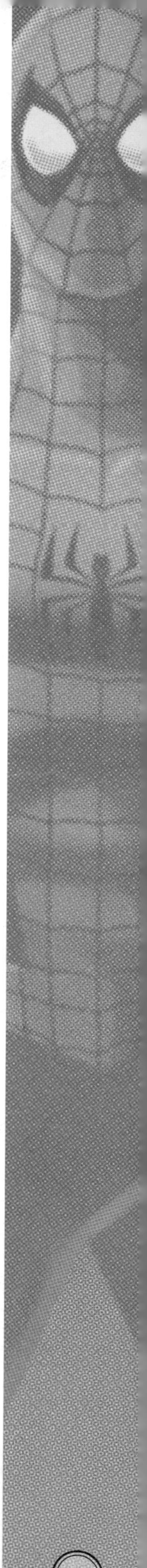

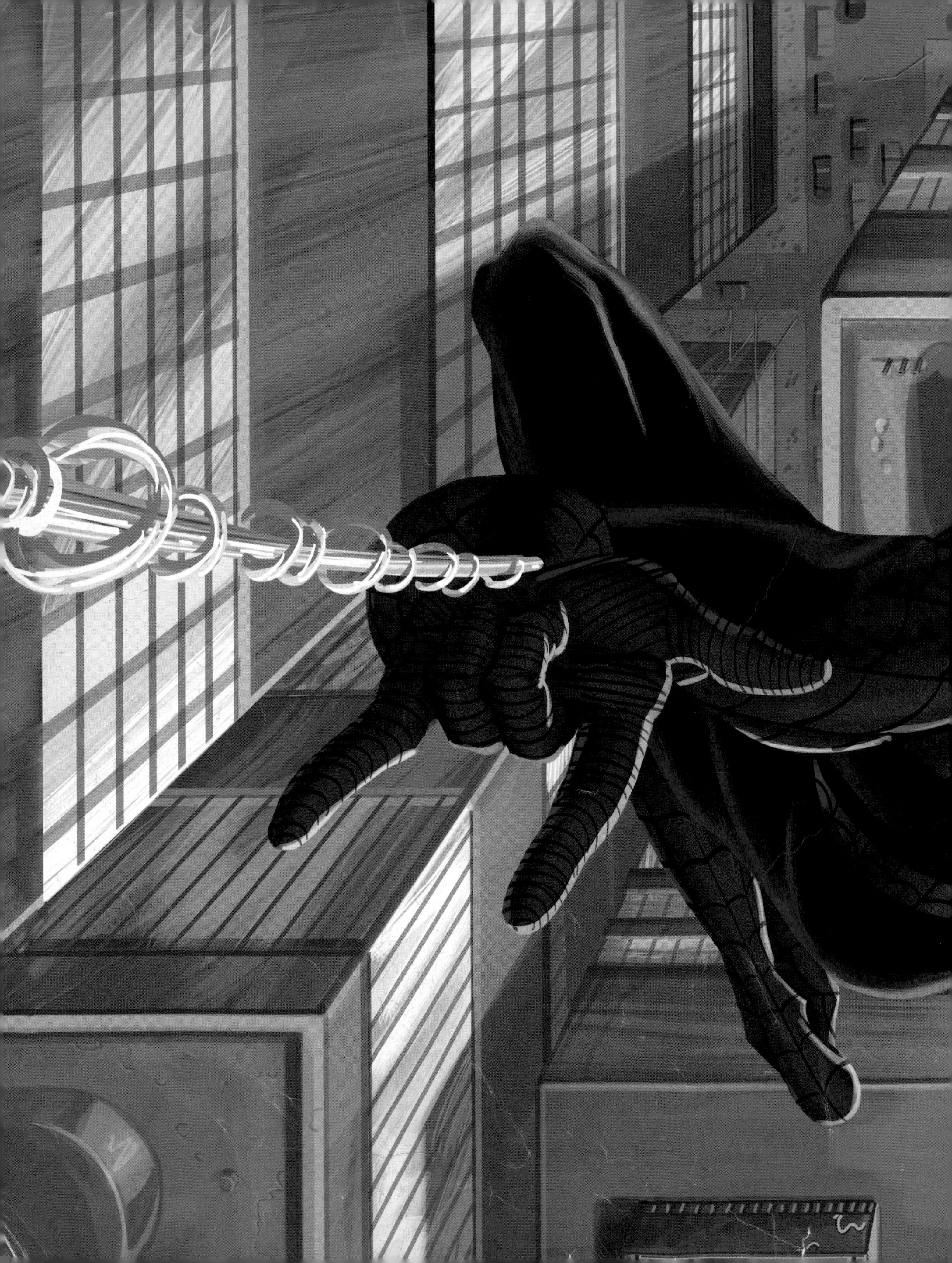

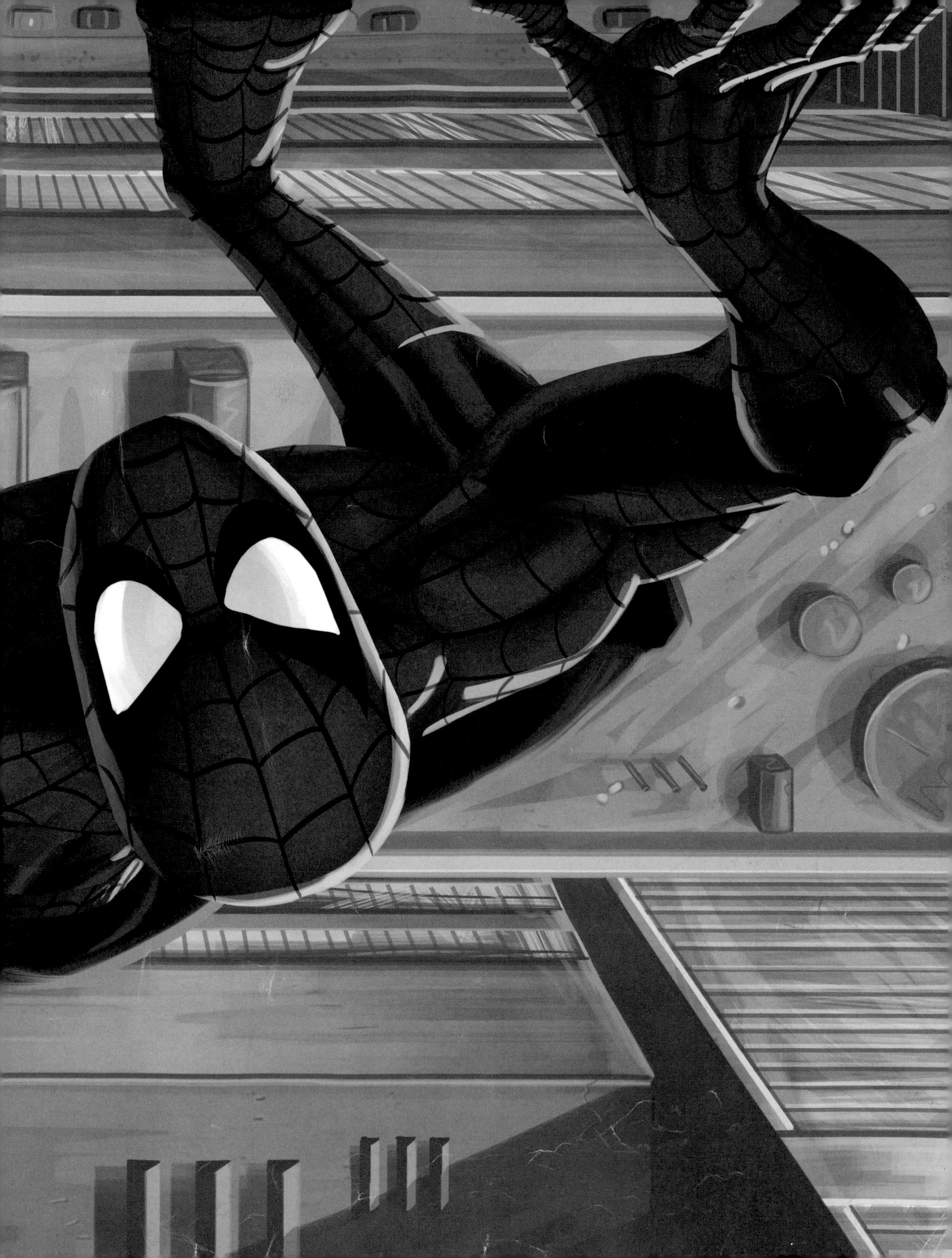

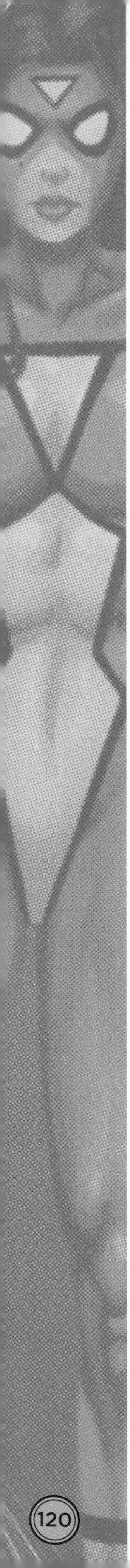

SPIDER-WOMAN

WHEN 10 YEAR-OLD JESSICA DREW became sick with radiation poisoning, her scientist parents invented a special machine that would inject her with spider DNA. She instantly felt better. But the spider DNA altered her own, giving her the ability to leap and jump farther than anyone could possibly imagine. Jessica could stick to surfaces and possessed the ability to shoot power straight from her hands. Using her new abilities for a good cause, Jessica Drew helps those in need under the name Spider-Woman.

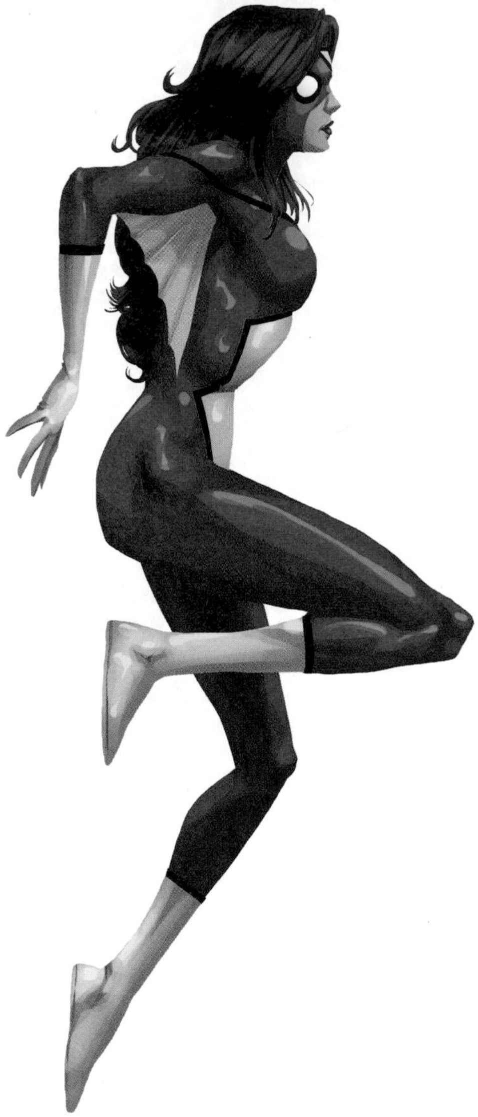

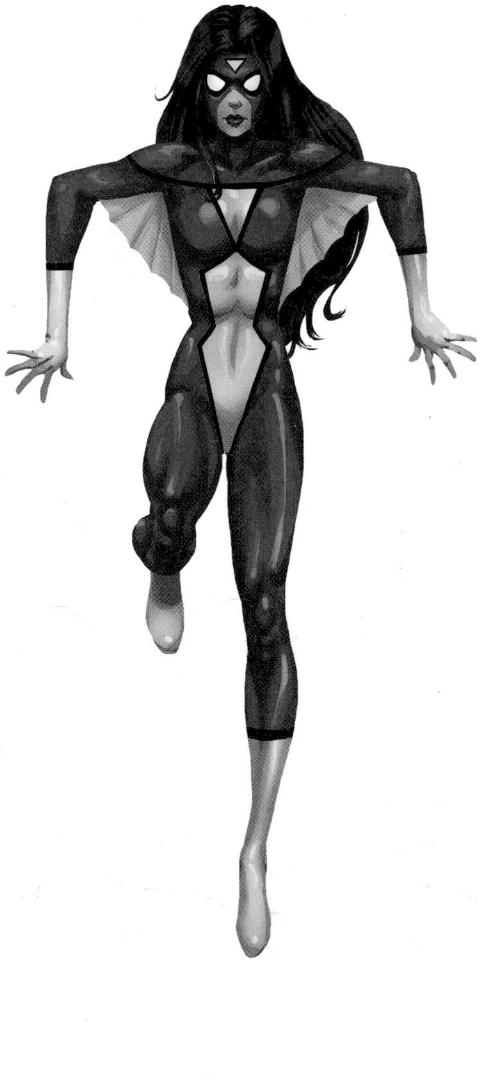

SQUIRREL GIRL

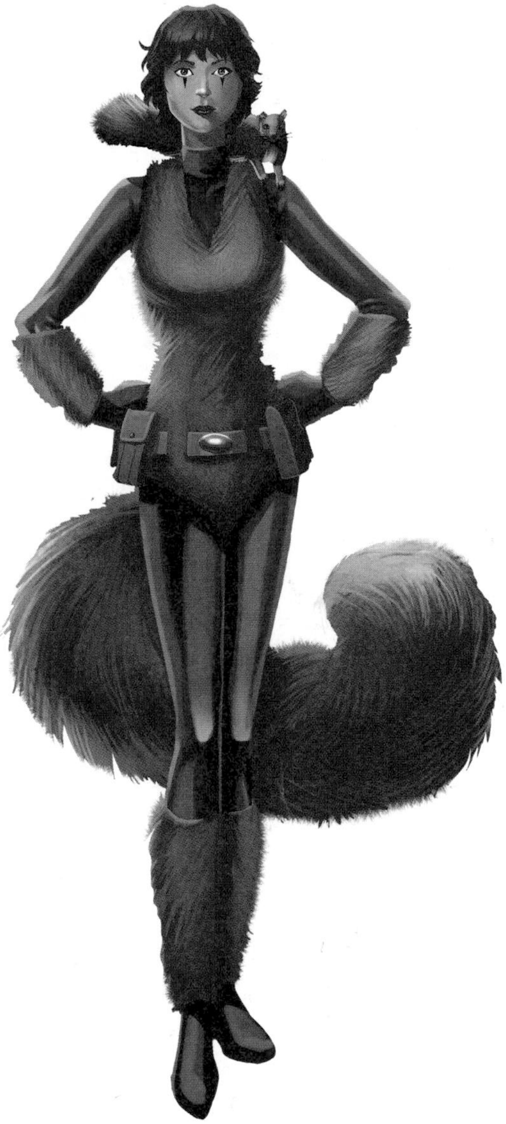

DOREEN GREEN just wanted what any kid wants: to be a Super Hero based on a rodent. So she ambushed Iron Man, hoping to impress him. He was not impressed.

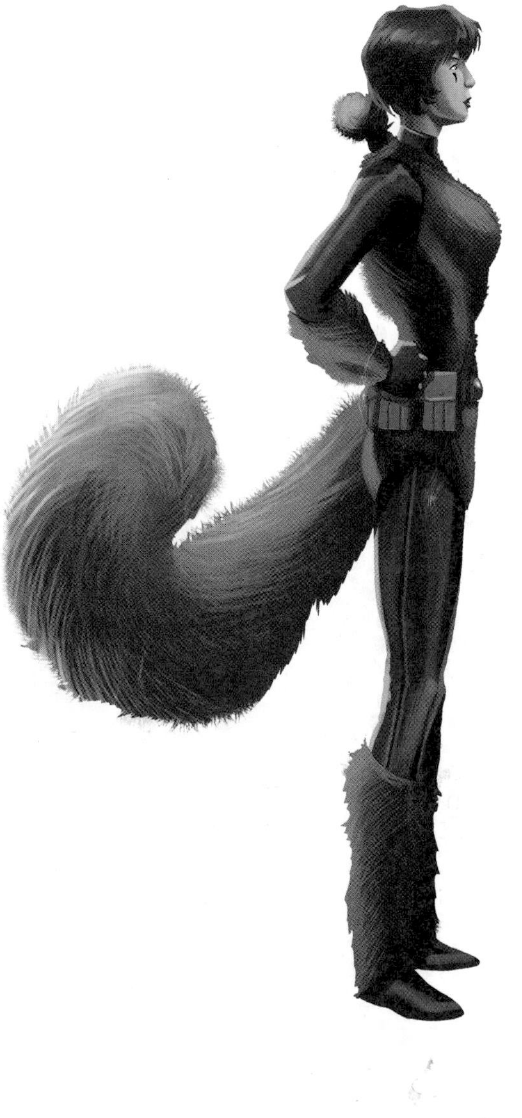

When Iron Man was later captured by Doctor Doom, however, Doreen came to his rescue—and that did impress him. Too young, in his opinion, to be an official Super Hero, Squirrel Girl has used her ***SQUIRREL-LIKE MUTANT ABILITIES***—abnormal leaping ability, a knuckle spike, and a big, bushy tail—to defeat Super Villain after Super Villain.

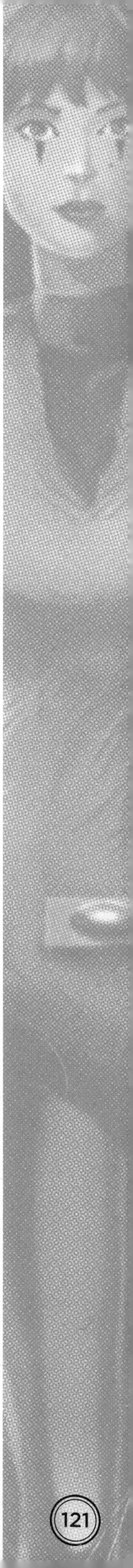

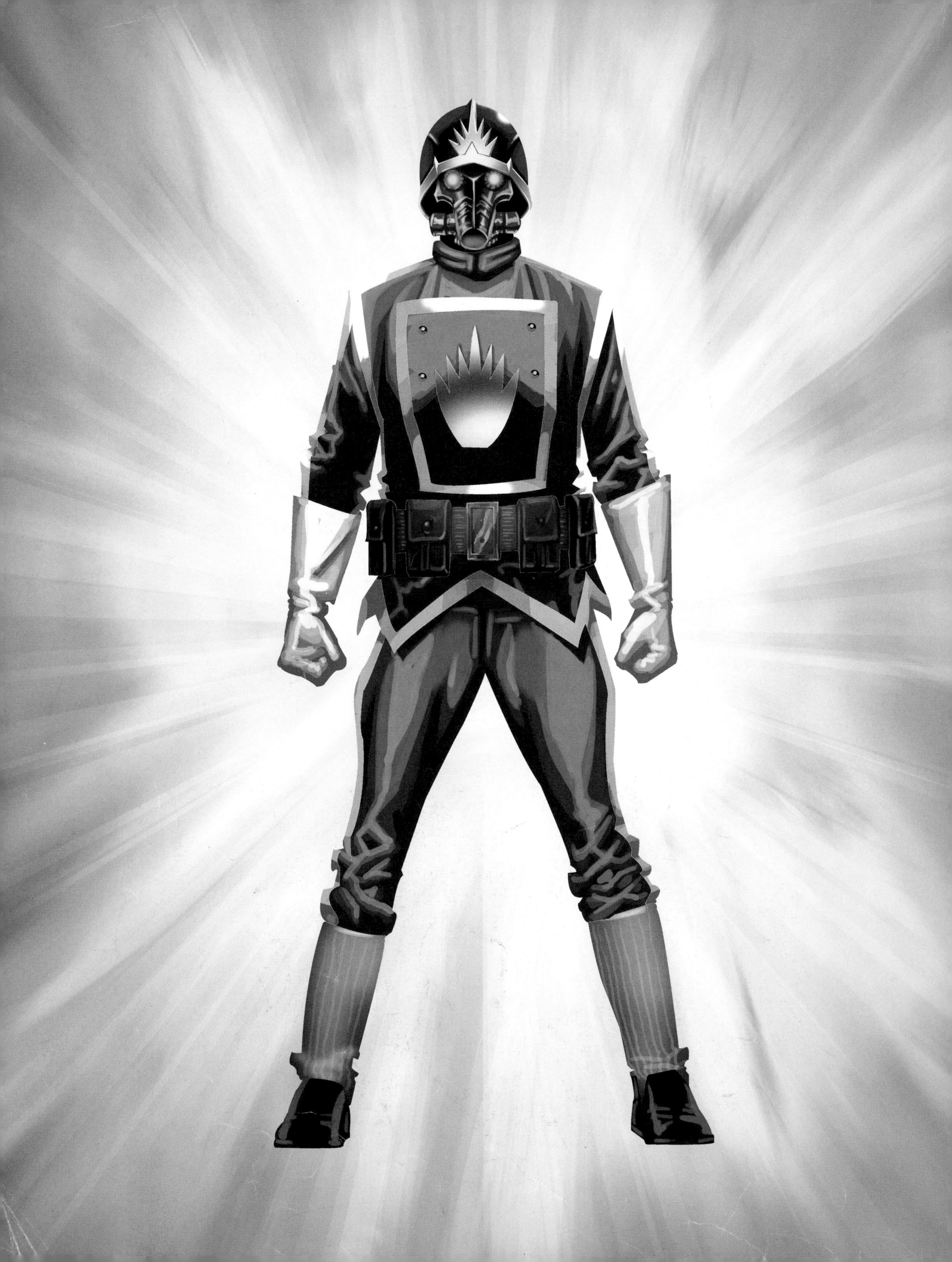

STAR LORD

WHILE ON HIS FIRST MISSION, Peter Quill and his fellow astronauts were visited on their space station by an alien who was looking for a new Star Lord: a kind of intergalactic policeman. Peter immediately volunteered . . . but he wasn't chosen. Showing his ingenuity—and less-than-total respect for rules—Peter took the place of the astronaut who'd been selected. And that's how Peter Quill became Star Lord, **LEADER OF THE GUARDIANS OF THE GALAXY,** with a living spaceship, a spacesuit that gave him special powers, and an element gun, able to shoot any of the four elements.

STORM

ORORO MUNROE is the daughter of a Kenyan princess. Born with white hair and blue eyes, like her mother, she always stood out—especially since they both had the magical ability to **CONTROL THE WEATHER.** When Ororo was older, Professor X contacted her and asked her to join the X-Men. He explained that Ororo's powers weren't really magical: she was actually a mutant. Curious about this new information, Ororo not only joined the team but even led the X-Men for a while. Given her ability to command lightning and tornados, rain, hail, and snow, it's fitting that she would take the codename Storm.

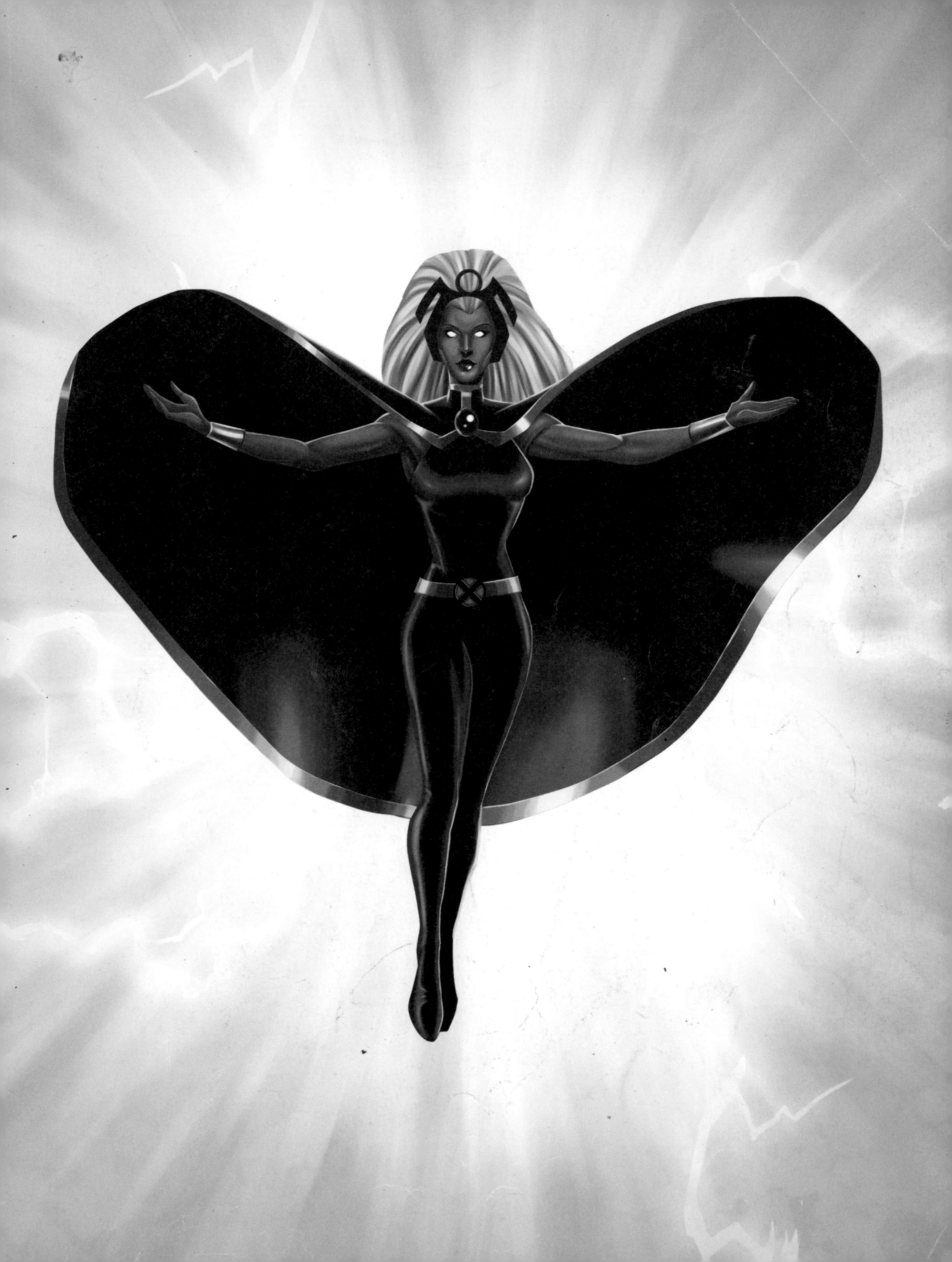

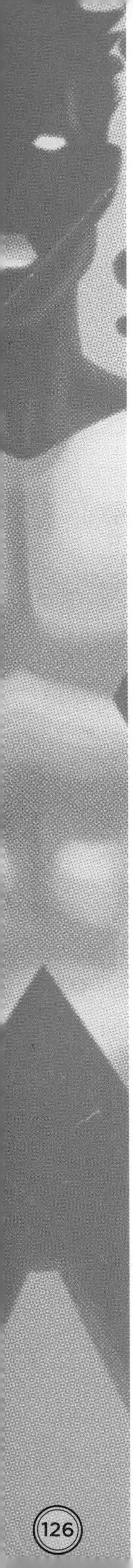

SUNSPOT

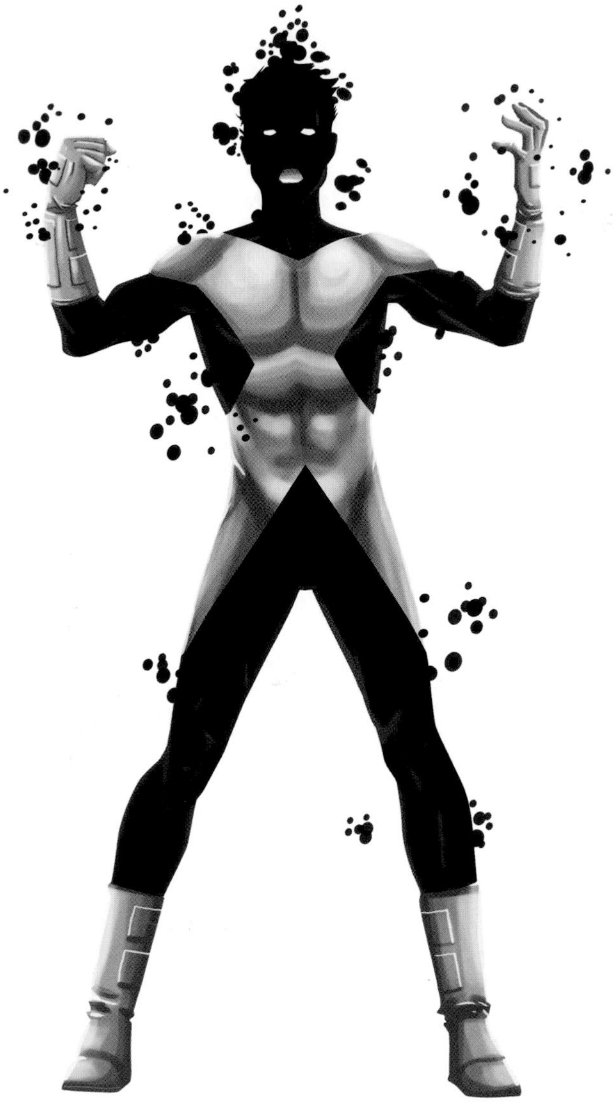

ROBERTO DA COSTA loved to play soccer. But his playing days came to an end the moment his mutant abilities erupted during a fight in the middle of a game in Rio de Janeiro.

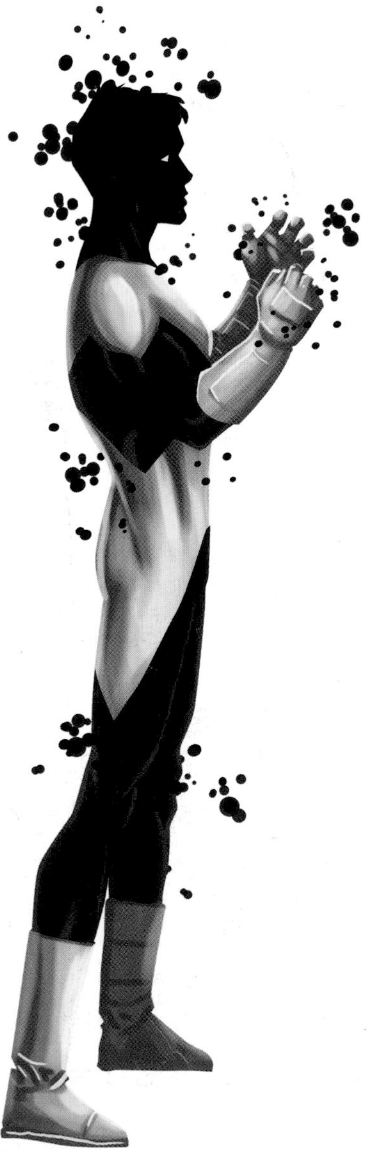

Changing into a being of **DARK SOLAR ENERGY,** he came to the attention of an evil group of mutants. Saved from their diabolical ways by Professor X, Roberto became Sunspot, one of the first New Mutants. Using his mutant abilities, Sunspot is superstrong, can fly, and project blasts of heat and light.

THE THING

BEN GRIMM NEVER HAD IT EASY. His home life was hard, and he fell in with a gang at an early age. Fortunately, he got a football scholarship to college, which is where he met Reed Richards, who became his best friend. After school, Ben joined the Air Force, where he learned to fly jets. That's how he became the pilot on a spaceship Reed designed—and that's how he ended up getting hit by cosmic radiation. The radiation gave Ben superstrength . . . but it also changed him into something that looked like a **ROCK MONSTER,** with superhard skin. The Thing may not be pretty—but it comes in handy as a member of the Fantastic Four.

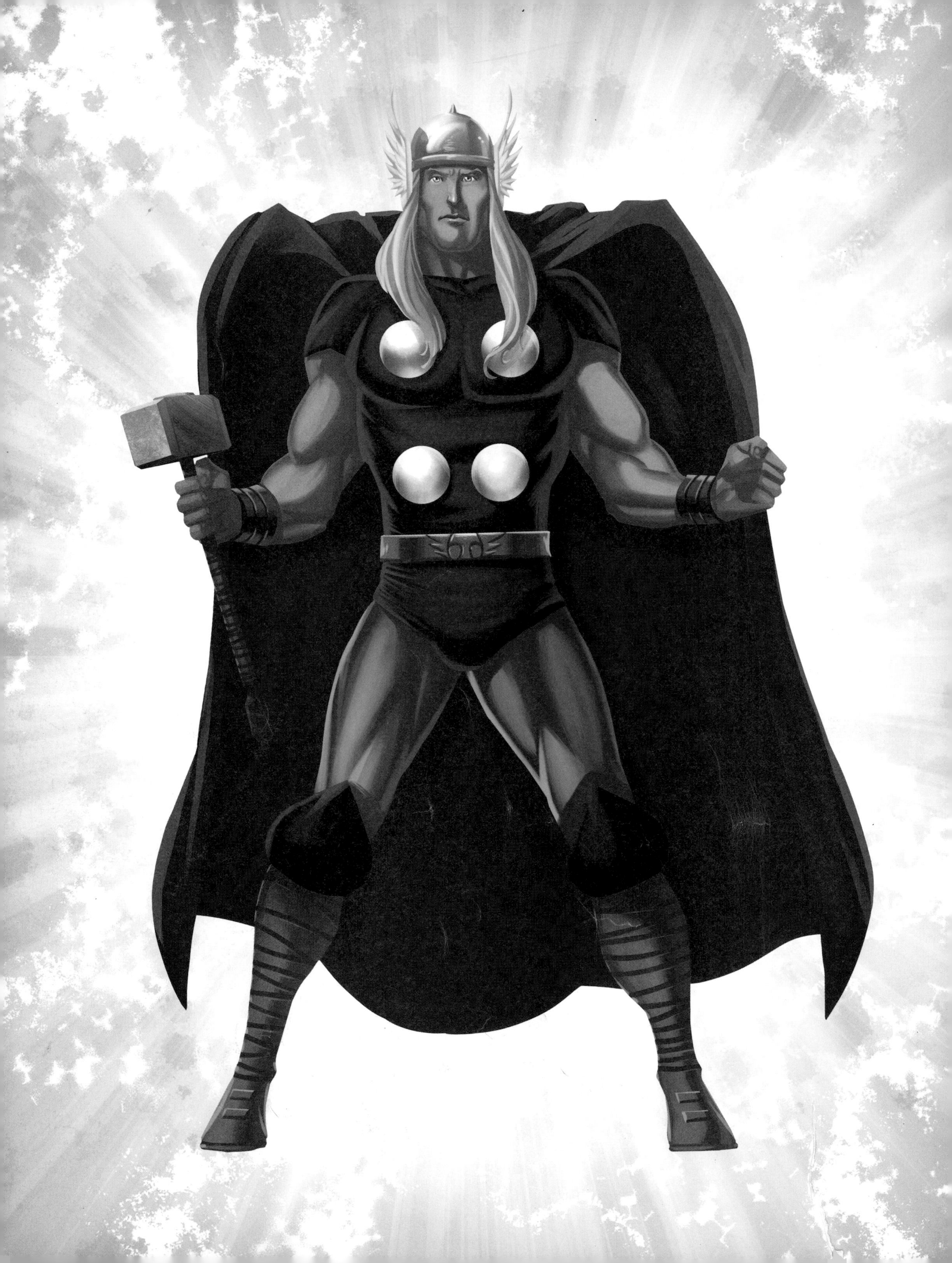

THE MIGHTY THOR

AS SON OF ODIN, king of the Norse gods, Thor was proud—too proud. To teach him a lesson, Odin sent Thor away from their home in the magical Realm of Asgard. The King stripped Thor of his memory and forced him to live on Earth as a human until the proud young prince learned how to be humble. With his memory gone, Thor believed he was Donald Blake, a poor orphan putting himself through medical school. Despite a bad leg, Donald became a wonderful, caring doctor. When Odin realized his son had finally grown up, he returned Thor's memory and powers. Odin also gave Thor back **MIGHTY MJOLNIR,** (myol-neer) the magical and unbreakable war hammer that Thor—and only Thor—is able to use to call down lightning and wind. Proving he was truly a worthy hero, Thor decided to stay on Earth and fight for those in need.

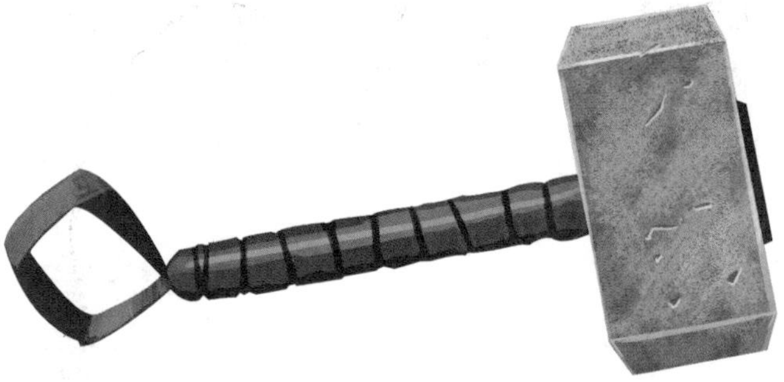

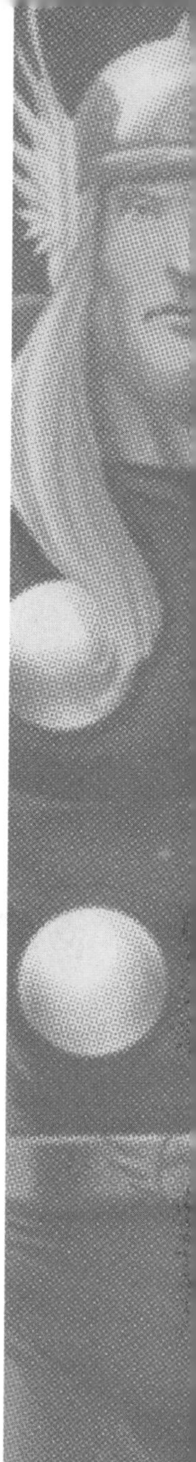

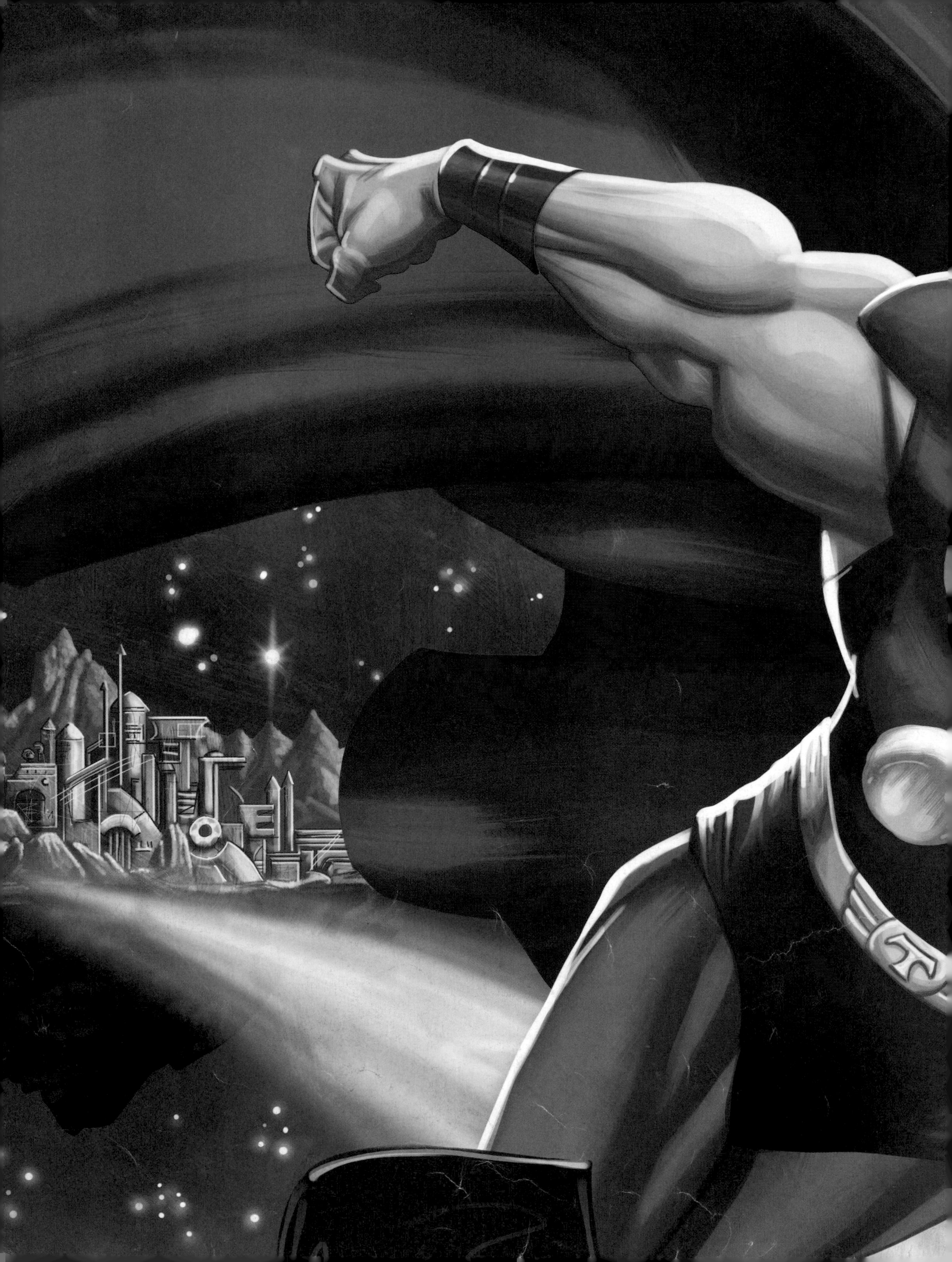

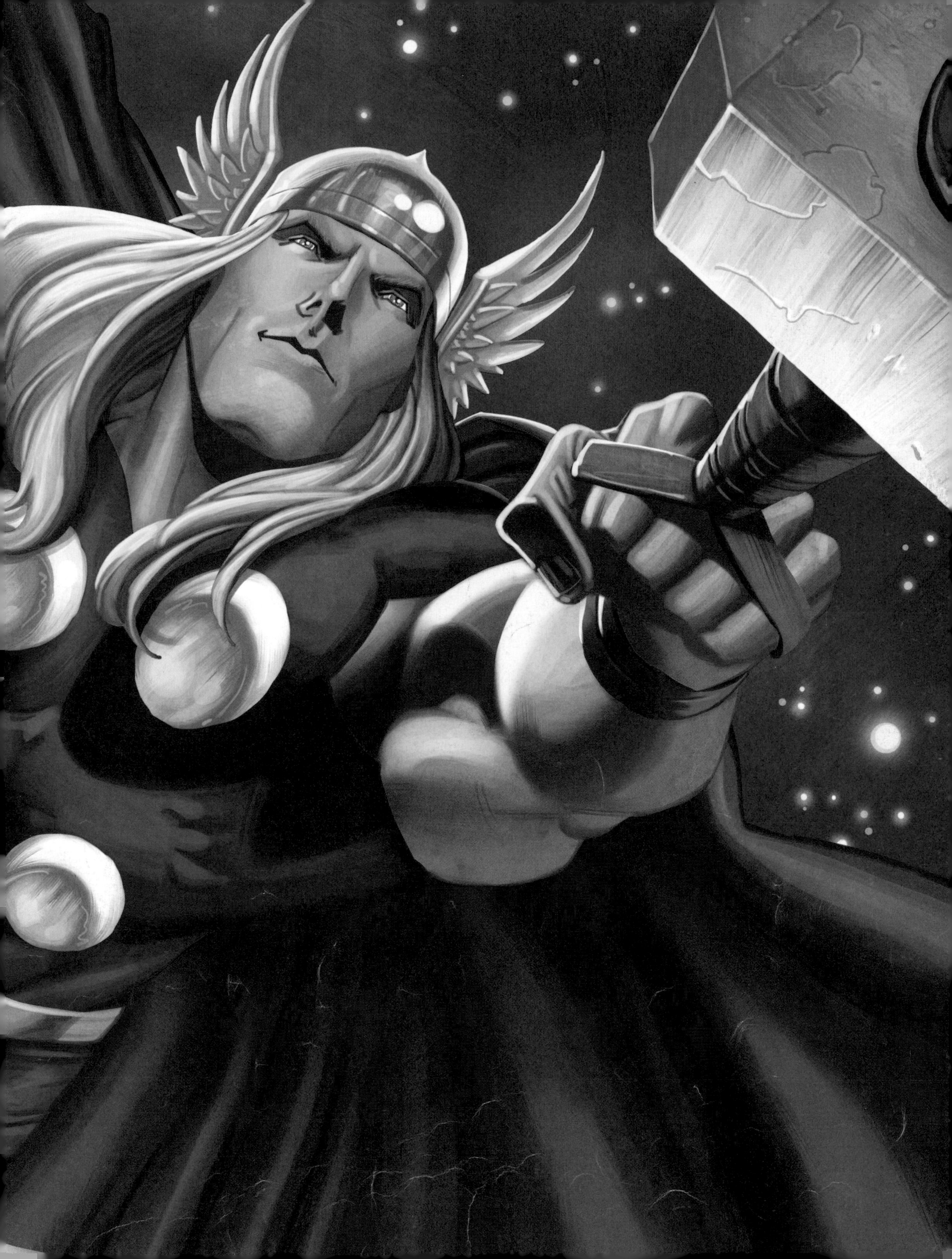

US AGENT

JOHN WALKER wanted to be a hero in the worst way. He underwent a special treatment to make him a professional wrestler, but he soon realized his new powers could enable him to be the hero he always dreamed of becoming.

Superstrong, tough, and flexible, he took the codename US Agent and uses his abilities to, as he sees it, **PROTECT HIS COUNTRY.**

VALKYRIE

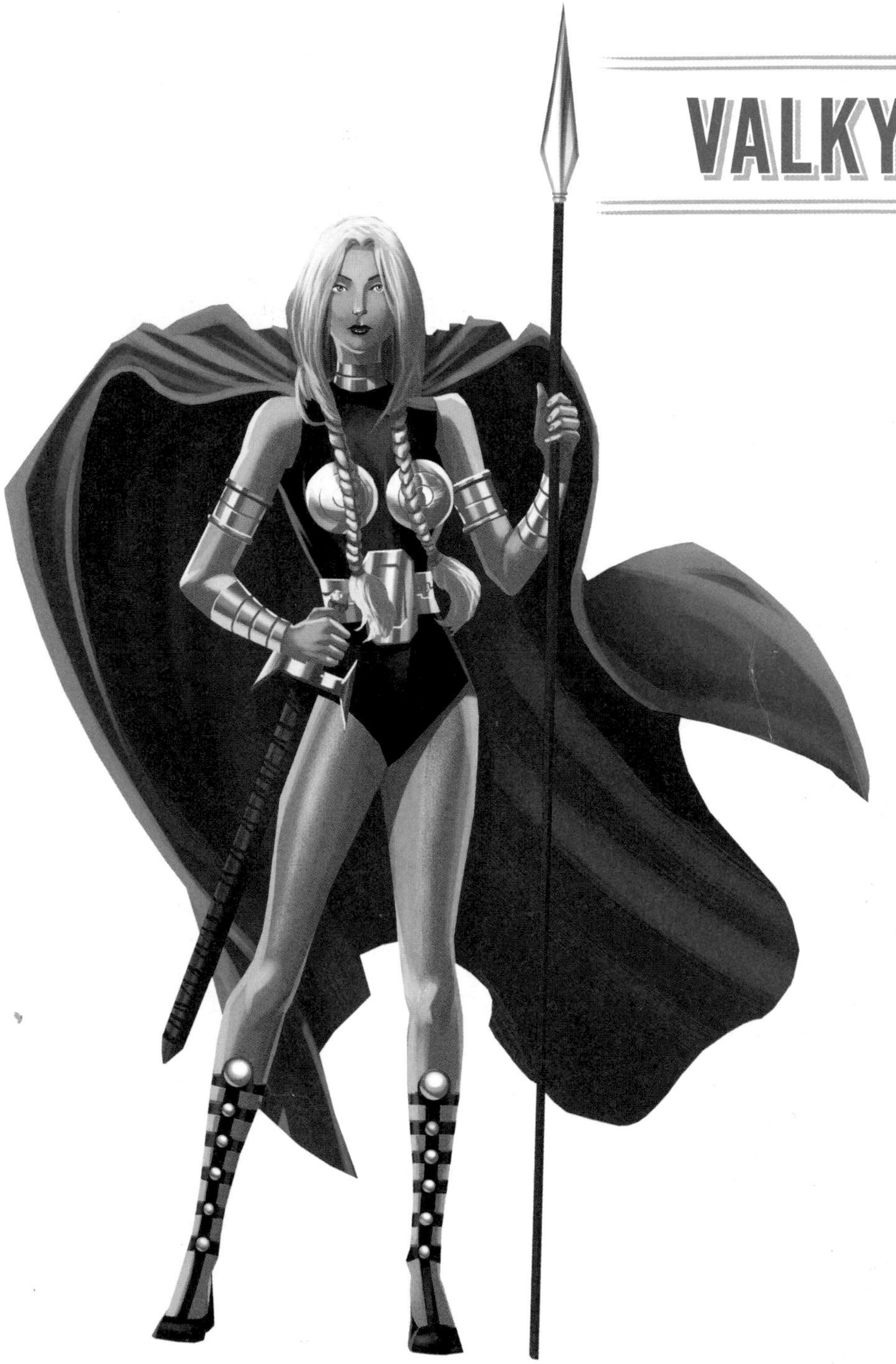

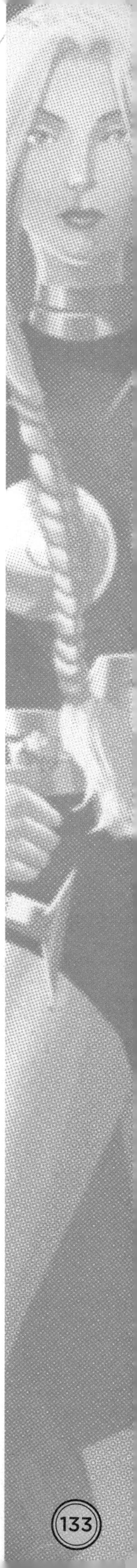

IN ASGARD, there is a race of warrior goddesses called the Valkyrior. Proud and noble, their leader is Brunnhilde. Known as the Valkyrie, she is her people's most powerful warrior. Perhaps because of her ability to see Death approaching, after uncountable millennia, she passed her powers onto Samantha Parrington, an idealistic young woman who had befriended the Hulk. Able to turn into the mythical Valkyrie at will, Samantha becomes superstrong and wields the mystical sword **DRAGONFANG** as a member of the Defenders.

VISION

THINGS DON'T ALWAYS WORK OUT quite the way you expect. The android called Vision was created by the robotic Super Villain Ultron to destroy the Avengers. It was a good plan, since Vision was so incredibly powerful. He's able to fly, pass through solid objects, become hard as diamond, and use heat vision to melt through steel. Vision was more than a match for the Avengers. But, using his logic, Vision realized the Avengers were the good guys and joined them. He became a **LOYAL AND TRUSTED MEMBER** of the team. Funny how things turn out.

VOLSTAGG

IT'S NOT EASY being a member of the Warriors Three. You never know when you're going to find yourself in a death-defying battle alongside the Mighty Thor. But Volstagg wouldn't have it any other way. Older than the other Warriors, and more prone to brag about his adventures, Volstagg's actually the one most likely to get them all in trouble.

But there's not a **BRAVER OR KINDER** Asgardian anywhere. Superstrong and tough, like all Asgardians, Volstagg is not quite as fast as he used to be (thanks to his ever-expanding belly), but he's still more than capable of watching Thor's back.

WAR MACHINE

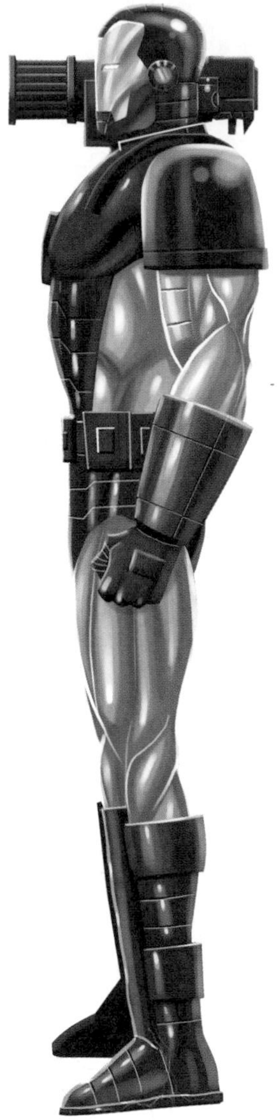

LIEUTENANT COLONEL

James Rhodes has long been one of Tony Stark's closest friends, meeting him almost immediately after Tony created the very first Iron Man armor.

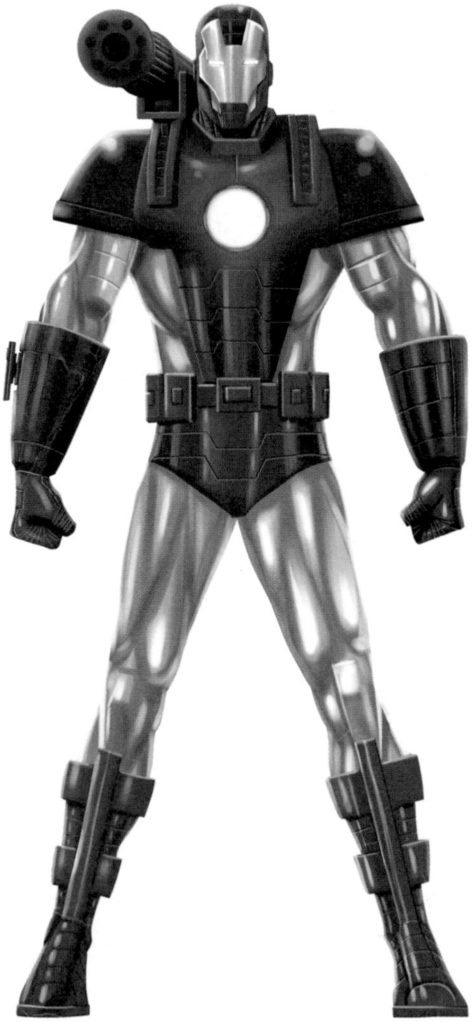

Later, Rhodey went to work for Tony at Stark Industries. So when Tony needed someone to fill in as Iron Man, Rhodey—a former Air Force pilot—was a perfect fit. After Tony became Iron Man once more, he designed a ***NEW SUIT*** just for Rhodey. Like the Iron Man armor, it's superstrong, can fly, and has an enormous number of weapons. Behold the War Machine!

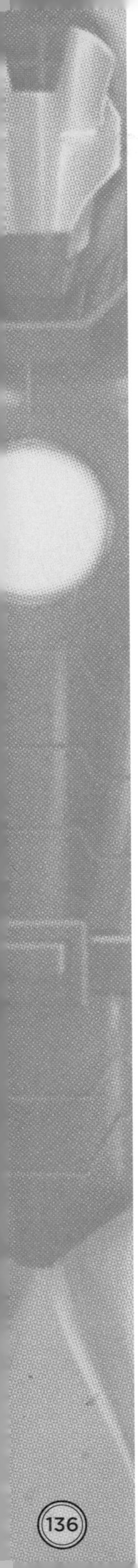

WARLOCK

CREATED BY SCIETISTS, the artificial human known as "Him" came to life and learned of his creator's evil intentions for his existence. He rebelled against them and fled into space. Now known as **WARLOCK,** he possess superhuman strength, speed, agility, and the ability to manipulate cosmic energy for energy projections.

THE WASP

THE DAUGHTER of a famous scientist, Janet van Dyne was determined to avenge her father's murder. She convinced Henry Pym, a scientist friend of her father's, to help. Henry—who was also secretly Ant-Man—gave her the same Pym Particles which granted him his superpowers. Like him, Janet gained **THE ABILITY TO SHRINK DOWN** to the size of an insect. She grew wings and the power to shoot blasts from her hand, like a bee's sting. After a while, like Ant-Man, Janet gained the ability to grow, as well as shrink. Calling herself the Wasp, she not only joined the Avengers, she was the one who came up with the team's name.

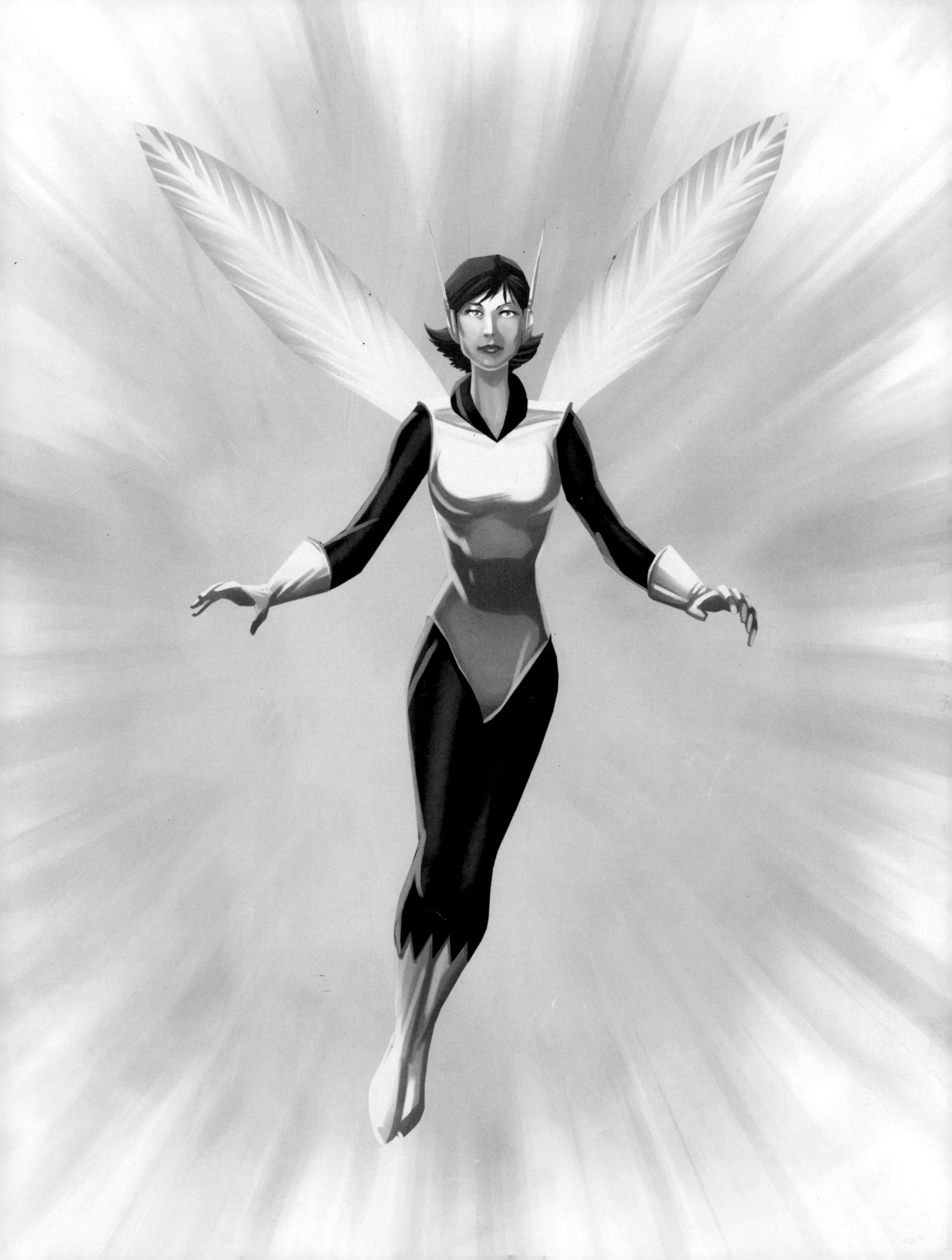

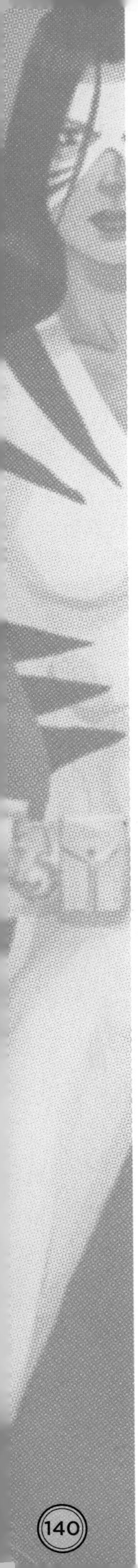

WHITE TIGER

BORN IN PUERTO RICO, Hector Ayala was a college student in New York City when he found three mythical tiger amulets. Wearing all three of the amulets gave Hector superstrength and amazing martial-arts abilities. As the White side with heroes like Daredevil and Spider-Man. Unfortunately, he was framed for a murder he didn't commit and shot trying to escape. After his innocence was proven, his niece **ANGELA DEL TORO** took up the amulets and became the new White Tiger.

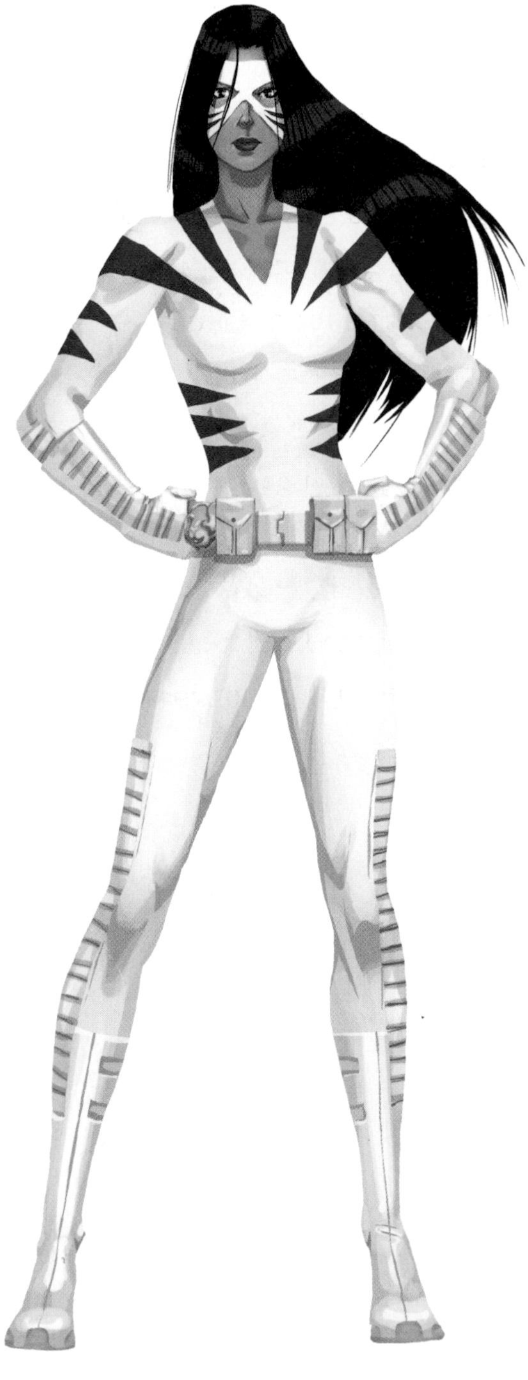

WOLFSBANE

WHEN RAHNE SINCLAIR first developed mutant powers as a youngster in Scotland, she was mistaken for a werewolf—understandable, considering she was able to turn into a wolf. After being chased across the Scottish highlands, Rahne fell unconscious and reverted to her human form in front of Doctor Moira MacTaggert. The scientist brought Rahne to America to be taught by the one man who could help her: Professor Charles Xavier. As a member of the **NEW MUTANTS,** Rahne embraced her true nature, proudly taking the codename Wolfsbane.

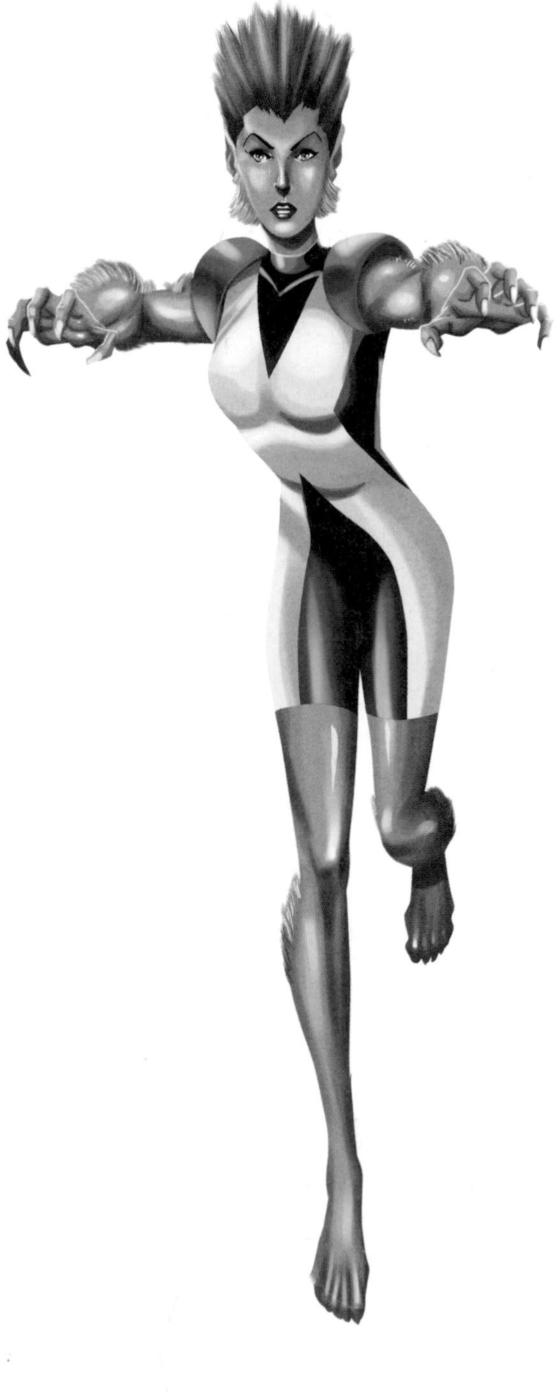

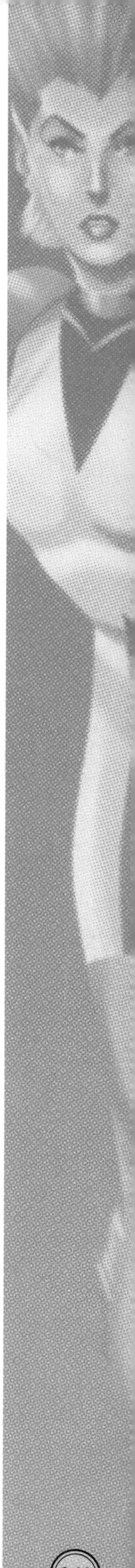

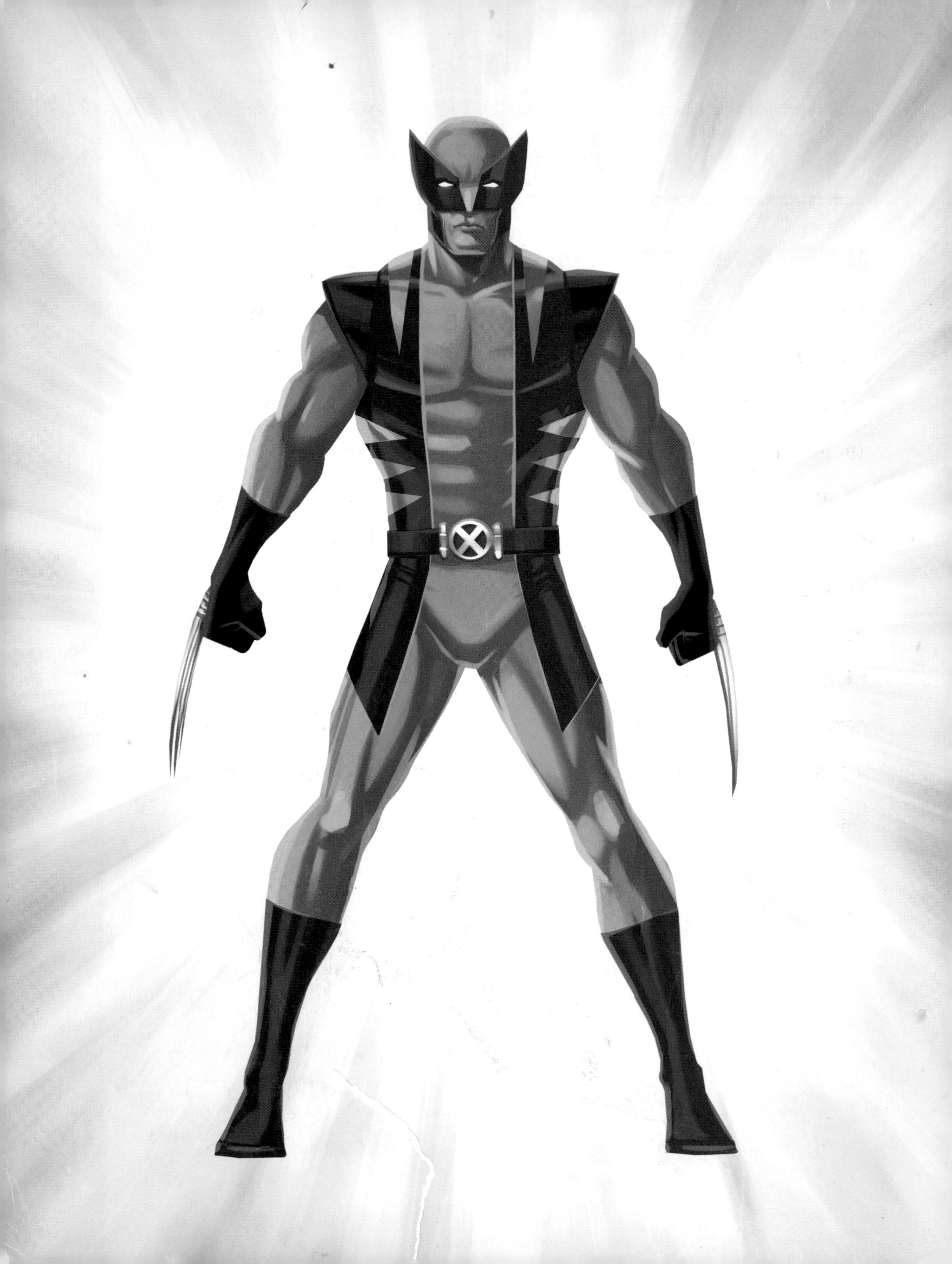

WOLVERINE

HE'S THE BEST THERE IS at what he does. So maybe it's not surprising that the story behind the hero known as Wolverine is a strange one. Born in Canada way back in 1882, his mutant ability is an amazing healing factor. This enabled him to recover from horrible injuries, as well as to live much, much longer than normal humans. But again and again, enemies have managed to capture Wolverine and erase his memory, leaving him little clue as to his true past. Now, Wolverine also has a skeleton made of the indestructible metal, **ADAMANTIUM,** and claws he can pop out when he needs—or just wants to. Although a loner by nature, even Wolverine will sometimes admit he has finally found a family in the X-Men.

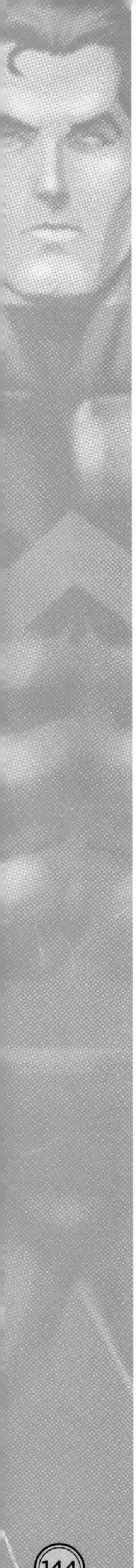

WONDER MAN

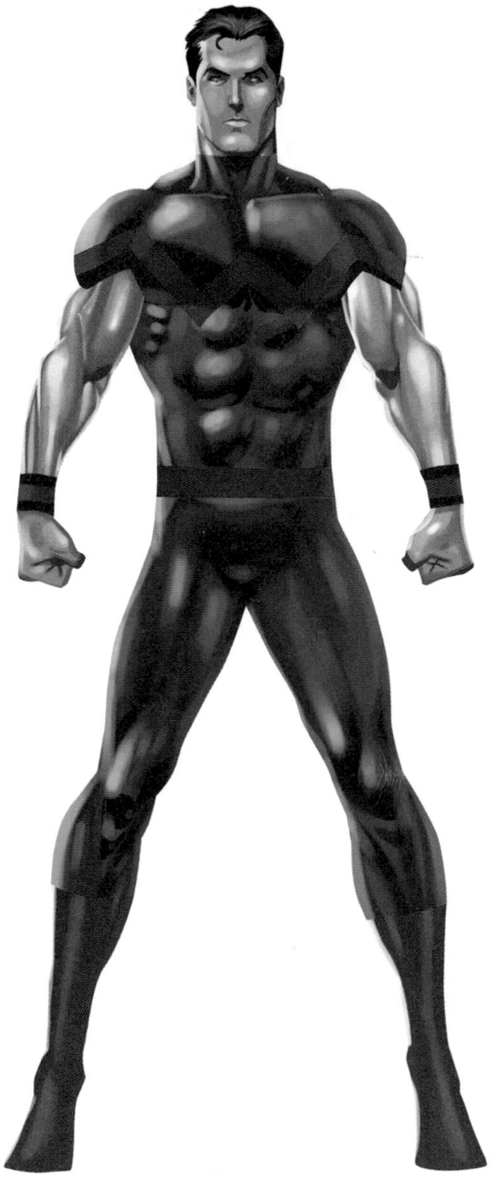

A BUSINESS RIVAL of Tony Stark's, Simon Williams hated Iron Man so much he agreed to radiation and chemical treatments from evil Baron Zemo. The treatments made Simon superhuman, giving him superstrength and superspeed.

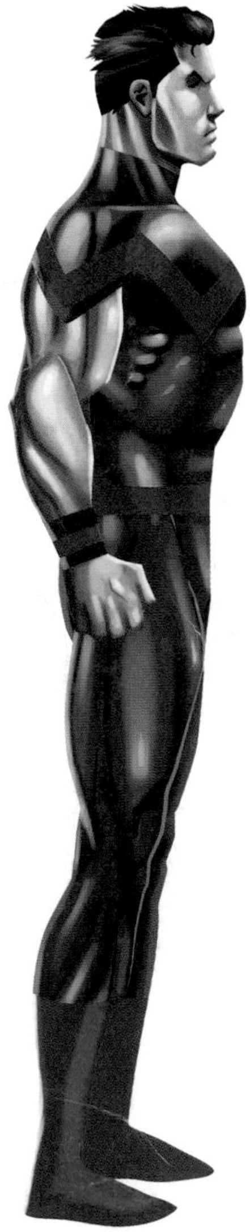

Calling himself Wonder Man, he set out to attack the Avengers. He lost so badly that he slipped into a coma. When he woke up, the Avengers helped him get better. Wonder Man was so **GRATEFUL** that he not only changed his ways, he actually became an Avenger. Now *that's* wonderful.